LOVE U…
ADVENTURERS

The Lusty, Texas Collection

Cara Covington

MENAGE EVERLASTING

Siren Publishing, Inc.
www.SirenPublishing.com

A SIREN PUBLISHING BOOK
IMPRINT: Ménage Everlasting

LOVE UNDER TWO ADVENTURERS

ISBN: 978-1-62740-113-5

First Printing: May 2013

Cover design by Les Byerley

Printed in the U.S.A.

PUBLISHER
Siren Publishing, Inc.
www.SirenPublishing.com

DEDICATION

No one is an island and that is particularly true for authors. I count myself very lucky and blessed by the people who are in my world, and in my corner.

To my friend John, who is always ready to help with any questions I may have with regard to police procedure (he is one), fire fighting procedure (he was one), life in the service(he was in the Air Force) and EMT knowledge (yes, he was one of those, too). Thanks for your help, your patience and for making me assemble a Henry AR-7 blindfolded. Thanks for showing me how to safely fire several different types of guns, including a Glock 9mm so that when I write of them, I don't sound completely stupid.

To my very good friend Heather Rainier. Often, my friend, chatting with you online or on the phone is the highlight of my day. You are a complete joy to work with. I love our cross-overs, and I look forward to many more get-togethers between the folks of Divine and Lusty.

David, we've been married for a long time. I wouldn't be where I am without you. Thank you for being you, and for loving me.

LOVE UNDER TWO ADVENTURERS

The Lusty, Texas Collection

CARA COVINGTON

Chapter 1

Lusty, Texas, December 25, 2004

"I'm surprised those artsy-fartsy friends of yours aren't here, gobbling up free Christmas turkey and booze."

Rebecca Jessop blinked, the only outward sign she was willing to give that she'd even heard the "barb" in the words Greg had just tossed her way.

His brother, Kevin, who'd been chatting with him as she'd come upstairs, just sighed, shook his head, then took the stairs down to the ground floor.

"I don't have any artsy-fartsy friends, and if I did, I'm quite certain they would desert me for you."

She walked away from him, and peered inside his sister's bedroom. Julia wasn't there, and when she turned around, she caught a look in Greg's eyes, one she'd seen there briefly from time to time. It was a look of interest, not enmity. She held back her own smile. Rebecca Jessop burned for Greg Benedict today hotter than she'd ever burned for him before. And he was here, now, at home. As if from the heavens, he'd dropped in the day before from Jakarta, of all places.

No one had known he would be home for Christmas. *She* hadn't known he would be home.

Who knows when I'll see him again? Who knows when I'll get another chance?

The families all thought they were oil and water, that all they ever did was bicker. Everyone thought they didn't like each other much, because all it seemed they ever did was snip at each other.

Rebecca knew different, deep in her soul where her artist's heart pulsed out the very essence of her being.

And so, too, did Greg. She understood that in a flash as emotion, and, *thank God*, heat, flared in his eyes.

"Brat."

"Cretin."

"Shortie."

"Beanpole."

With each new insult, the distance between them eroded. They were upstairs in the Big House while music played and family partied below. She really hadn't known he was up here, and certainly hadn't planned this encounter. She realized, in that slow way one did after having a couple of glasses of wine, that she was standing in the hall just outside his bedroom. She didn't stop to think. The moment, the circumstance, cried out to her. The wine emboldened her. The alcohol had the added benefit of stoking her fires. She was horny as hell, and decided it was high time she did something about that.

She took one little half step closer. "You've always been a beanpole with way too big an opinion of yourself, Mr. Benedict."

"You know, Ms. Jessop, someone ought to shut that sassy little mouth of yours."

His breath bathed her face and she inhaled the scent of his beer and the scent that was pure Greg. Her hormones began doing the happy dance, and she felt moisture gather between her thighs.

"Oh, yeah? Now, who d'ya figure ought to do that?"

"Me."

Rebecca wasn't certain which one of them moved first. But finally, *finally*, with his body pressed close to hers, Greg covered her lips with his own and, *yes*, he kissed her.

She felt the ability to think fly away as every bone in her body seemed to melt in response to the heat and the fire that only *this* man could ignite in her.

Hot and heady, long and lush, his tongue stroked hers, a seductive salsa that lit her up more splendidly than the Christmas tree downstairs in the Great Room. She kissed him back, the taste of him more delectable than chocolate, the effect of him more potent than the strongest wine.

For one instant she felt a nudge in her back and realized the doorknob to his room was poking her back. And then that sensation was gone—gone, because he'd opened the door of the room behind her.

He wrenched his mouth from hers. "Hang on to me, baby."

She didn't argue, and she didn't speak. What she did was wrap her arms around his neck, and when he lifted her, she wrapped her legs around him, too.

The sensation of being carried made her head swim. She thought the wine was making her dizzy, but no, he'd brought her into his room, kicked the door closed, and laid her on his bed. He came down on top of her and everything inside her shivered with arousal, with the need to have this man on her and in her.

"*So long*. I've wanted you for so *fucking* long." Greg fastened his mouth on hers again and plundered.

Rebecca returned his kiss, her lips and tongue frantic to taste all, to know all. His fingers combed her hair then held tight, and she mimicked the gesture, holding tight.

He lifted his mouth from hers. "You're so damn beautiful, Becca. *My* Becca."

Rebecca couldn't explain the desperation that overwhelmed her as she looked in his eyes. Urgency filled her, the urgency to have him in her now. *Now, before he changes his mind.* "Don't talk. Just take me. Do it. Do it now! Oh, please, Greg!"

"Shhh, baby. Don't beg. Don't worry, we're going to take care of each other."

In a blur of movement fueled by greed, colored by a passion too long denied, and tinted with the alcohol so recently consumed, Rebecca pulled and tugged at Greg's clothing as he pulled and tugged at hers. They were naked in mere seconds.

Hurry, hurry, hurry. She gasped at the first kiss of his flesh on hers. Hot and heavenly, he settled on her, and made a place for himself between her legs. She wrapped around him, a vise to clamp him where she wanted him the most. She stretched up and locked her lips to his, inviting his cock to plunge by rolling her hips against him, rubbing her wet pussy on his hot cock and thrusting her tongue in his mouth.

Greg slid against her then yanked himself back in a sudden, jerky movement.

"No! Please, Greg, don't tease me! Don't leave me like this!"

"Not teasing, not leaving. Condom."

Rebecca didn't let herself consider that she maybe should have thought of that, nor did she wonder if her subconscious had wanted him naked inside her—naked and giving her his seed.

She whimpered as he fiddled with his pants, swore, and then seemed to recall they were in his bedroom. He yanked the bedside table drawer open, and his "*yes*!" told her he'd found some there.

Then he was back, and the feel of his latex-covered cock against her wet pussy nearly made her come right then and there.

Who knew the sensation of a man's cock could be so different from my own touch?

The shivers, the thrill, the soaring of arousal gripped Rebecca in a fevered clasp. She rolled her hips again and caught his hot hard cock between her pussy lips, and began to pump so that she was rubbing up and down his hot shaft. The head of his cock brushed her clit and she whimpered, and cried out. "Please, Greg. Fuck me!"

"*Becca!*" Greg covered her mouth with his and then pulled back, just enough to center his cock at the opening of her pussy.

He plunged, pushing into her in one forceful thrust. His mouth devoured her scream as the pain, sharp but not unexpected, cut through the haze of arousal and alcohol.

Greg pulled his mouth from hers. "Jesus, *Jesus*!" He went totally still, his body rigid as if frozen in time. "*Becca*...baby. Damn it, you should have told me."

"It doesn't matter. I want this. I want you. I've always wanted only you. Don't stop. Oh, please, don't stop."

"Hush, now."

She felt him relax. He placed tiny kisses on her face—she felt her tears under his lips—and then he nuzzled her neck.

"If I had known you were a virgin I would have made that moment better for you, baby."

"It couldn't be better. It's you. That's all I've ever needed. You."

"Then you'll have me, sweetheart. But we'll do it my way, now." Greg gave her the kind of look she'd longed for from him—aroused, tender, *loving*. She fell into his aqua gaze and knew she could never regret ceding her innocence or the control of her body to this man.

He kissed her, softly, thoroughly, until the fires that the sting of losing her virginity had doused were lit once more. When he moved in her, slowly at first, she felt the thrill of him, the joy of union, and moved with him.

She erupted in orgasm, the best she'd ever had. Rebecca sobbed his name as wave after wave of ecstasy washed over and through her. Greg held her, and cooed to her, and made her feel as if she was the only woman on the face of the earth. When he stiffened and followed her over the edge Rebecca tasted for the first time in her life the singular satisfaction of having pleasured the man she loved.

He left her only briefly, returning with a warm, wet cloth. Though she blushed as he cared for her, he didn't notice. He returned again and lifted her, pulled the blankets down, and climbed onto the bed beside her. He covered them both and drew her close. Lying in his arms once more, she snuggled in, and kissed his chin, and his chest, and let her hands play over him.

Rebecca dozed lightly, satiation cradling her, and when Greg turned to her in the night, she let him set the pace. She fell in love with the way he loved her, gentle yet oh, so hungrily.

She slept again, and opened her eyes as the bedroom door closed quietly. Morning light filtered through the curtain-covered window. Alone in the bed, she grinned, and figured he'd gone downstairs to get them some coffee.

More happy than she knew she could be, more in love than she'd believed possible, Rebecca settled down and waited for Greg—for her *lover*—to return.

* * * *

I never should have touched her.

Greg Benedict turned at the bedroom door and looked back toward the bed. The smile that stretched his lips came without his consent. His cousin, Rebecca Jessop, when she slept, slept deep, but not necessarily pretty.

Cousin is a misnomer, because she isn't my cousin, really. Of course that wasn't the only thought he'd just had that wasn't quite true. Rebecca was the most beautiful woman he'd ever known.

He closed his eyes in response to the swift kick from his conscience. He really never should have given in to temptation.

If he'd known before he brought Rebecca to his bed that she'd been a virgin, would he have stopped himself?

Damn me to hell and back, no. Greg had been just emotional enough, just needy enough, and just tipsy enough that he'd stepped away from his better conscience and taken what he'd craved for so very long.

Craved, and needed, but had been afraid to claim, because at heart he was a coward. How could he expect the only woman he'd ever loved to accept him as he was? Not only flawed, though he was that. But *different*.

Hell, who would have guessed she could have still been a virgin? She was twenty-three years old, for God's sake. She'd been away to college. At college and since, she'd hung out with that artsy crowd of hers, too.

Everyone knew those characters were…what? Loose? Free? *Jesus, Benedict, when the hell did you become a self-righteous prig?*

Greg quietly left the room, pulling the door of the bedroom closed as he did. He stopped and listened, but could hear no one up and moving about in the Big House on this early morning after Christmas. He wouldn't be surprised if everyone slept very late today. That had been one hell of a party yesterday. He smiled when he recalled how happy his Grandma Kate had seemed. It was good to see her smiling and happy again. Losing both of her husbands—his grandfathers—within months of each other three years ago had been very hard on her.

As he crept down the stairs, he turned his head and let his gaze linger for one more moment on the closed door to the room he'd just left. Making love to Rebecca Jessop had been everything, and more, that he'd dreamt it would be. But he really never should have touched her. Not without telling her everything about himself—and not so soon on the heels of his massive fight with Daniel.

Daniel. His heart squeezed tight when he thought of the man. They'd been together nearly a year, and had been getting along fine, for the most part. They'd been happy, for the most part.

And that was the problem, it was all only *for the most part*. Dr. Daniel Montrose had some pretty dominant genes in him—as well as a propensity for always wanting to have his way. Greg had grown up in a large, extended family, and he knew the best relationships—the happiest and most enduring relationships—were ones where all parties concerned were equal partners, and where no one got their way all of the time.

He had some serious thinking to do—about Daniel, and his future, and hell, about Rebecca, too. And it would best that he do that thinking before he make any more life-altering moves.

If he wanted Rebecca, then he really needed to end things with Daniel. Not that he was averse to having a true ménage, himself. But he had no idea what Rebecca would think of that, once she got over the shock of his bisexuality.

Of course, the crux of the matter was that Daniel would *never* share, period.

I've put myself in a hell of a mess, and all before breakfast. His stomach growled. Greg grinned as he hit the bottom of the stairs and hit upon a great idea. He'd head on over to his Aunt Samantha's. He was as at home there as he was here—or over at the ranch, with his Aunt Bernice and Uncles Caleb and Jon. He frowned when he thought about the news the family had served up when he'd arrived on Christmas Eve after spending several months in Indonesia.

Benedict International was opening an office in New York City. Most of his immediate family would be moving there, likely sometime in the next few months. The Town Trust had hired a manager to head up the office of Benedict Oil and Minerals in Houston. His father, Carson, would commute a couple of times a month to oversee that manager until Josh and Alex were ready to take over for him in 2006.

Everything was changing, but then home did that to you if you weren't paying close enough attention—or if you stayed away too long.

My God, the geeks are going to be running one of the companies in just over a year! He didn't waste any time thinking about the very real fact that Josh and Alex were two and four years younger than he, respectively.

Those particular cousins who were *actual* cousins had grown up always knowing what they wanted to do—and, he'd bet, they'd be damn good at it, too. For his own part, Greg wanted nothing to do with the corporate life. He was grateful, actually, that between the geeks and his triplet older brothers, the corporate arm of the family would be well taken care of.

It didn't take Greg more than a few minutes to make his way over to the New House. If he knew his Aunt Samantha, she'd be in the kitchen with his Uncle Taylor and maybe his Uncle Charles, cooking up a huge breakfast. Uncle Preston would have set the table and by now be sitting in the kitchen, reading a law journal of some kind, ready to fetch and carry as needed as his contribution to the cooking process.

Those were images ingrained in his brain from all his growing-up years, part of the myriad memories he took around the world with him.

Greg bet he'd be able to tell, as soon as he opened the door and walked in, what would be on the breakfast menu this morning.

He grinned in anticipation. But when he opened the door and stepped inside, he could smell nothing cooking at all. Nor could he see anyone, but he could hear…*something*. Voices, but not the voices of the family.

Kind of odd to have the television on so early in the morning.

He headed down the hall toward the family room, where he knew the television was located. His Aunt Samantha stepped into the hall from her office.

"Sweetheart, I just tried to call you at the Big House."

He'd never seen her look so somber. She said nothing more, just held her hand out to him and then led the way back into the den.

When he entered the room, his attention was captured by the sight of so many of the Kendalls gathered in front of the television screen.

His heart dropped as the images being shown and the words of the announcer bombarded him. It took him long seconds to understand exactly *what* he was looking at.

"Sit down, boy. Thank God you decided to come home for Christmas. But you've some good friends there, I reckon." Uncle Preston eased him into a chair. Greg's attention was riveted to the breaking news story.

"Yes. I…I know a lot of people there." He stopped short, of course, because no one in the family knew his secrets. He felt a searing stare brush him and turned to meet Jordan Kendall's gaze. Well, Jordan knew one secret he had—it was something they shared.

He hadn't even told Jordan about Daniel. The expression on that man's face now told him he knew, anyway.

The words of the newscaster didn't seem connected as his subconscious fought with reality. "*Subduction earthquake…9.1 on the Richter scale…the third largest earthquake ever recorded on a seismograph…*"

The pictures he was seeing were of something *more* than just an earthquake. The word at the top corner of the screen finally registered.

Tsunami.

He recognized the map being shown, of course. Indonesia laid spread out before him, so much of that fascinating, complicated land familiar to him now. The red patches—areas of the worst devastation—were farther away from Jakarta, the area he'd spent the better part of his time in. They illustrated the worst hit areas with a stark, searing red. Most of the red had been painted along the northern end of the island of Sumatra.

Greg mentally pulled himself out of his shock. He reached into his pocket and pulled out his cell phone.

Shit. When did I turn the fucker off? He pressed the button, impatient for the device to power up. Finally it did, and he quickly dialed the number for the clinic. He got a busy signal, which told him that either the clinic itself was inundated—*well, duh, of course it would be*—or that phone service to the city was out. That was more than possible, as well.

The infrastructure there wasn't of the same quality as here in the States.

He listened to the announcer on ANN—the All News Network—as the sober-faced man spoke of the rescue efforts already underway and the recovery plans that were even now being drawn. Tens of thousands of people were missing, and feared dead.

Tens of thousands!

Greg quickly calculated the time line of the disaster. Disaster had hit at around eight thirty in the morning, Jakarta time. He did the math quickly—seven thirty in the evening last night.

Hours ago. There was talk on the screen of refugee camps already being set up. *That's probably where Daniel is, treating patients as they arrive.* As a member of the relief group, Médecins Sans Frontières—Doctors Without Borders—he was in the country to offer his talents and services to the people who needed them most.

Dr. Daniel Montrose was the second son of the Earl of Warrington, and had no need to make a living. It was one of the things they had in common, and one of their bones of contention.

Greg's family had always treated him as if they knew he was just searching for his place. Daniel accused him—often—of being a spoiled, trust fund baby.

Some truth in that, I suppose, as I haven't settled down to a single goal.

"Most of your friends are in Jakarta?" Jordan asked.

"Yes. Although I've been to Sumatra a few times. I know some…relief workers there. I've lent a hand now and then."

Because Daniel insisted he needed to help. True, he was no doctor—hell, he was not much of anything, truth be told. But he could drive a truck filled with supplies and he had a back strong enough to move things. He'd split his time between Daniel's group and another well known, international charity—*Maria's Quest*—that could also almost always be found in the most depressed and needy areas in the world.

He still held his phone in his hand when he felt the vibration. He'd turned the ringer off when he'd left Jakarta, and hadn't bothered to turn it back on again. He looked down at the display. He had a message in voice mail.

The number was unfamiliar but the country and area code were not.

Greg retrieved the message.

"Greg." There was a pause, and he heard the sound of a sigh. "Christ, I made a mess of things, didn't I?" Daniel's voice sounded tired. He always overworked himself when he was stressed. "I wanted to call and say Happy Christmas, but I was in surgery most of yesterday. I miss you. I'm sorry for…" He gave a sound of derision and Greg could picture him so clearly, could see him run his hand through his short, blond hair. "Bloody hell, I'm just sorry. Look, it's not even dawn yet, Boxing Day." Greg still didn't get that, why the British had an extra holiday named for a sport the day after Christmas. "I'm in Medan, they had a hell of a mess here on Christmas day so I came up to lend a hand. I should be leaving for home just around noon. I just want to check on my two patients, first. You can call the hospital here before that, or reach me at the clinic tonight. I need to hear your voice. I want us to work this out." Daniel recited the number he'd called from. "Take care, love." That last had been said quietly. Daniel wasn't very comfortable using terms of endearment, and never when someone else might hear him.

Greg didn't realize he'd sobbed out loud. Medan was a city on the northern end of Sumatra.

"Greg?"

"Sweetheart?"

Jordan and Samantha had spoken at the same time. He met Jordan's gaze, and then looked at his aunt.

He couldn't tell them, couldn't find all the words. "I…I have to go. I have to get back there." *Daniel.* He inhaled deeply and knew he was quaking, inside and out. "My…my friend. My best friend. He's there. I have to go."

There was too much to do for the numbness to set it. It took planning, and pull. It meant cutting short his time with family, but that didn't seem significant just right then. It meant a hasty, sloppy good-bye to Rebecca. He filed away the look of shock and hurt in her eyes, to think about later.

Later, after hours of travel and paying thousands of dollars in bribes to get to where no one was supposed to be able to go. Later, when the numbness, the horrible, empty numbness finally set in.

Later, when he stood on muddy ground where Daniel's Medan clinic should have been and looked out over devastation so complete, no one could possibly have survived it.

Chapter 2

March 2013

The damn dream never changed.

Rebecca Jessop tossed aside the blankets and set her feet on the floor. The chill of the burnished wood helped pull her all the way out of sleep. With the fingers of her left hand she combed back her long, black hair so she could at least see. With her right hand she scooped up her cell phone and pressed a key. She guessed it was too damned early even before her eyes focused on the illuminated, digital time display. *3:15 a.m.*

Rebecca knew from experience she'd never get back to sleep—not for a while, at least.

Not for the first time, she wished she smoked, or drank, or *something*. Not for the first time she wished she could tumble all the way into an old cliché of the *artiste*, become a creature given to excesses, driven by her great, raw, overpowering talent, pushed to the very edge of sanity…

Yeah, right. She'd actually met some artists who fit that old, worn-out stereotype. She thanked—and occasionally blamed—the grounding she'd received as one of five children growing up in the small, well-insulated, and disciplined town of Lusty, Texas. Because of the way she was raised, and despite earning her living with canvas and pigments and brush, she was actually a fairly normal woman.

For all that her family tended toward the politically correct term of living "alternative lifestyles," and that every last one of them had more money than they could ever spend in *two* lifetimes, the people of Lusty were conservative, ordinary, and really just plain folk.

She could recite the precepts she and all her cousins, and near-cousins, had been raised on—probably even in her sleep. *You don't live rich, you don't think yourself better than others, and you sure as hell don't act like a trust fund baby with a sense of entitlement.*

Or an over-arrogant *artiste* with one.

"I must be desperate to get those damn dream images out of my head, if I'm reaching back that far." The sound of her voice echoed in the darkened bedroom. Rebecca reached over, turned on the battery-operated bedside lamp, and reached with her hands for her robe and her feet for her slippers.

Hot tea. A nice pot of hot tea and a cookie were what she needed. Darjeeling, as it was one of her favorites. If exhaustion didn't return so she could go back to sleep, she'd pull out her sketch pad and make her time out of bed productive.

She stood and took one step away from the bed and started to put on her robe. A flash in the full-length mirror on the wall caught her attention and she froze, transfixed by the image of the tattoo that stared back at her, an image that she still wasn't quite used to seeing.

The vines, graceful and fluid, in charcoal black, looked as if they'd been gathered and sculpted to grow into a shape, the shape of an arrow shaft. Beginning on her left hip bone, the shaft angled down and to the right, until the vines gave way to an arrowhead, intricately drawn of delicate flowers in shades of blue with tiny pin-points of red, the details so meticulous, that Rebecca—an accomplished and sought-after artist in her own right—felt awe whenever she looked at it.

The arrow pointed *directly* at her pussy.

"Why bluebells?" Seth Carter, tattoo artist extraordinaire, had asked as he drew the sketch that he would then re-draw on her skin.

"I like them." Her answer had been true, but not all.

Greg Benedict had once told her not to "bat her pretty little bluebell eyes at him." Of course that was before they'd had their one-night stand, for which he'd had the nerve to apologize for the very next day.

The dream unfolded in her mind again, just like always, only now she was awake as it happened.

It always started out so happy, so joyous. They'd made love, beautiful, wonderful love, and she'd been in seventh heaven, having finally given him the gift of her virginity. Then the dream turned dark, and hurtful.

"I never should have touched you, Becca. It was wrong. I'm sorry."

"What?"

"Look…I don't have time…I'm sorry, I have to go. We'll talk later."

Rebecca pulled herself out of the past, out of that horrible dream she kept having over and over and over again. Of course it hadn't ever been just a dream, but a real memory. And they'd never talked later. Greg had rushed off back to Indonesia, and she'd headed for all points—any points—west.

Rebecca focused her eyes in the mirror once more, on that tattoo she'd had inked on her body just weeks ago, specifically *for* Greg. She exhaled, and then put her robe on.

The truth of the matter was their not talking "after" had been her fault, not his. She'd shunned every attempt he'd made to communicate, until, finally, he'd given up trying.

She shook her head. She was older and wiser now, and when she'd left Seattle to come home, she'd made herself face some hard truths. Or rather, one specific hard truth.

She'd been a self-centered, immature child at twenty-three, and had handled the entire situation between her and Greg Benedict totally wrong.

While no woman would want the man she'd had a crush on all her life to apologize for finally making love with her—and taking her virginity—she was old enough now to understand that in all likelihood, and for whatever reason, she'd never gotten the whole story there.

At the time she'd thought he was apologizing because he regretted making love with her, as in, it had been a horrible experience. Now she figured that her immature, knee-jerk reaction likely had been completely off base.

Everything between Greg and her had gone from hell to heaven to hell again during about a thirty-hour period. Not coincidentally it had been a period of time when a part of the world had been devastated by a horrific natural disaster. When he'd left so hurriedly, she understood he was heading back to where he'd been living for the last several months—Indonesia.

She'd held a grudge for a lot of years, but the truth was if she'd loved him as much as she thought she did—or rather, if she'd been more mature and generous in that love—she would have admitted to herself that likely someone, or several someones who he cared about had been in peril. And although, as far as she knew, he'd never spoken about that time afterward, she believed that he'd lost someone he loved in that tsunami.

In the aftermath of that disaster, according to most in the family, Greg Benedict had become a changed man. Oh, he was still a self-described adventurer and still refused to settle down in one place. But now his wanderlust took him to places in need, and rather than challenging himself to climb higher, go faster, or reach farther, *now* he challenged himself to do more, to dig deeper, and to make a difference.

Since Rebecca had never been able to cure herself of this love she had for the man, there was only one thing left for her to do.

She needed to face him straight on, confront him about the feelings she had for him, and have that long overdue talk.

She did know he'd met someone several months before. A friend of a friend had run into them in New York, and Greg had introduced the friend of a friend to the man. His name was Cody Harper, he was a photographer and, like Greg, he was bisexual.

That may have complicated the situation, but it didn't really change things. Rebecca needed to see if something between them—hell, between all *three* of them—could be possible. She thought of her cousin Tracy Alvarez-Kendall, and how happy she was in her marriage to her two men, who were also married to each other. She'd asked her once if it was difficult, balancing time with her two husbands, with time for the two men to spend alone. She'd shrugged, and grinned, and finally had declared it was definitely worth it.

If they weren't interested in her, if there truly was no hope for her to have her heart's desire, then she needed to finally and at last let go, and move on with her life. All she had to do was finish gathering her nerve, find out where they were at the moment, and then make arrangements to get there.

When Rebecca had made the decision to stay here in the family's cabin several months ago, she'd moved herself into one of the two downstairs bedrooms. It had never occurred to her to use the master bedroom, and trekking upstairs whenever she wanted to rest didn't appeal to her, either. Not when she was all alone and there was nothing else to do in that very big bed but sleep. She much preferred the downstairs rooms, because of the set up of the cabin. The downstairs bedrooms were down a short hall from the great room. That sprawling space, by virtue of not only the large panoramic windows facing the southeast, but the fireplace tucked into the corner, had become her temporary studio. Standing by those windows, her easel awaited, the canvas upon it bearing, as yet, only the very early stages of a portrait.

She'd taken down the other piece she'd finished the day before. She'd wanted to leave that painting out, so she could look at it and hope on it, but in the end had been afraid it would serve as a jinx. She'd called it *Forever Lovers*, and she hoped the name wasn't a jinx, either. At the moment the painting was stowed carefully in her bedroom closet.

She'd never met Greg's lover, although she had looked him up online and knew what he looked like. But not having actually been face to face with him she hadn't felt comfortable creating a still life. So she hadn't painted a picture of the three of them together, exactly. She'd painted basic shapes, three nudes caught in the fluid and flowing throes of lovemaking, giving just a subtle smudge to represent motion. If one stared long enough, the faces became visible and, she thought, fairly recognizable.

It had been the first time she'd ever painted her deepest, most desperate wish.

She let her eyes scan the new portrait. Much safer territory, this one. And maybe by focusing on Grandma Kate, that woman's optimism and can-do attitude would somehow bolster her for the days or weeks ahead.

She turned away from the canvas and headed out to the kitchen. It took only a moment to light the two-burner propane stove used for light cooking and put the kettle of water on to heat. While she waited, she wandered over to the door, and looked out over the dark, Central Texas landscape.

It had never bothered her to spend time in remote locations. So when Detective Dwyer of the Seattle Police Department suggested, for safety's sake, that she take herself off to someplace remote, someplace outside of Seattle, that wasn't a problem for her. Unlike some of her acquaintances, she wasn't an avowed urbanite.

She was an avowed artist, and cherished her alone time. Rebecca shook her head. Alone time had been at a bit of a premium just lately. The last week or so had seen her driving into Lusty twice—once to attend her brothers Grant and Andrew's engagement party—she smiled when she thought about Chloe Rhodes becoming her sister.

She liked the woman, a lot.

Then, at that very same party, two of her cousins had gone into labor. So of course, she'd had to go back to town to visit the moms and the babies. Tracy's son, Cameron, reportedly didn't particularly like to sleep, much. Fortunately mom and both dads divided the baby care equally so that all three were able to get some rest. Julia's *three* babies on the other hand—sons Darien and William and daughter Madison—enjoyed sleeping a great deal.

Julia had confessed this was a good thing, and if they could keep it up for just another couple of days, their fathers could recover from the shock of the multiple births.

As far as Rebecca knew, it was the first time in the history of the families that a triplet birth had included a girl child.

Grandma Kate liked to talk about cycles. She often said that they were all connected, from the first of them to the last. Just lately, especially after the bizarre happenings in Seattle, Rebecca was beginning to believe her grandmother knew what she was talking about.

She took one last look out the window, satisfied that she was alone in her part of Texas. Her gaze flicked down just for a moment. One of the two rifles kept here at the cabin stood against the wall beside the front door, within easy reach.

The other was at the back door. On her bedside table, beside the light, her Walther PPK lay like an odd sort of knickknack.

All three were loaded, and ready to fire. If anyone else were at the house, Rebecca would have to find a different way to protect herself. But she was alone, had been well trained in how to handle and store weapons, and understood that while keeping a gun by the door or lying in plain sight next to her bed didn't fall under the heading "how to store weapons *safely*," it fit right in the box labeled "use in case of attack by deranged stalker."

The kettle whistled, and Rebecca left the door to go and make herself a pot of tea.

* * * *

Greg debated for one moment taking a hotel room for the night. There were certainly a lot of them near DFW International Airport. But at this hour—just past one thirty on a Wednesday morning—the drive to Lusty shouldn't take all that long. He'd dozed lightly on the flight and wasn't as tired as he might have been, otherwise.

In fact, he felt energized, and knew that feeling came from finally being on home turf, in control, and *doing* something.

The deciding factor whether to get a room or push on, of course, was Cody. He thought his lover had suffered through quite enough of strangers and crowds for a while.

He kept saying he was fine, but Greg, quite frankly, didn't believe him.

"You didn't sleep on the plane, love," he said now, looking over at the man sitting in the passenger seat beside him.

The blond hair that hung close to Cody's shoulders seemed to lack its usual luster. Exhaustion had replaced intelligence as the dominant feature in his brown eyes. "I couldn't sleep with all those people…" He let the sentence drop. Greg reached over and squeezed his hand—and sighed in relief when Cody turned his hand over and accepted Greg's touch.

"You'll like the cabin," Greg said then. "We're surrounded by Benedict land there, and the nearest neighbor is miles away. The only inconvenience is that for the last twelve miles of the route, we have to travel over what's little more than a dirt path, so it'll be a bit rough."

"Ah, so that's why you rented this kick-ass Jeep," Cody said.

Crap. There were a lot of things about himself he hadn't told Cody. They'd known each other for almost exactly two years—and had been lovers for just over six months. Greg had moved slower in this relationship than Cody had wanted to, and he still tended to hold things close to the vest.

That was a habit he'd developed not long after college—not long after meeting Daniel—and still hadn't lost.

Now, he said, "Actually, this is my Jeep. I had it stored in Dallas, and then brought to the airport for us."

"Oh, yeah?" Cody looked around the vehicle as if seeing it for the first time. "Naw, can't be yours. It's too clean inside."

Greg laughed, delighted and relieved at that glimpse of the Cody he knew and loved. He just prayed that the damage the man had suffered in the last month—both physical and psychological—could heal here, in central Texas.

"You forget I had it stored and attended." Then he tilted his head and shot him a sly look. "It's amazing what you can have others do for you, if you have the means to pay for it."

Cody exhaled, and relaxed in his seat. "I grew up going to the Hamptons every summer," he said. "It's okay. I think neither of us mentioned to the other that we come from money for roughly the same reason."

"Because we're both paranoid, closemouthed jerks?" Greg asked.

"You're not paranoid," Cody said quickly. "It's foolish to let on how wealthy you are when you travel to untamed and foreign lands. And pretty hard to be open about who and what you are on the inside when those around you will judge you saint or sinner by their own whim."

Greg didn't miss his lover's backhanded barb. "Then I *am* a jerk, because my family sure as hell would never have judged me. Not my mother and certainly not either of my two fathers."

"*Two* fathers?"

Greg really had been a closemouthed jerk where Cody was concerned. He'd thought to hold some of himself back, and not only because he worried that Cody would deride his family as being *amoral philistines*. No, he'd thought that if he kept a chunk of who he was hidden, he wouldn't fall all the way in love, wouldn't open himself to the pain of losing that love, as he had with Daniel, or abusing that love, as he himself had done with Rebecca.

Great plan, asshole. He'd fallen in love, anyway. And he'd died a thousand deaths, anyway, waiting for word on Cody, on his whereabouts, on whether or not he could be found and then freed from his kidnappers before they killed him.

Rebecca. Damn it, he needed to tell Cody about Rebecca. He'd had enough of her evasions. As soon as he got his hands on her, he was going to give her a good shake—and then kiss her senseless.

He was going to love her so long and so well she would never turn her back on him again.

Things he and his lover had talked about in recent months gave Greg hope that he'd be able to count on Cody's help with that little thing.

First, though, it was time to go for a little more transparency. And since they had a long drive ahead of them, he thought here and now would be the perfect place, and time, to begin.

"Remember how you told me about your brother, Gene, up in San Francisco?"

"Which part?" Cody asked. "The part about how mom and dad disowned him? The part about how he founded a commune outside of 'Frisco? Or the part about him having a husband, *and* a wife?"

Greg grinned. Yep, Cody's acerbic wit was back, and with a vengeance. "The last part."

"You said it didn't bother you that my brother was in a happy—a *very* happy—monogamous ménage."

Acerbic wit, check. Defensive edge, check. Looked like his man was on his way to a full recovery. *Now if only we can do something about those damned nightmares.*

"It sure as hell doesn't bother me. In fact, I'll see you one brother and raise you an entire town."

He felt Cody looking at him. The man was so smart, sometimes it was scary. He'd bet at that very moment Cody was rifling through everything he knew about him, not just from the time they'd been together, but all the myriad bits and pieces he'd have learned in the beginning when he wanted to know more about Greg Benedict.

"You're shitting me. An entire *town*?"

"I'm not shitting you." The familiar words came to his tongue easily. "Let me tell you a story about an 1880s Chicago businessman, his new wife with expensive tastes, and his daughter, whom he sold into marriage to a man whose heart was as black as sin…"

For the first time in a long time, Greg let himself feel the pride and the adventure and the sense of history that was his heritage.

Cody kept silent all through the telling of the Benedict, Kendall, and Jessop family saga. He didn't interject smart-ass observations, nor did he fidget in his seat. That meant Greg had his attention, and he was letting his mind fully take in everything he was saying.

The telling ate up a lot of miles, and when it was done, Greg waited to see what his lover would say.

Cody took his time. "So your folks…they'd be okay with me? With *us*?"

"Yes." Greg exhaled heavily. "Yes, they would be." And with the wisdom of age, he understood—maybe for the very first time—that they all likely knew already what his sexual preferences were. That would explain why not even Grandma Kate or Aunt Samantha had ever chided him about taking a wife.

"So…why am I going to be the first lover you've ever brought…*almost*…home?"

Good question. "I guess the answer to that was that I was always the one who felt…I don't know, different, I guess. Even though I knew my cousin Jordan was also bisexual."

"I can see why you would be a man who felt at odds. Didn't you tell me you were the only one among your five brothers who didn't have a womb mate?"

Greg had forgotten he'd said that. "Yes, I am."

"Do you know what I think? I think the reason I'm the first to come home with you has nothing do with your sexual orientation, lover. I think it has everything to do with your deep fear of commitment."

Greg snorted. "You and Rebecca. Both delusional." He hadn't meant to let that slip. His only excuse was that he was in shock over Cody's insight.

"*Now* we're getting somewhere." Cody sat up straighter, rubbed his hands together, and nailed him with his patented smile. "Tell me about Rebecca."

Greg didn't know where to start. He explained that she was a cousin, but not really a cousin. That she was bratty, but not really bratty. And then, holy hell, the words just flowed. He talked about her bluebell eyes and her ability to see beauty in just about everything. He told him about her accomplishments as an artist, and his pride in her.

He talked about wanting her, and resisting her, until that one time, and he told him how he'd pretty much fucked everything up.

"You're more screwed up than I am, pal," Cody said. "But now I understand so much more than I did."

"What? What do you understand?"

"Not what, but who. *You.*" Cody sighed. "I wish my body would bounce back, for God's sake. I hate feeling weak and exhausted."

"You have to be patient and cut yourself some slack."

"I don't feel like being patient."

Greg felt something snap inside him. "You fucking damn near died from that infection because those bastards let you sit in one cold dank cell after another for six days with a Goddamn bullet in you. You just got out of the hospital three weeks ago, so you damn well better be patient!" Greg pulled in his exasperation as he stopped on the county road, right turn signal on, and edged toward the fencing. He inhaled deeply and exhaled the same way. Clearly, he hadn't dealt with all of his anger yet.

"Ah, Greg? There's no road here, babe. There's just a fence."

"Watch and be amazed."

Greg pulled down his sun visor to reveal what appeared to be a garage-door opener. When he pressed a button, the gate, which was barely discernible in the fence, swung open. He navigated his Jeep carefully over a track that was seen as much in the memory as it was by his eyes with the aid of the Jeep's headlights.

He took it easy as they drove over the somewhat bumpy and uneven pastureland. Greg could see the path, of course, and he could tell by the way Cody relaxed that he could see it, too. The clock on the dash read three twenty. He watched the odometer, and knew they weren't more than fifteen minutes out.

He was grateful that the Town Trust inspected this path every month. He thought that might have been done very recently as it seemed to him as if the path was more worn than usual. *Likely Robert would have seen to it once I called him to let him know I'd be coming.* March typically wasn't the time of year when family vied for time here at the cabin. Good thing, because he was looking forward to giving Cody and himself this break—for Cody to heal, and for him to figure out what the hell came next.

He pushed aside the whisper of thought that suggested holing up here had all the earmarks of "settling down." They weren't *settling down*, they were just taking an extended and very necessary time-out.

Memories from the last few weeks flashed through his mind. From the moment he'd heard that Cody and that dipshit reporter had been kidnapped just inside Syria until he'd gotten the call to wait on the Turkish side of the border crossing at Bab Al-Salameh for Cody's return, Greg Benedict had lived in near-paralyzing fear. He'd barely slept, hadn't eaten much, and prayed more than he had in all the years since losing Daniel.

"Fuck me. That is a *cabin*? It looks more like a freaking manor house."

Greg returned to the present and grinned. He parked his Jeep near the front of the building, not far from the porch. He'd never brought anyone here before, but he guessed the word "cabin" really didn't jive with the structure the families had built here.

"We'd call it a vacation lodge, but that sounds pretentious, and if there's one thing Benedicts, Kendalls, and Jessops are not, it's pretentious."

"Does it have a pool?"

Greg thought of the en suite bathroom off the master bedroom. The spa tub might qualify as a pool. But he knew what Cody meant, so he said, "No, not yet."

"I'm beat." Cody looked over at him. "Let's go inside. I want to fall face-first onto the first soft surface I find."

Greg knew Cody hated to admit to any weakness. *He must really feel like shit*. It had been a long day of travel for them, beginning early in the morning—yesterday morning—from Ankara.

Since he also balked at having Greg do anything for him, he said, "Sounds like a plan. I'm beat, too. Let's just grab our travel bags for now, and get the rest in the morning."

They'd taken two steps toward the house when the door burst open. Light spilled out the house, silhouetting a woman. The sound of a gun being readied to fire shouted into the night, and a voice he heard in his dreams said, "Hold it right there."

"Jesus, Becca. Give a man a heart attack, why don't you!"

"*Greg*?"

His brain had trouble responding because standing the way she was with the light behind her emphasized the fact that Rebecca Jessop was gloriously naked beneath her light robe.

"*That's* Rebecca?" Cody asked.

Greg gave the woman credit. She immediately disarmed the rifle and pointed the barrel toward the ground. The way she'd sometimes treated him these past several years, and all things considered, he thought she might rather just have shot him.

Then she tilted her head to one side. "You must be Cody."

How the hell does she know that?

"Yes, ma'am. And thank you for lowering that gun. They make me kind of nervous, especially lately." Then he looked at him, and Greg had the first sense, in a good long while, that maybe things might work out for him, after all. "Hey, there, lover? Can Rebecca count as the first soft surface?"

Chapter 3

This is not the way I imagined this scene would play out. But then what the hell do I know? I'm a painter, not a writer.

"Becca? Can we all go inside, please, sweetheart? We're exhausted." Greg flicked a quick look at Cody. "Seriously exhausted."

Rebecca realized three things at once. The first was that she was standing in the light in what could be considered a diaphanous gown. The second was that all her female parts covered by said gown were reacting with hormonal glee at the sight of both men. But the third realization was the one that galvanized her.

There was something seriously wrong with Cody.

"Yes, of course. I've just made a pot of hot tea…and of course, there's brandy in the house."

"You are an angel," Cody said. "I thought I recognized you."

She wanted to reach forward and help the man, but a lifetime of living in a town populated by super-Alpha macho men had her holding back, and instead leading the way inside.

"I've got the lower bedroom on the southeast side of the house. Why don't you two take the master, upstairs?"

"Would it bother you if we bunked across the hall from you, instead?" Greg asked.

Rebecca blinked and wondered if the request came because he wanted them to be close to her, or if it was to save Cody the stairs.

Does it matter?

"No, of course not." She looked at Cody. In the minimal light in the cabin—they subsisted on battery or oil lights at night—Cody looked pale and in distress. "I'll get the tea and brandy. There's a fire burning in the great room."

"Perfect."

Both men headed off toward the great room and the bedrooms beyond. Rebecca was happy to have something to focus on. Inside, she felt the quaking that only Greg Benedict had ever stirred in her. She couldn't think about that now. She'd serve them tea, and then likely—very soon after—they'd retire for what was left of the night. She'd have time to shore up her defenses—or plan her strategy, depending.

She reached for two extra mugs and couldn't help but notice her hands shaking. *This would never do.* Every other time, she'd been able to wear that cold-as-glass mantle around the man. She felt confident that she'd done a good job of convincing him she couldn't stand him. They'd still sniped at each other, as they'd always done when they came face-to-face from the time they were teens—or in her case, a preteen. She supposed to the rest of the family it had appeared the same as ever between them. But she knew different, and so had Greg.

So she reached for that cold, that armor. And discovered it no longer existed.

Well, hells bells.

She loaded a tray with teapot, mugs, and brandy, and carried them into the great room. The men were just coming back from the hall to the bedrooms.

"Hell of a place," Cody said.

Rebecca could see he was drawing on his last bit of strength, and determined to wear his own armor—humor.

"It's not much, but we manage."

Cody laughed and Greg looked…he looked grateful, and worried.

"Gentlemen, libations have arrived."

Two love seats faced each other, but angled toward the large built-in fireplace. Rebecca had been sitting on one, nursing her tea, when she'd heard the sound of tires on the stones and small rocks outside. She'd been thinking about Seattle, and the fear that had chased her from there, and had simply reacted. She'd flown to the door, grabbed the gun, determined to get into the face of her fear, come hell or high water.

The men clearly saw her cup positioned on the low table between the small sofas, and sat on the opposite one.

Rebecca set the tray down before them and then resumed her place. Needing something, she picked up her cup and cradled it in both hands.

Greg poured out, and put a fair dollop of the alcohol in Cody's cup. When he offered to pour some in her cup, she held it out to him.

The brandy couldn't hurt.

"You'll pardon me for saying, but y'all look as if you've been rode hard and put up wet."

"I love the Texas accent," Cody said. "Greg's isn't as pronounced, but yours, darlin', sounds like music."

"I don't have an accent, Mr. Harper. You do. And it's a Yankee one, at that." She grinned so that he knew she was teasing him.

"We've been on the go since early yesterday," Greg said. "And we had a longer than expected delay in London."

"You flew in from England?"

"No, we started in Ankara," Greg said.

Beside him, Cody had quietly sipped his beverage. Now, he carefully set it on the table.

"I think I'll go to bed now." He got to his feet, and when Greg moved to do the same, Cody put his hand on his shoulder. "No. You stay and finish your tea…and other things." He looked up at Rebecca then, and the smile he gave her touched her heart.

Clearly in pain, and beyond exhausted, the man seemed determined not to let either show. Rebecca was an artist and accustomed to seeing what others thought they'd masked.

"Thank you for the hospitality. I look forward to getting to know you better, tomorrow."

"Good night, Cody." Rebecca looked at Greg, and knew she'd raised her one eyebrow. She got the gesture from her mother and every once in a while, it emerged.

Greg seemed to get the message. He got up and easily slid his arms around his lover.

Cody sighed. Clearly grateful for the hug, he returned it, though Rebecca thought his stamina was damn near depleted. But it was Greg's expression that captivated her.

Greg Benedict clearly was in love with Cody Harper.

Cody ambled off toward the bedrooms and Greg remained standing, his attention focused. When he nodded, Rebecca guessed that Cody had entered their room. The soft sound of a door closing confirmed it.

Greg turned back to her and resumed his seat. "Thanks for not fussing over him."

"Maybe I'm not the fussing sort."

Greg snorted. "You're the most sensitive and caring member of the families, period. Well, except maybe for my grandmother."

The silence stretched between them. Silence, when she experienced it on her own, felt soothing. When sitting across such a small space from the only man she'd ever loved, a man who'd arrived on her doorstep with another lover, that silence felt oppressive.

She battled the need to fill it with chatter—or worse, by digging at him, as she usually did.

Then she looked up at the exact same moment he did, and their gazes locked. Her little imp, the one that usually got her into trouble, decided to wake up and begin shouting. *You were going to try, remember. What other signs do you need that this is the time? You didn't even have to traverse the globe to find him. Karma brought him—and Cody—right here to you. What the hell more do you need, dummy?*

She said, "What happened, Greg?"

"When, baby? Then, or now?"

She saw then what she'd missed because she'd been focused on Cody. Greg Benedict looked…world-weary. She might even say he looked shattered, but just thinking that hurt her heart. "Either. Both."

He nodded. "Both, yeah. Because I seem stuck in a weird kind of time loop, where some things feel like they keep repeating, and I think it's because I made a mess of things, before. All the way around."

"Maybe it's time for us to have that conversation we never had, before."

"I think maybe it is."

"So tell me."

* * * *

"We never found his body."

Greg slowly emerged from the corridors of the past he'd walked, needing more than anything to tell Rebecca everything. At some point during the telling, Rebecca must have gotten up from her spot across from him because she was beside him now, and their hands were clasped.

"I am so sorry. I wish—I *really* wish I had known what you were going through, then." She gave a half laugh, but Greg knew there was no humor in it. "I wish I'd been mature enough to look beyond my own selfish need and pain."

"No, baby. You weren't being selfish." Greg had spent a great deal of time thinking about things. He was older and wiser than he'd been then, so he knew what was what. "You were a young woman who'd just taken her first lover—but not any first lover, one she'd been in love with for a long time. You deserved a hell of a lot better treatment than what I gave you."

"I imagine that when you woke up you were attacked by guilt. Because you'd had a fight with Daniel, but you hadn't broken it off with him. In your mind, you would have considered that you'd been unfaithful to him."

"I *was* unfaithful to him." Greg sighed. "Daniel would never have welcomed a woman into our relationship. He didn't have a very nice opinion when I told him about the family, either." Greg sincerely hoped she didn't tug any harder on this particular thread. Only in the last couple of weeks had Greg begun to look back on his relationship with Daniel with new, fresh eyes.

There was a tendency to build up deceased loved ones, sometimes, as being almost super human. He realized that, to a certain extent, he'd done that with Doctor Daniel Montrose.

"Tell me about Cody. He's been hurt, hasn't he?"

"Fuck, yeah." Greg laid his head back against the love seat. Then a thought occurred to him. "How did you know about Cody? Did Robert tell you?"

He was looking at her so he saw her shock. "Robert knows about him?"

"Well…hell, I'm not even sure now if I mentioned his name, or not. I called Robert about a week ago, told him I wanted to come here, to the cabin. I told him that I was bringing a friend who needed to recuperate, and that since I knew he was familiar with gunshot wounds that I wanted to bring my friend by the clinic, too."

"Why that arrogant, bossy Dom!"

Greg raised one eyebrow. He didn't know that Rebecca knew her brother was a Dom. She must have taken his look for one of confusion about her outburst itself.

"I've been living here for a few months, which he very well knew when you called him. I bet he didn't tell you that."

"No, he didn't." Clearly, Robert had engineered things so that he and Rebecca would be together.

He owed the man one. And since Robbie had gone out on a limb with his sister—so fiery at times he swore she should have been a redhead—he decided to make his case for them all to stay right where they were.

"I'm glad you're here. Maybe Robert was being an arrogant, bossy Dom—though, baby, I have to tell you that's an oxymoron if ever I heard one."

Rebecca chuckled. "Well, he and David are the only ones I know, and David wouldn't have done this."

Greg kept his opinion as to whether David Jessop was a true Dom, or not, to himself.

"I'm glad you're here," he said again.

"Tell me about what happened to Cody."

"As soon as you tell me how you knew his name."

"I ran into Freddy Maxwell a while ago, back when I was living in Seattle."

"Ah." Freddy was a friend of Greg's from his college days, and someone Rebecca knew as well. He and Cody had run into him at the release party for Cody's book that his publisher had hosted for him in New York City a couple of months before.

It feels like that was a lifetime ago.

"Just after that book release party," Greg said, "Cody was made an offer he couldn't refuse."

"I think we all need to be aware, we humans, if we are presented with such a thing that we should run, not walk, away." Rebecca also relaxed back against the sofa.

"Amen." Greg decided to take a chance. He released her hand and put his left arm around her. Instead of stiffening against him, she laid her head on his shoulder. He took up her right hand again, with his right.

"The publisher who'd published Cody's book, *Aftermath*, wanted him on another project. Drummond Pierce, former talking head for the All News Network, had been signed to write a book on the Arab Spring slash summer slash fall."

"He'd been their chief foreign correspondent, hadn't he? Pierce? For a lot of years, if memory serves."

"Yeah, the fucktard."

"Oh oh."

"Oh, oh, indeed. Of course, Cody said yes. So we all headed off to Turkey. The best way to gain access into Syria is through Turkey. I have to tell you, I didn't like Pierce on first meet."

"What happened?"

"We had to cool our heels while the great journalist made arrangements. It was all hush-hush. He guarded his contacts as if they were the fucking crown jewels. It was Pierce's plan to meet with some of the rebel factions in Syria, the ones working to end the Assad régime. While there, I hooked up with some folks I know doing relief work in the region, a charity group I've worked with before."

"Which one? Doctors Without Borders or *Maria's Quest*?"

Greg smiled. "*Maria's Quest*. I've come to know quite a few folks working with both groups." He shrugged, not really wanting to toot his own horn. "I usually get in touch with both groups when I land somewhere I know they're active. No big deal, I just help when and where I can. Anyway, the day came when Pierce finally announced he had a meeting set up. A member of one of the factions was going to pick them up and drive them into Syria, to the super-secret meeting place. I had a shipment of medicine and supplies that also needed to find its way to a small town outside of Damascus. So we went our separate ways. Pierce assured Cody that they'd only be gone at the most, overnight. But the next night came, and they hadn't returned. Or the next. On the third day, Pierce showed up—looking no worse for wear, I might add—and claimed they'd been kidnapped. He'd escaped, but whatever group had taken him still had Cody."

"The bastard left Cody behind?"

"Yeah. He *claimed* he didn't know where Cody was, and there might be some truth to that, because Cody says after they were ambushed, and driven to the first place they were held, they were separated."

"You don't believe him, this Pierce character."

"No, I don't."

"What do you think happened?"

"I think Pierce didn't even give a single thought to Cody. Hell, maybe he even hoped he was dead."

Rebecca wrinkled her nose. "Why, for God's sake?"

Greg knew he was a lot more cynical than most of his family. He guessed that was a natural result of having lived so much of the last decade out in the wider, uglier world. "Would sure as hell put a premium on his book, wouldn't it?"

"That's just sick."

"Baby, it's the way a lot of people in this world think, and operate. For his part, Pierce didn't stick around and try to find Cody, either—which kind of lends credence to my theory. He was on the next fucking plane out, headed back to New York. I think he was hoping to put a rush on finishing his book, then getting that book out to soak up on the publicity following the death of an up-and-coming photojournalist."

"How did you get Cody back?"

Greg shrugged. He wasn't one to boast, ever, and this wasn't that, exactly—even if it did feel like it.

"I'm not a stranger to that part of the world. I've lent a hand, now and then, with more than one relief agency, as I said. As well, a couple of times when the rebels in that area were in need of medicines and other supplies and couldn't get any, I stepped in and got them some."

"So when they heard a friend of yours had been kidnapped, they put their ears to the ground?"

"More or less. Six days after he was captured, my contacts found him. Cody says there was firefight, and he didn't know what was happening at the time. They'd…" Greg needed to take a moment to steady his voice, to beat the tears that threatened.

Christ, I'm more exhausted than I thought.

"They'd moved Cody around a couple of times, and the last move, they'd shoved him into what he thinks was a basement cell. He'd been shot the day of the kidnapping, but they hadn't tended to his wound at all."

"Oh, my God. That's horrible!" Rebecca hugged him, her left arm slipping around his waist.

He wrapped both arms around her and held tight.

"Yeah. They brought him to me, and we rushed him to one of the clinics. The doctors got the bullet out, but he'd developed an infection. We nearly lost him."

"But you didn't. He's here, and alive. And well?"

"Getting there. He keeps saying he's fine, and he hasn't really talked much about what happened."

"I hear a huge 'but.'"

"You really are one of the most intuitive members of the family, you know? And yes, you heard a large 'but.' *But*, he doesn't sleep well, and he has nightmares."

"That's why you wanted to be here. You figure staying in this cabin, away from noise and civilization, can help him."

"This cabin, yes. And Lusty. And the family. And you. Especially, you."

He moved, then, so that he could look into her eyes. "Daniel was gay. He never would have been interested in or even considered a ménage. But Cody and I are both bisexual. Before this—before he was kidnapped—we'd discussed the possibility of finding a woman to be with. I hadn't told him about you yet, but in my mind and in my heart, you were the only woman I wanted. You still are. I know I'm asking a lot."

"Will you kiss me?"

Greg thought he understood her request. The last time, when he'd moved on her, when he kissed her, it had been like the Fourth of July and the millennium's New Year's celebration all rolled into one. He couldn't blame her for wondering if it would be like that again.

He laid his lips on hers, his touch tentative, gentle, because he wanted to cherish, he wanted to treasure. And he found himself yanked down into a vortex of wild, churning passion and heat.

Her flavor hit his system, awakening his heart, thickening his cock, and making his blood race and his body shake. She was sweetness and light and every good thing he'd ever known in the world.

She was also as deep into him, as awakened and turned on, as he.

It took every bit of strength he possessed to end their kiss. He eased back from her just a little and ran his thumb over her lips. "What do you say, Rebecca?"

She rested her forehead against his. "I've been in love with you—with the memory of you—forever. But I think I need to see. I need to know if I love the man you are now, or if I'm only still in love with a fantasy. And I need to know if I could come to love the man you love. I won't settle, Greg. I won't settle for anything but everything. I'd rather be alone than settle."

"All right, baby." Her words hurt, but really, hadn't he been afraid that she would just simply say no and walk away? She was being more generous than he deserved. As long as she was willing, they had a chance.

He would *not* let this chance elude him. "I think that the best way for us to do that is to stay here, together. Get to know each other, together. Don't you think?"

She lay against him for a long moment, and he wondered if maybe she'd fallen asleep. Then, she said, "Yes. We'll stay here and get to know each other, together."

Greg had been as conciliatory as he needed to be to win Rebecca's cooperation. But he already knew the truth and he finally allowed himself to acknowledge it.

Rebecca Jessop was *his*. Cody Harper was *his*. And by God, he'd do anything, *anything*, to keep them.

Chapter 4

Rebecca hadn't slept well, but that really was nothing new. She was used to being tired, used to being a restless soul.

The morning sun would eclipse the great room's windows soon, and she'd only begun to apply some color to her canvas.

Her gaze flicked to the side, a quick look to verify what she knew. The bedroom door across the hall from her own hadn't opened yet this morning. She hadn't really expected either of the men to be up very early anyway. Everything was fine with them. They were just getting the rest they needed. She would *not* worry about them.

Rebecca had heard a shout as she'd lain in bed, a plaintive kind of noise that had sounded muffled, yet frightened. She'd been up and standing at the door to Greg and Cody's room in a heartbeat. She hadn't gone in, but she had listened—shamelessly—with her ear gently pressed to the wood of the door.

"Shh, it's okay, babe. I'm here with you. You're safe. Wake up now, Cody."

"What…oh. Sorry. Goddamn it, Greg, I—"

"Enough of that. Next time maybe I'll wake you with my *nightmares. Go back to sleep, now, sweetheart. I've got you. I'm right here with you. I'm not going anywhere."*

"Don't let go of me."

"I won't."

Rebecca made a note to let Jake Kendall know the rooms here weren't as soundproof as they should be. She didn't feel guilty, having listened in. She'd only wanted to ensure that everything was all right with Cody.

She'd heard that some people who suffered from post-traumatic stress disorder could have violent nightmares, or react severely to sudden sounds, or crowds. How seriously was Cody suffering from the malady? Had he seen a psychologist? She thought maybe the answer to that last question was "no."

She wouldn't interfere, or try to push her opinion on him. Men were strange creatures, often refusing to admit to their weaknesses, or their failings.

Rebecca had plenty of both. She didn't see how, being human, she could have avoided collecting them.

She turned her attention back to the canvas, and the image she was attempting to create, from memory. And she thanked whatever fates there were that it was *this* subject that had captured her attention for the last few days, and not the other one she'd found herself painting a lot, lately—Greg. She was also very glad she'd hidden *Forever Lovers* in her closet.

She used a white pigment first, into which she blended just the barest hint of blue, because when she thought of this person, the color white came to mind—but not a vapid white. In western cultures, white signified purity, and oddly, that quality also belonged to her subject.

She imagined many would disagree, but then her definition of purity was the one that counted, as she was the artist.

The work caught her, and she let herself fall into it, let the subject on the canvas reveal herself to her, brush stroke by brush stroke. A person was made up of myriad moods and facets, angles and shades, the whole changing from time to time, and dependant—always so dependant—on the perception of the observer.

Her style—impressionism—lent itself, in her opinion, to many other styles. Rebecca had been classically trained, of course. She'd even spent a year in Europe, surrounded by some of the greatest art ever created.

But in the end she painted what she felt, and often surprised herself in the doing. Those were the moments she loved best, when she stepped back from her work, especially if the subject was a familiar one, and saw something new, some aspect she'd never noticed before.

She stepped back now and felt her mouth slide into a smile.

"Christ, she zones out just like you do."

Rebecca started, and then looked over to her left. Greg and Cody bracketed the entrance to the corridor leading to the bedrooms, both men leaning against the wall. She guessed they'd been there for a while, based on Greg's very accurate comment.

She'd recognized Cody's name the first time she'd heard it. She'd bought his book, *Aftermath*, and found his photographs stunning in their edginess and enlightening in their honesty.

Just then she noticed she'd lost the sun, and that her shoulders felt stiff.

"Good morning," she said. "I was about to check to see if y'all were alive, or not."

"Sure you were, right after you came out of your trance," Greg said. Then he nodded toward her canvas. "Can we look?"

She appreciated that he'd asked. She mostly didn't mind, depending. But she knew some artists who hated to have anyone look at their incomplete work.

"Sure. I've only been at this one a couple of days. There's not a lot filled in yet."

The two of them approached together. They ranged themselves behind her, one by each shoulder.

"Oh, now she's a sweetheart," Cody said. "Who is she?"

"Grandma Kate." Greg's tone had softened. Rebecca heard a wealth of love in his voice. Then, "Is she still in town?"

"She is, indeed." Rebecca grinned. "And she's been a very busy woman."

"I heard she was the one who set up the triplets with Maggie," Greg said. "I have to say, Maggie Morrison was an excellent choice for the three of them."

"*And* she brought your sister back together with her Navy SEALs," Rebecca said, and then, because he hadn't mentioned it at all the night before, she added, "Uncle Greg."

"Shit! Julia's had her baby? When?"

"I told you to keep that cell phone charged last week," Cody admonished.

"Once you were out of the hospital I didn't need to because I never left you. Come on, Becca, spill it. When did Jules have her baby? And is it a boy, or a girl?"

"She went into labor at Grant and Andrew's engagement party—at the same time that Tracy did, by the way."

Greg laughed. "Hell, you had to figure," Greg shook his head. Then to Cody he said, "Tracy is our cousin, but the two of them always called each other 'sister.' Okay, the rest of it? Boy or girl?"

"Both," Rebecca said. "You have two nephews, Darien and William, and a niece, Madison. Mother and babes are fine. The daddies, however, are not so fine. I think Dev and Drew had a minor nervous breakdown during delivery."

"My God. Triplets, and mixed, too!"

"It would seem multiple births run in your family," Cody said.

"They sure as hell do. In all of the families," Greg agreed. "I can imagine my brothers-in-law might have felt a bit overwhelmed if they came from small families."

"I think they're 'onlys,' both of them. Apparently they thought there were only going to be two babies. Julia suspected triplets, but kept that to herself."

"Still a troublemaker," Greg said.

Just then a sound, discordant and sudden, spilled into the silence. Greg's hand moved to his stomach and Rebecca laughed. "Someone's hungry. I'll cook breakfast—*this* time."

"I'm starving," Greg and Cody said at the same time. Then they looked at each other and grinned.

Rebecca knew she wouldn't get any more painting done for the day, anyway. But she *could* begin her newest, most important mission ever—getting to know both Greg and Cody.

"Follow me to the kitchen, please, and prepare to be amazed."

* * * *

Greg put a pot of coffee on to brew while Rebecca busied herself at the stove. Cody refused to be idle, and set about looking for the things he'd need to set the table.

"Cody, do you like hot sauce on your eggs?"

"No, sorry. Is that a strike against me? Because I have to tell you I have many other, *very* fine qualities to compensate for that sad lack."

When Rebecca turned to look at him, he wiggled his eyebrows, suggestively.

Greg watched the two people he loved interacting. The vibes felt right. *She has the prettiest smile.* He settled in to be an observer, at least for a few moments.

"I don't think it's a strike, but there are some in the families who would be scandalized. So perhaps for the time being, we should just keep that little thing to ourselves."

"So noted." He wandered out of the kitchen and was back moments later with a small, decorative vase that had been on a shelf in the great room. Made of fine china, the ornament held what appeared to be bluebells in various stages of bloom. Cody set the figurine at the center of the kitchen table. "There." He nodded and then sat down.

"Now that's a nice touch." Rebecca turned her attention back to the stove.

Greg brought the coffee to the table, and placed cream and sugar there, as well. Before long they were sitting down to a nicely prepared breakfast of eggs, sausage, and toast.

“Given more time, I could make biscuits and sausage gravy,” Rebecca said.

“I’ll make you some French toast tomorrow,” Cody said. “You haven’t had breakfast until I make you my signature French toast.”

Greg said, “I can testify, it is damn good.” Then he smiled. “Y’all both know I’m not much of a hand in the kitchen. I can grill steaks and chops, and given the right equipment I can smoke a ham or a brisket. But that’s about it.”

“You don’t need to feel inadequate, lover,” Cody said. “You have some other fine qualities, too.” And damned if he didn’t give Rebecca that same teasingly lascivious look as he had a few minutes ago.

“Hey! You have *many* fine qualities, and I only have *some*?”

“These are the best eggs I’ve had in a long time,” Cody said.

Rebecca laughed at their banter, and Greg sensed that she’d finally relaxed. He suspected that she’d been a little unnerved to look up from her work and realize they’d been watching her for a while.

“I may not be much of a cook, but I have been told that I have a first-class mind,” Greg said.

“That’s kind of hard to argue,” Rebecca said, “since you graduated from college at the age of twenty-two with *two* degrees.”

“You do seem to have a talent for logical thinking and problem solving,” Cody said.

“I do. For example, when I see something out of place, or that doesn’t make sense, I can logically deduce that there’s a problem.”

Cody frowned. Greg knew the man wasn’t following his line of reasoning, but knew him well enough to sense a trap. “I suppose that could be a logical assumption.”

“It’s never good to make assumptions,” Rebecca said. “Because you could always be missing a pertinent piece of the puzzle. Remember, logical premises can lead to an invalid conclusion.”

Bless her heart, she has no idea that she just gave me the perfect opening.

"You're absolutely right, baby. It is always best to ask." He sat back from his plate and picked up his coffee cup. He met her gaze and asked, "Would you care to tell me why you have loaded .22 caliber rifles at the front and back doors, and that pretty little Walther PPK that our Uncles Charles, Preston, and Taylor gave you when you turned Sweet Sixteen sitting there on your bedside table, within easy reach?"

Rebecca didn't blink, she just said, "Not particularly, no."

Greg could see he'd surprised Cody. Thankfully that man stepped up to the plate. "You have to know, Blue Eyes, that is *not* the way we play 'getting to know you' where I come from." Cody raised his hand. "Now, I know, I know, I'm one of those damn *Yankees* your momma probably warned you about. I can't help where I was born. But it seems to me that there are certain rules that would be universal when people are setting out to start something intimate between them." Cody stopped and met Greg's gaze before he looked back at Rebecca. "One of those rules is, you don't keep important secrets from the ones you're about to become involved with."

Greg noticed that Rebecca seemed inordinately fascinated by the food on her plate. For his part, Greg didn't miss that stare Cody had just given him. He, too, had kept a few things back, and Cody was letting him know, in his own way, that he didn't much appreciate it.

Greg waited a beat, and then said, "Rebecca Jean? Do I have to have a talk with Robert?"

That got her attention. She jerked her head up and met his gaze. He caught the slight blush, and knew the color to be a mixture of embarrassment and anger.

His Becca could be prickly and incredibly easy to piss off, when she set her mind to it.

"You just leave that damn bossy brother of mine out of this."

Greg sat back and simply looked at her. He could no more prevent his right eyebrow from going up than he could stop his next breath.

"Fine. Okay, fine. If you nosy parkers *must* know, I had a little trouble in Seattle. Detective Dwyer thought it would be a good idea for me to leave the city for a while, that's all. As a purely precautionary measure, I might add."

Greg kept his gaze on Rebecca. "Detective Dwyer. What department did you say he was in?"

"I didn't."

There was some comfort in learning that his woman hadn't changed overmuch during the last eight years. Greg sighed and said, "I can get the information I want another way, baby. The fact that you're doling it all out as if you were Ebenezer Scrooge is not giving me—is not giving *us*—any peace of mind, here. Why not just spit it out? It will only taste bad for a moment, I promise you."

Rebecca scrunched her nose at Greg. "You, sir, are a bully."

"He's not, sweet thing." Cody leaned forward. "Tell us, please. We can't take care of you properly if we don't have all the information."

"Look, yes, we are getting to know each other, but you don't have to take care of me."

"Of course we do," Cody said.

"It's what men do." Greg reached over and took one of her hands. Cody grasped the other. "Spill it."

Rebecca sighed. "All right. Detective Dwyer is a homicide cop. About four months ago, a man I barely knew—he was in charge of publicity for the gallery where my last showing was held—ended up being the victim of a fatal hit-and-run. An accident, by all accounts. But then I had the feeling that I was being watched, and followed, and things started to happen. My apartment was broken into, as was my studio. Fortunately, all my work had been moved to the art gallery. Then one day, someone tried to run *me* down on a busy street. Thank God for the kindness of strangers."

"I take it there's a connection?" Greg asked.

"The cops think so, now. I saw the stalker a couple of times—and I'd seen her once when I was with Brady—the man who died. It seemed to me she was lusting after him and shooting daggers at *me* at the time. I was able to give the cops a sketch, and they've been working at trying to identify her, and tracking her down, ever since."

"Her?"

"Yeah. He never told me her name, but Brady dated her—once. Apparently, she became fixated on him. Detective Dwyer said that he didn't think what she'd done matched the pattern of any other attacks on file, but he couldn't be sure. Anyway, he felt certain it would only be a matter of time before they found her. Coming here seemed like a good idea. And that is all I know, except for one thing."

"And that is?"

"I looked into that stalker-chick's eyes. That bitch is bat-shit crazy. And she scared the living hell out of me."

Chapter 5

Mel Richardson sat back in his chair, laced the fingers of his hands behind his head, and thought. He and his partner, Connor Talbot, had been hired a couple of months ago by the Lusty Town Trust to look into a crime committed some years before.

In the wake of a devastating tornado that left sisters Chloe and Carrie Rhodes orphans in 1998, the man appointed as executor of their parents' estate had made off with their entire inheritance.

The crime was about the lowest thing he'd ever heard of, and he'd heard of some shockers, both in his years working as a private investigator and previously, as a member of the San Antonio police department.

"The real problem, of course, is that fifteen-year span between then and now," Connor said.

Mel Richardson sat forward again and picked up his pen and ran it through his fingers, working the piece of plastic around each digit in a dexterity exercise. He and Connor had been combing the Internet looking for background information on Ralph Baxter, Donald Rhodes's former business partner and Neil Jackson, the public defender hired by the courts to protect the interests of the Rhodes sisters. They'd also tried to dig up information on the real estate business Donald Rhodes had operated with Baxter. They'd had better luck pinpointing the moment when the millions that Baxter had stolen went missing. The money had been transferred to a bank account in the Cayman Islands, and that was where the trail ended. The funds had been sent somewhere else, but no record seemed to exist for that second transaction.

That was the only clue they had that Neil Jackson had been murdered, and it was only a clue, not evidence.

"The Internet wasn't as prevalent then as now." Mel certainly understood the problem. "You know, we rely on it today for so damn much, we forget it hasn't been around all that long, really. And no one was interested in posting the kind of information we need, after the fact." Richardson scowled at the pen in his hand and set it down.

"Precisely. Today, so many businesses use the Internet that it's pretty easy to trace just about anything at all. And if you have decent hacking skills, very little remains hidden from if you want to find it out."

"After Baxter flew the coop, the business folded, of course." Mel shook his head. "You know, it really pisses me off that the cops didn't press for answers at the time."

Connor shrugged. "You would know more than I how police department resources can be stretched thin. This was really a case of theft and fraud—white-collar crimes. Once it was determined that in all likelihood Baxter had gone to ground voluntarily—that there was no foul play involved—then the 'missing persons' case would have been closed. With no one to make a lot of noise, there would have been no incentive for them to find the man."

Mel let his mind wander for a moment. There had to be a way to at least get a hint of where Baxter could have gone. Of course, with five million dollars at his disposal, he could have bought himself not only a new identity, but a new face. The guy could be married with a passel of kids, living in any one of the fifty United States or, hell, maybe over in Europe somewhere, and they wouldn't ever find him.

But Mel didn't think so. He had the feeling that Baxter didn't do what smart money would advise. The plan to steal the young orphans' inheritance had been a plan born out of desperation and opportunity. If indeed he had murdered Jackson on top of it all—Baxter could have ended up more than a little traumatized when all was said and done.

It was one thing to go after and find professional, lifelong criminals. It was quite another to trace a man who ended up in desperate straits as a result of bad decisions he'd made because of an addiction.

"Once we have a sense where he *could* be, I can start looking at Internet gaming sites," Connor said. "The guy is a gambler. That's what he is at his core. He'd have sought out the familiar, in person at first—I'm thinking race tracks, casinos, what have you. But I'm willing to bet—pardon the pun—that before long he'd be too nervous to be seen out and about more than now and then—and certainly, not at any illegal casinos. Unless, of course, he got that new face. But I really don't think he did that."

"Your thoughts echo my own," Mel said. He thought for a moment, about one thing that had struck him as odd. Then he said, "The person who reported him missing was Sofia Torres. She was the secretary who'd worked at Rhodes and Baxter for the two years before the death of Donald Rhodes. She was the one who, according to the police report, packed up the office and the files, and arranged for them to be stored when the bank foreclosed on the building—with Baxter still missing."

Connor sat back, his brow furrowed. "That's a little above and beyond, don't you think?" Connor asked. "I mean, she would have been left high and dry with no job. Baxter likely would have stiffed her for some wages owed, too. She also would have had the cops looking at her, at least initially. Who does something like that? And how'd she manage to do that? Did she pay for the file storage out of her own pocket? And if she did, for how long, and, more to the point, *why*?"

Mel said, "Huh. Good points, every one of them. Maybe a lover who expected to hear something, down the road? Do we have a whereabouts on her?"

"Not at the moment," Connor said, "But we will have."

He turned his attention back to his keyboard, and Mel knew it wouldn't take him long to come up with something. His gaze drifted to the clock.

They'd been at it since early this morning, just after 6:00 a.m. They'd had some background checks for another client to complete. Tomorrow, Mel would be meeting with a new potential client—a private clinic—to discuss their security needs.

The best decision he'd ever made was to hire Connor Talbot. Of course, they didn't really have an employer-employee relationship anymore. Mel had made the man a full partner in his business within weeks of hiring him.

They'd certainly clicked on a personal level, right from the start. Mel had been looking for someone to be a partner for some time.

His stomach growled, reminding him that it was approaching lunchtime. "You hungry?" Mel asked.

Connor shot him a glance and said, "I could eat." Then he stopped and turned to face him. "Especially if it was whatever the daily special happens to be, served with a particular smile."

"Emily Anne Bancroft." Mel sighed. "She hasn't worked there all that long. But she lives in Lusty, which to me indicates she isn't bothered by the way most of the folks there live their lives."

"I'm not, either." Connor looked like a man on edge, and as he sat forward, Mel realized that their thoughts had been coalescing on more than just case lines.

"I've been intrigued from the start—from the moment I realized my former comrades in arms shared more than a career. Since then, I've paid attention whenever I've been in Lusty. It's not just the women who are happy and contented there. It's the men."

"I've noticed that, too. Happy, contented, and relaxed. I've known some of the folks for a long time, and I have to be honest. I think the fact that I'm still single owes itself to two salient truths. The first, of course, was that I hadn't met a woman who 'lit me up' on the inside." Mel looked away from Connor for a moment, inhaled, and then met his gaze again. "And the second, was that I hadn't met anyone I could consider a partner."

"You used the past tense in both instances," Connor said.

"So I did."

Connor Talbot did something Mel hadn't seen very often. He smiled. "What do you say we take a drive to have some lunch—and talk along the way?"

Melvin Richardson exhaled and smiled. "That, my friend, sounds like a plan."

* * * *

Connor didn't think he'd ever get tired of making the drive to Lusty, Texas. From the first moment he set foot in this town he'd known it was different. Despite having received a punch in the face from Richard Benedict his first time in town when he hadn't been incognito—he *had* earned it, even if inadvertently—being in this town gave him a sense of peace.

If he were the fanciful sort and believed in reincarnation, he might believe he was coming home.

They found a parking spot about a block away from *Lusty Appetites*, in front of the *Lusty Glow Day Spa*. The big plate glass window displayed the reception area, with its shelves filled with sparkling jewelry and bottles of brightly colored nail polish and other female accessories. It was practically impossible to see much beyond the front door, but the movement of several people inside said that Ms. Rhodes's business was prospering.

"While we're here, we can touch base with Jake Kendall," Melvin said. "Let him know where we're at in our investigation."

"I feel like we should be further along." Connor's gaze took in his surroundings as they walked to *Lusty Appetites*. He didn't think he'd ever be able to go anywhere or do anything when he wasn't completely aware and on guard.

"So do I," Mel said. "It's frustrating as hell. But I think that if we can locate and then talk to Sofia Torres, we might find ourselves on the right path."

"God, I hope so." Connor reached the door to the restaurant first and opened it. The aromas that wafted out made his taste buds water and his stomach growl. He scanned the inside of the restaurant and immediately located Emily Anne. He couldn't help the grin that spread, and welcomed the sense of relief he felt.

Emily Anne is as much a source of that sense of peace and home as this town is.

Michelle Grant made her way quickly over to them. "Welcome back, gentlemen. If you follow me, I'll seat you. I hope you don't mind if I put you in Emily Anne's section." Her laughing eyes gave her away, and Connor winked at her.

"Much obliged, Michelle," Mel said.

Michelle's smile widened to match her eyes. Connor hadn't thought they'd been that obvious in their interest in pretty Emily Anne the couple of times they'd been here in the last few weeks. He supposed women had a sixth sense about those kinds of things.

Soon they were seated, with menus in hand. Emily Anne approached their table, and because he had been watching her, he saw the flash of emotions that swept her when she saw them. By the time she was reaching for their glasses to pour them some sweet tea, she seemed to have herself in hand.

"Good afternoon, gentlemen."

"Hello, Emily Anne. You're looking lovely today."

The color that kissed her cheeks made Connor think that not many men had complimented Emily Anne in her life.

"Um…thank you." For a moment she seemed to be at a loss for words. Then she looked down at her order pad and back up at them. "Thank you," she said again.

"You're welcome." Mel kept his voice low. "We both think you're a beautiful woman."

Emily Anne blushed. “Are y’all flirting with me?”

“Yes ma’am, we are.”

“We don’t mean to embarrass you, but we do mean for you to understand we’re—*both* of us—very attracted to you.” Connor kept his tone gentle, too.

“Oh!” Emily Anne’s mouth formed a perfect little *o* in astonishment, and Connor tried not to think what he’d love to do with her mouth shaped just that way.

He angled his body so she wouldn’t see the evidence of his arousal.

“Are you spoken for, Miss Emily Anne?” Melvin asked.

“N–No.” She tilted her head to one side. Connor caught the quick little glance down at their hands. “Are either of you?”

“No, ma’am.” Mel answered her first. “I was engaged once, to a woman who thought I should aim toward being the mayor of San Antonio, and thought starting out as a cop for the city was good strategic planning. When I decided to leave the force and go out on my own, she left me.”

“She couldn’t have loved you.”

Connor knew she hadn’t meant to say that. Mel gave her a smile that to him looked a little goofy. “You’re right, of course, but it took me a little while to understand that.”

When she turned her attention to Connor, he said, “I was married for about a year, just before I shipped out the first time.” He shrugged. “I was in the Army Rangers, which is a Special Forces group. That meant I couldn’t give anyone any details of where I was going, or when I’d be back—not even my wife. I came back early, to what sounds like a cliché. My wife had fallen in love with a coworker. She says she didn’t cheat on me, and I believe her. She asked for a divorce, and I gave it to her. I haven’t been involved in a serious relationship, since.”

“I guess we all have that one thing in common, then—being dumped.”

Connor could see that he wasn't the only one who wanted to pursue the topic further, but Emily Anne blinked, and shook her head. She clearly hadn't meant to say that, either. It seemed to Connor that she'd just realized she was at work. He really couldn't blame her. While they'd all been speaking very quietly, this was hardly the place for a serious, private conversation.

"I'm sorry. I don't mean to be taking up your time this way." She looked as if she was having a hard time reining in her emotions. Finally, she inhaled deeply and held her order pad and pen at the ready. "Do y'all know what you want for lunch?"

"We're both very glad to chat with you, Emily Anne, so no apology is needed. As to lunch, why don't you surprise us?" Melvin asked.

"That sounds like a fine idea," Connor said. He took Melvin's menu and handed it, with his own, to the startled waitress.

"Surprise you?"

Connor smiled. "That's right. Bring us whatever you think we should have for lunch."

"Y'all sure are in a funny mood today," Emily Anne said. "I've never had customers tell me to surprise them before."

"Don't worry, Emily Anne," Mel said. "You'll discover that we're not very hard to please."

Emily Anne looked from Mel to Connor. She closed her order pad and slipped it into her pocket. All teasing left her expression. "I used to say the same thing. But just lately, since coming here to live and work, I've been thinking that wasn't right. I think I am going to be hard to please from now on."

Mel nodded. "You're precious, Emily Anne Bancroft. You *should* have high standards. And you certainly deserve to have your expectations met."

"We'd like the privilege of trying to do just that," Connor said.

"Well, now. That's certainly something to think about, isn't it? If y'all will excuse me, I'll go see to your lunch."

Connor followed her with his gaze until she disappeared into the kitchen. A quick scan of the restaurant showed him no one had been paying attention, particularly, to their conversation.

A man takes the first step toward changing his life, there ought to be some sign that it happened.

He sat back and exhaled. Then he turned and looked at Melvin. “That woman is going to keep us on our toes—*if* she decides to try us on.”

Mel shrugged. He looked over at the door to the kitchen, still shivering a little from Emily Anne’s momentum as she’d entered. Then he looked back at Connor. “I wouldn’t have it any other way. Would you?”

Connor didn’t really even have to think about it. “No. I don’t want easy. I want it to be hard. And I want it to be right.”

Melvin Richardson sighed. “Me, too. I want it to be right. So maybe, after lunch, after we update Jake, we’ll go visit your friends. Do you think they could give us some pointers—answer some of our questions?”

Neither he nor Mel had ever shared a woman before. They really didn’t know what to expect. They were old enough and realistic enough to understand that just because they wanted to do something, didn’t necessarily mean that they’d be able to.

He thought of Dev Wakefield and Drew James, and of not only how crazy in love they were with their wife, Julia, but how happy, too, now that they’d welcomed their triplets into the world. Connor supposed he trusted only three people. One was sitting here at Lusty Appetites with him. The other two were in a cozy little Victorian on the other side of town.

“Yeah. I think they’ll tell us anything we want to know.” It would be a first step. One that he thought they were both, now, more than ready to take.

Chapter 6

Life was a funny business. It could take a man from terror to tranquility in the blink of an eye. All a man had to do was hang on tight to his sanity until the memory of the terror faded enough, and everything would be all right.

Cody stepped outside onto the porch of what Greg referred to as "the cabin." He stood and took in the slightly rolling land that seemed to go on forever, in every direction. There was no traffic, no city noises at all. No city noises equated to no other people, and that suited Cody just fine. Not a building could be seen, and nothing but nature filled his personal camera lens. He didn't find it difficult at all to imagine that this place was the only oasis of civilization left in the world.

That was a comforting thought just now.

The sky sparkled blue overhead, with white fluffy clouds looking as if they'd been spewed out by a bubble-blowing giant.

It was pleasant here, and he certainly couldn't complain about the amenities. He'd just toured the house, with the final stop being the master suite.

Good God Almighty, I have never seen such a big bed. And the shower, tub, and Jacuzzi are pretty damn prime, too.

Cody felt almost giddy with relief when the thought of sharing all those hedonistic spaces with Greg and Rebecca brought a twitch of interest from his cock. He'd been just about convinced, over this past month, that his dick had forgotten what it was best at.

He'd also been convinced, as Greg had arranged their travel and shepherded him here, that he was going crazy and that the next step was going to be the loony bin.

Maybe he wasn't going insane, after all. Maybe all he really did need was rest.

"You need to talk about what you experienced, Mr. Harper. Until you do, those flashbacks, nightmares and that sense of disorientation you're suffering from will only continue, and escalate."

Cody pushed away the memory of his one and only meeting with Doctor Headcase. *Fucking shrinks always think that you need to be "treated."* Cody didn't believe in shrinks, and he didn't necessarily buy that he was suffering from PTSD, either. He'd only been imprisoned for six days, for God's sake. But he did think that if he could just be away from *there*—from that part of the world and that hell—then the memory of what had happened to him would fade.

It wasn't a total bad experience, after all. Cody's being kidnapped, shot, and then damn near dying of an infection had served one very vital purpose.

It had given Greg Benedict a much-needed kick in the ass.

Up until his misadventure in Syria his lover had been content to keep him at arm's length, emotionally speaking. That had frustrated the hell out of Cody. He'd wanted nothing more than to find a way to breach that distance.

Be careful what you wish for, asshole. Cody ran a hand through his hair and nearly laughed out loud.

"How would you photograph that?" Rebecca's soft voice behind him damn near made him jump right out of his skin.

"I'm sorry. I didn't mean to startle you." She approached him, not cautiously, exactly, but maybe carefully.

Christ, do I have to analyze everybody's every move?

"No, I'm sorry. I'm a little jumpy."

"Who could blame you?" Rebecca crossed her arms in front of her chest and rubbed each elbow with the opposite hand. "It must have been hell."

"It was." Cody sighed. "But it's over, now. I survived, thank God—and thanks to Greg." He gave her his best smile. "Did you know that he's been to that area and helped some of those folks so much, when they heard I'd been taken, they mounted a full-scale operation to find me? Talk about the rewards of paying it forward!"

Rebecca tilted her head to one side. "Actually, I haven't known much about what Greg's been up to—at least not until last night."

"He does tend to hold everything either close to the vest, or way out to here." Cody extended his arm.

He turned his attention back to the view. There were clusters of trees here and there as the land gently sloped to the southeast. He'd surfed the web, just after he'd first met Greg, filled with curiosity about the area in Texas the man he loved was from. He knew they were on the very edges of the Texas Hill Country, and on a piece of the continent called the Edwards Plateau. He'd learned facts and figures, but nothing compared to this view.

The trees weren't the kind of trees he was used to, having grown up in New York State. The ground appeared rocky and uneven, covered in scrub grass in some places, and bare dirt in others, with bits of rock poking through.

Before he'd known Greg, before he'd looked it up, he'd been certain that *all* of Texas was dry, barren, and flat.

Rebecca's question echoed in his mind.

"I'd use filters to even out the light, maybe shoot it in sepia. This view doesn't need anything to enhance it, to make it special. It just is."

"Hmm." She seemed to be focusing with singular attention on what for her must have been a very familiar view.

He knew she wasn't humoring him. She, like him, was an artist working in a visual medium. He'd seen some of her work in New York, and in Paris.

Rebecca Jessop's paintings were highly sought after—but more, she was a damn good artist.

"I think I might use mostly muted colors. The trees, of course, would be blurs, and I'd put flecks of color on the ground, to hint at the wildflowers yet to come. We get a few, here and there." She met his gaze and grinned. “It’s a shame I’ve never felt compelled to paint this.”

Cody leaned against one of the porch posts, and studied the compelling view Rebecca represented.

“Now *you*…I think if I were to photograph *you*, I’d do what I rarely do, and pose you.”

“You would?” Rebecca leaned against the opposite post and gave him a sweet smile.

“I would. I think I’d have you kneeling on top of a round hay bale, in autumn, with the eastern sky before you, about an hour before sunset. Maybe I’d go for a bit of sun shining on you. I see you in cut-off denim cheek shorts, a tied-off gingham shirt, and a straw cowboy hat. Arms akimbo, you’d be looking off toward the north—or maybe at your lovers who were headed your way.”

“Really? You wouldn’t pose me as a Goth?”

“Hell, no. You’re brimming with life and color. Who the hell sees you as a Goth?”

“Well, pretty much everyone. I tend to wear black sometimes.”

“You’d shimmer, even in black.” Then he focused his gaze on the cabin. “I’ve been picturing you in that hot tub, upstairs wearing nothing at all but that sexy smile of yours.”

“Is that right?” Rebecca blushed, which told Cody that despite her being such a big deal in the art world, she likely didn’t have as much experience between the sheets as either he or Greg could boast. Not only was his cock beginning to perk up and notice that he was still alive and there was a sexy, very attractive woman nearby. His emotions began to stir as well. *Maybe I can take one step in that direction, test the waters, so to speak.*

“So tell me, Blue Eyes, do you kiss on the first date?”

“We haven’t been on a date,” she said.

“I beg to differ. We had late-night drinks, and breakfast this morning. By my reckoning, that’s two dates.” He reached over and caught her hand in his. When he tugged gently, she came to him.

Greg came to the open door. He leaned against the doorframe, folded his arms in front of his chest, and nodded.

"This is kind of a watershed moment for us, Blue Eyes. I think Greg is a hot kisser, and I bet you do, too. If this is going to work, there has to be that same kind of heat between the two of us."

Rebecca loped her arms around his neck. "I'm glad you realize that. I haven't kissed very many men, because quite frankly, not a one of them has come close to Greg." She looked over her shoulder, then, telling Cody that she'd felt Greg's presence. "I realize that might give you an even bigger head than normal, darlin'."

"As long as it's the one below the waist, darlin', you can only benefit from that." Greg grinned and for the first time in a good couple of weeks looked relaxed, lighthearted, and *interested.*

When Rebecca turned back to face him, she was smiling. He didn't waste a moment, but bent down and captured that smile with his lips.

Heat surged, a heady kind of heat that told Cody all systems were definitely a go. His arms tightened around her as he drew her up and drew her in. He drank her, using his tongue to slide against hers, to gather her essence, to indulge.

Her flavor aroused him, seduced him, and Cody knew he needed more. The wet slide and wonderful glide, the inhalation of scent and taste fed him an elixir he'd dreamt of, but never sipped.

Her nipples pebbled against his chest, her hips surged against his, and *God*, he could smell her arousal.

Slowly he tapered the kiss, needing to see passion in her eyes, needing that visual to confirm what his instincts were telling him—that here in his arms was the final part to himself that had been missing all his life.

As he raised his head, he felt Greg close in, stand between and beside them both. His lover stroked a hand down his back and he shivered. Rebecca's eyes drifted open and yes, passion had turned those already hypnotic orbs of hers a deep, shimmering, violet.

"Christ, you two just got me hot as hell." Greg ran a hand down Rebecca's head.

When she looked at him, he said, "One more thing we need to know, baby." He turned his head and met Cody's gaze.

Cody felt Greg's fingers fist in his hair, and his cock pulsed in response to his lover's primal grip.

Cody met him halfway, opened his mouth under Greg's, and dove. Always hot, always delicious, with the remnants of Rebecca's flavor on his tongue, Greg's essence evolved, and there, yes, *there*, was the holy grail of Cody's personal quest. That taste, that wonderful, nectar-of-the-gods taste filled him up, heart and mind and body and soul.

Cody's tongue danced with Greg's, following his partner's lead, and the heat between them neared the flash point.

Greg eased back, and Cody felt his heart turn over. For the first time he understood how deeply Greg had been worried about him, and how much he'd missed their intimacy.

Because they were standing, all of them so close, Cody felt Rebecca shiver and heard her gasp the same as Greg did. With Greg, he turned his attention on her. Eyes closed, Rebecca seemed to be struggling for breath.

"Why, darlin', did you just *come*?" Greg's tone, affectionate and maybe a little cajoling, brought a smile to Cody's face.

"I didn't mean to." She opened her eyes and met his gaze, and then Greg's. "It just sort of happened."

"Well that certainly answers all of our questions, doesn't it?" Greg said.

"It certainly answered all of mine," Cody said.

Rebecca blushed. "This is moving fast, and I need a chance to think."

"It was only a couple of kisses, Blue Eyes. *We* weren't moving that fast." Cody thought he might enjoy learning how to tease Rebecca Jessop.

"You're a cautious woman, Becca. You always have been." Greg leaned toward her and gave her a brief, though delicious-looking kiss. *Just like tossing a cherry bomb into my fire.*

"I can't help that."

Cody could practically see the nerves on her. "No one wants you to help that, Rebecca. Neither one of us wants you to change."

"Maybe what we need to do is head into town. You only would have had supplies on hand for one, not three. How about if we go in, get some things, and have lunch." Greg ran his hand over Rebecca's hair again so that she looked up at him. "We'll visit cousin Adam, and tell him all about the scary stalker chick."

"Damn it, Greg."

"Damn it, Rebecca. You know that we have to."

"Who's Adam?" Cody asked.

"Lusty's sheriff," Greg said.

"Yep, we're definitely stopping in to see the man." Then he reached over and lifted Rebecca's chin so that she could meet his gaze. "It's what men do, honey. They take care of their women. But most importantly…"

"It's what your men do," Greg finished for him. "So get used to it."

Cody was certain he saw not only resignation, but relief in Rebecca's eyes. Those were two emotions he could certainly identify with.

* * * *

Rebecca relaxed against the passenger seat, taking a moment to try and shore up her defenses and put everything that had just happened into perspective.

I had an orgasm watching Greg and Cody kiss.

She never would have guessed something like that could happen. And speaking of kissing, there was no doubt in Rebecca's mind right now that whatever it was Greg possessed that got to her, Cody had it in equal measure.

Rebecca realized she stood at the very precipice of achieving her heart's desire—and she felt a little afraid to take that next step.

"You really should have let Adam know, as soon as you came to town, that you had a problem," Greg said.

"I'm staying on family land in a cabin that's about as remote as it's possible to be. I figured that was good enough."

"Well we don't think so," Cody said. "Look, I know you think this is overkill, but you're not looking at the situation the same way we are."

"I'm glad you feel that way, sweetheart," Greg said. Rebecca knew he was addressing Cody in the backseat, because his gaze kept flicking up to the rearview mirror. "Because our second stop of the day will be the Lusty Clinic."

"Well, hell and damnation, Greg."

Rebecca turned around. "Hey, if it helps, you could just think of it as meeting some of my family."

Cody's mouth was turned up in a kind of snarky smile that Rebecca thought was cute as hell. He met her gaze. "Someone who works at the clinic is in your family?"

Rebecca laughed, "*Everyone* who works at the clinic is in my family." Then, because it just occurred to her, she said, "And no telling my big brother Robert about the crazy stalker chick."

"Well now, Blue Eyes, this seems to be one of those moments in life that calls for a bargain."

"It does, at that," Greg said. "So tell me, darlin', what's it worth to you? Our silence where Doctor Robert Jessop and your crazy stalker chick is concerned?"

"That's not a bargain! That's blackmail!"

"A rose by any other name…" Greg said.

From the backseat, Rebecca recognized the sound of smugness in Cody's laughter.

She sighed. Actually, she wasn't as peeved as she sounded. *It never hurts to hold on to a little bit of negotiating space.* Besides, this was a good way to introduce something she hadn't known how to broach. "Fine. I seem to be saying that to y'all a lot, but fine! If you don't tell Robert about the crazy stalker chick, then when we get back to the cabin I'll show you my tattoo."

"You have a tattoo?" Greg looked as shocked as he sounded. "When the hell did you get a tattoo, and do I have to break some guy into pieces because of it?"

"I've got your back, lover. Even if the dude's a six-foot, three-hundred-pound biker dude named Killer, I've got your back."

Rebecca wanted to laugh, but held on to her aplomb. "All right, let me see if I cover all your questions. Yes, a few weeks ago, and a lot of folks around here would prefer that you didn't because they like him. Besides, Seth is a total professional—a real artist. And he is very much in love, and happily married to a woman I consider a friend."

"Only a few weeks ago? What were you thinking of to put yourself in that kind of danger? Tattoo shops can be dangerous."

Rebecca shrugged. They'd just entered Lusty, and Greg pulled to the curb across from the sheriff's department. "Maybe tattoo shops can be dangerous in the part of the world you've been inhabiting, but I can tell you without a doubt that Seth Carter runs a very clean place over in Divine. Actually, Robert knows him, and was okay with it. As to what I was thinking of, it's not what, but whom."

"What do you mean, 'whom'?" Greg asked.

Rebecca reached for the door handle then looked over her shoulder. "Why, lover, when I got that tattoo, I was thinking of you."

Chapter 7

Rebecca wanted to crawl into the nearest hole in the ground and disappear.

Adam Kendall had just given her a very pissed-off look, and then laid down his pen and covered his face with his hands. She heard the scratching sound of his palms brushing over his morning's beard growth and wondered if that action—rubbing his hands over his face—was his way of counting to ten.

Finally he looked up and skewered her with another very potent glare.

"Do you know what I would like to do? I would like to travel back in time, to that moment in our families' history when Warren Jessop was detailing the setup of the Town Trust."

"Oh yeah? Why's that, Adam?" Matt Benedict, sitting over at his desk, looked and sounded like he was having entirely too much fun at the moment.

Rebecca wasn't sure she wanted to know the answer to his question.

"I'm glad you asked that, Matt. It would be so that I could beg him to add a few 'thou shalt nots' specifically aimed at the women of Lusty. As in, *thou shalt not grab the sword and the shield and prepare to slay the fucking dragons without the help of the men.*"

"Well, at least you don't mind us handling the swords and shields every once in a while." Rebecca said that as sweetly as she knew how, but it could very well be she was out of practice at being sweet because her cousin just scowled at her.

Cody snickered, Greg made a different kind of noise altogether, and Adam just shook his head.

It occurred to Rebecca, at the sound of Greg's choked-off laughter, that her words could have been taken another way. Heat suffused her face.

"All right. Now that I got that out of my system, I need a complete report from you, young lady. Why don't you tell me about the first time you saw that stalker chick?"

"*Crazy* stalker chick," Rebecca said.

"I stand corrected."

Rebecca sighed. "It was the opening night of my last show in Seattle, at the Eugenia Carstairs Gallery. That's a small and prestigious private gallery owned by the people behind that big hotel chain. They always showcase only the crème de la crème in the art world. I was tickled to be offered a show. In preparation for the event I worked with Brady Alexander, their private shows manager.

"Anyway, during the opening, we were standing in front of one of my paintings, you know, smiling, talking to guests, sipping champagne, the way you do at these things."

"No, I don't know, but I'll take your word for it," Adam said.

"You were working," Cody said. "It's all a part of the 'face' you put on for the art-buying public. Some folks are into your art, and some are just into being seen talking to artists. Waste of time, and generally you wish you were *anywhere* else, but it's the penance you pay for being an artist, and having talent."

"Exactly!" It was kind of nice to have someone there who got the whole art scene. "Anyway, I got this really uncomfortable feeling, like someone was staring daggers at me."

Remembering the moment now, she couldn't help but shiver. She had never seen such hatred on a person's face before.

Cody, who was sitting beside her, took her hand in his, and Greg, who'd been mostly pacing, came to stand by her other side and set his hand on her shoulder and squeezed. The feel of their touch steadied her.

"I finally looked around and I saw this woman—makeup and clothing *so* 1980s—and she was *staring* at me. You know that old saying, if looks could kill?"

Cody squeezed her hand and Greg inched just a bit closer.

"Yes," Adam said. "Then what happened?"

Rebecca thought his tone had softened, somewhat. "Anyway, Brady looked to see what had captured my attention. He got this scowl on his face, and headed toward her. Wow, when she looked up at him, her entire countenance changed."

"Like he was the man of her dreams?" Adam asked.

"Exactly. Until he reached her. I don't know what he said to her, but it was as if she simply deflated right before my eyes. Then he took her arm and walked her to the door." Rebecca inhaled, and worked to put that entire scene out of focus in her memory. She didn't like the combination of images, in light of what had happened since.

"Did you and Alexander get involved, then?" Adam asked.

Rebecca didn't miss the warning glance he sent Greg and Cody, and she didn't think they missed it, either.

She appreciated the gesture, but there was no need.

"He did ask me out—had a couple of times already, in fact. I finally had to tell him—" She paused and looked up at Greg. "I finally had to tell him there was someone else in my heart, and that I couldn't see him, or anyone."

Rebecca shrugged, and tried to ignore the heat in her face. She'd hoped to keep a little back from the man standing beside her. He could be as bossy and arrogant, sometimes, as her big brother. "After the show was over, I was already getting ready to come home when I heard Brady had been struck and killed in a hit-and-run accident. It really upset me, because he was a genuinely nice man. I went to his funeral, and there again I had a feeling I was being watched. I looked around, but saw no one. I had that feeling a few times after that. Then, my apartment was broken into. So was my studio—I rented a separate space for working in. Fortunately, since I was planning on moving home, I'd already crated up all my work and sent it to the gallery. They've offered to ship home what doesn't sell."

"Trashed your studio, did she?"

"Oh, yeah, though I didn't know at the time who it could have been, who would do such a thing. I called the police to report both incidents, of course."

"And they chalked it up to desperate people looking for drugs or money?"

"More or less. And then." Oh boy, just remembering how close she'd come to getting killed gave her shivers.

"That's it." Greg reached down, picked her up, and then sat in her chair with her on his lap. He wrapped his arms around her. "Go on, baby. Finish your story. I've got you."

I've got you. Those were the same words she'd heard him say to Cody through their bedroom door that first night. Somehow, she thought Greg Benedict was the kind of man who would always say, and mean, "I've got you."

"A few days before I was scheduled to leave town, I was on my way to have lunch with friends. We were to meet at a trendy restaurant—O'Malley's, where they serve great lobster. I looked both ways when I stepped off the sidewalk, of course. No one was coming. But a car pulled out from the curb, about a half a block up the street. I heard a squeal of tires and looked up. I recognized the woman behind the wheel from the gallery in a split second. I thought I was going to die, but at the last minute a man I didn't even know yanked me back, out of harm's way."

"*Jesus.*"

"*Fuck.*"

Greg and Cody had spoken at the same time. Adam looked over at Cody, concern on his face.

"You all right, there, Harper?"

Cody had gone a whiter shade of pale. Since he still had her hand, she also had his. She covered their hands with her other one and squeezed.

Cody said, "Me? I'm fine. I guess being a photographer, I'm better than most at picturing things." Then he raised her hands and kissed the back of one. "We have to find out who your Good Samaritan is and send him a thank-you gift."

Rebecca wanted to challenge Cody's assertion that he was all right. But she understood the male ego better, she bet, than the average woman did. So she said, "I believe the police have his name."

"I'm going to contact the Seattle police department and have a chat with the man working the case," Adam said.

Like I didn't know that one was coming. "His name is Detective Dwyer, and he's with the homicide department. After questioning me, and then looking into Brady's death, they've reconsidered and ruled it murder. When I left, they hadn't yet identified the woman, but I did leave him my cell number. I haven't heard from him for a while."

"Ah, maybe because you went and stayed at the cabin where the reception is zilch." Greg didn't sound very happy with her.

Finally, something positive she could say. "Actually, the Town Trust put in a new cell tower out at the airfield a month ago. The cabin is no longer cut off that way."

"Good." Greg nodded once. To Adam he said, "We'll be staying with Becca, of course. We'd appreciate it if you kept us up to date. Before we leave, Cody and I will give you our cell phone numbers."

"Will do. I'm glad you're home," Adam said then, "and not just because you brought Rebecca in here to tell me about her stalker chick."

"*Crazy* stalker chick. Why can't anyone get that straight?"

Adam just gave her a smile that made her want to slug him in the arm.

"You've been through the wringer yourselves," he said, addressing Greg and Cody. "I'm glad to see you're recovered from your ordeal."

When Cody looked confused, Adam said, "It was all over the national news, about your being kidnapped. In fact, just hours before ANN broke in with the news of your release, some New York publisher had issued a press release saying they were afraid you'd been killed."

Cody snorted, and Rebecca found she was kind of getting attached to that derisive sound of his. "What was it Twain said? 'The reports of my death are greatly exaggerated.'" Then Cody shrugged. "I can hardly blame my publisher. As I have tried to convince Greg, Drummond Pierce, my companion in misadventure, likely believed I *was* dead—as I believed the same, myself."

"But you're not. And I aim to do all I can to keep it that way. Which is why we're on our way, next, to the clinic."

"Speaking of that"—Rebecca sat forward, well, at least as much as Greg's possessive hold would allow—"there's no need to tell Robert about this little thing, is there, Adam?"

Behind her, Matthew snorted. "She calls being the target of a stalker chick a little thing."

"Crazy stalker chick!"

This time, Cody and Greg said the words with her.

"Sorry, Becca." Matt didn't sound sorry at all, damn his hide. He sounded vastly amused.

Adam clearly fought the urge to laugh. Then he looked at Cody, and Greg, before meeting her gaze. "There's no need for Robert to know about your crazy stalker chick problem, *now*."

His message was clear to her, and it did surprise her some that her feminist genes didn't rise up even a little in protest.

As far as Adam Kendall was concerned, she'd been spoken for by Greg and Cody. They were her men, and because they were, they, and not her brother, were now in charge of her safety.

* * * *

She was very good at being overlooked, and very good at getting what she wanted, eventually.

Naomi Lake had learned a long time ago that what she'd cursed about herself for her first fourteen years on this earth—being so plain as to almost melt right into a wall—came in very handy from time to time.

Now was one of those times. With a little help from some simple, dollar store props, she was as plain as plain could be.

That boyfriend-stealing whore had left town before Naomi could make an example of her. Did she think running away was going to save her?

Not fucking likely. Miss Fancy Pants Artist would soon learn that no one crossed Naomi Lake and lived to tell about it.

At least not for long.

Naomi had spent the last month staying in someone else's house, someone she'd never met but who she knew was out of town. This wasn't the first time she'd done such a thing, just the latest time. She'd left that morning, knowing she would never return. She'd given the place a thorough cleaning, of course, making sure everything was exactly as it had been when she arrived.

Cell phone cameras were very useful devices.

It was never hard to find a place to stay when one had to leave a current address. There were agencies all over, in every city, which specialized in either subletting temporarily unoccupied places, or maintaining empty places as a service to those who traveled. There were several agencies in this city that provide both services.

Naomi had posed as a prospective client at a couple of them, asking about the opportunity for the former, and while at the second agency, had managed to steal a list of the addresses of the latter—addresses where there would be no one in residence for a time.

It was easy to then make use of such a house, because inevitably the "caretaker" agency did very little other than test the locks to make sure they were engaged.

These agencies had all the necessary info in their computer files, files that were easy to hack into if one knew how. The homeowner's travel schedule, alleged care-taking schedule, and even the in-house security codes were right there, ripe for the plucking.

Naomi would then choose her address—not too exclusive, and not too poor—pick the regular lock, disarm the security system—as if she was the caretaker who'd arrived to take care—and then she'd keep herself out of sight when the actual caretaker would arrive.

She was careful and kept her going out and thus coming back in to a minimum. There were twenty-four-hour groceries, and she was content to hunker down for a time and lie low.

She didn't worry really overmuch about the neighbors spotting her, though she took care not to be seen. Most people didn't give a rat's ass about other people, anyway. It was all easy, breezy, and Naomi Lake had brand-new digs.

She'd used her time wisely over the last month. She'd used the Internet at her new address—since the residents didn't password protect their computers—to do some research, and to keep abreast of the investigation into the death of that cheating bastard, Brady Alexander.

She supposed if she'd gone after that whore using a different weapon, the cops would still think Brady's death had been an accident. So the fact that they now knew differently and that she had to leave her cute little apartment was her just desserts for poor planning.

Daddy had always said that planning and timing were everything. *As a matter of fact, I do believe he said that right before he had me sent to that boarding school. He was just afraid I would tell on him. Faithless bastard. Cheating on momma that way. He was afraid I would tell momma, and so he had me sent away.*

Of course, momma had been no angel, either. She'd likely known what he was doing to her, and she'd let him.

She'd let him!

They both deserved what they got.

And Naomi deserved to be happy. She'd been so certain Brady was the one—the one who would make her happy. How could she have been so wrong?

Faithless bastard. He deserved what he got, too.

But it wasn't over. It couldn't be over until that whore got what she deserved.

Just like momma.

Naomi smiled even as she considered how well the brown wig and fake glasses disguised her. She knew how to blend in and she knew how to get the information she needed. Planning and timing. It had been long enough, now, that her mission would seem sincere. She knew how to act like the plain little mouse and elicit sympathy when she needed to.

Of course, she'd seen so many whores close up, she could pretend to be one of those, too, if she had to. But she'd rather not.

No, plain brown mouse worried about an acquaintance was what would do the trick. She'd choose her mark carefully, too.

They wouldn't even know what she'd done. Not ever. She was such a clever little girl. *Daddy always said so!*

Naomi looked up at the marble and glass building with the words Seattle Police Headquarters above the doors.

She knew how to get the information she needed, and she would have that information very, very soon. She would know where Rebecca Jessop had run to by the time she left this building again.

And then she would finally give that whore what she deserved.

Chapter 8

"Your wound has healed remarkably well, all things considered," Robert Jessop said. "It looks good."

Greg hadn't fully understood until that moment exactly how tense he'd been. He trusted those doctors in Turkey, of course.

But he trusted family more.

"I've always been a fast healer." Cody shrugged, and then slipped his shirt back on. Instead of a huge square pad of gauze, Robert had replaced the bandage with a much smaller square.

"You might want to keep it covered under your clothing for a while yet to prevent chafing," he said. "But you can shower, or bathe, without worry. And likely, just cover it for another week when dressed. If you'll pop back in next week, I'll look at it again."

"Thanks, Doc."

"Just Robert."

Greg said, "I want to say thanks, too, for an entirely different reason." Since Rebecca had opted to stay out and chat with her sister-in-law—Robert's pretty wife Jillian—Greg figured he was free to chat man-to-man with his "cousin."

He didn't have to say anything more. Robert clearly understood that Greg was referring to the fact that Robert had set Greg up with his sister.

"You're welcome," Robert said. "Just see that I don't ever regret giving you this opportunity."

Greg looked at Cody, before turning back to his cousin. "You *do* understand that I'm bisexual."

"Well who didn't know that? I've got news for you, cousin. We've all pretty much understood that you were bisexual, the same as we've all always known Jordan was. If you think that makes a difference to any of us as to how we feel about you, then you don't know us very well at all."

Well, hell. I always thought it was my big secret.

Greg decided to go for full disclosure. "Cody and I are lovers."

"That's not news, either, Einstein. Did you not realize that when ANN interrupted their regular programming with the breaking news that photojournalist Cody Harper had been rescued from his kidnappers in Syria, they showed you helping to get him settled onto the gurney and then getting into the ambulance with him? For those of us here, we knew when we saw the look on your face that he was yours." Then Robert proved that he was Rebecca's brother after all. "Is Becca okay with this?"

Greg and Cody exchanged a look and it was all Greg could do not to burst out laughing. He could see Cody was thinking about that moment on the porch.

I'd better not tell Robbie his sister had an orgasm watching us kiss.

"She says she is, and I believe her."

"No, she wouldn't lie about something like that," Robert said. "And frankly, I wouldn't have expected her to be otherwise."

"We'd know if her acceptance of us wasn't genuine," Cody said.

Robert looked at him. "Have you talked to anyone yet about what happened to you in Syria?"

Oh, he's good.

Cody shrugged, but Greg could see the change in topic threw him off-balance. "I spoke to a psychiatrist before I left the hospital in Turkey," he said finally. "I'm fine."

"If you need to talk to someone, talk to Greg. Or you can come here and talk to me."

"Thanks, I will. But like I said, I'm fine."

Yeah, right. Greg was more than a little concerned, because although Cody kept repeating that he was "fine, the truth of the matter was just the opposite.

Greg had seen flashes of the old Cody, but he'd changed, and Greg didn't know if those changes were permanent, or not. He didn't know if Cody was just in denial, or if the experience had fundamentally altered him.

Greg understood that living life changed people. How could it be otherwise? And if that was all that had happened, then that was okay. He loved Cody, and a few changes in attitude wouldn't affect that.

But if Cody was, in fact, suffering from post-traumatic stress disorder, then Greg wanted him to get help.

If he didn't, the situation would not get better, it would get worse. Cody's nightmares would get worse.

"What about you, Greg?"

"Pardon?" Oh, that sneaky, sneaky doctor. Who knew that cousins could be so damned sneaky?

"Someone you love has been through hell. How are you handling it?"

Greg very nearly brushed Robert off. He wanted to ask the man what right he had asking him a question like that when it was *Cody* who'd been kidnapped, *Cody* who'd been shot and had nearly died.

And then he got it. Trust Robert to dig back for one of the principles upon which they'd been raised. His dads—and everyone else's dads, too, for that matter—always said, "You don't lead by telling others what to do. You lead by example."

Greg didn't share easily. He always held his emotions close to the vest.

That kind of behavior was fine as long as I was a lone wolf. But now I'm a man with a lover—potentially two lovers—and if I want to build lasting relationships with them, I have to learn how to share.

"I was scared out of my mind. I was a basket case." He looked over at Cody. "When I got word that you'd been taken, it was like the

Boxing Day Tsunami all over again." He looked at Robert. "I lost someone I loved then—remember how I was home for that Christmas? 2004? We'd had a fight, Daniel and I. We were supposed to have gone to England together, to visit his family for Christmas. But we'd had a fight, and I came home alone instead." Greg sighed. "Daniel, being Daniel, decided to stay in Jakarta and work. He was a doctor, and working a term in Indonesia with Doctors Without Borders. The day before the disaster, he was called in to assist with an emergency on the north end of Sumatra."

"Where the worst damage was," Robert said. "Christ, Greg, I never knew."

"How could you? I never told anyone." Greg thought about that for a moment. "I never *told* anyone, and I suffered for it for a long, long time." He looked at Cody. "I was alone for a long time, and was going to stay that way until you came into my life. Hell, I'd even decided to *not* pursue the only woman I'd ever loved, too." Because he believed he didn't have a right. He let himself cling to the guilt he felt because he'd taken her when he was still technically committed to Daniel.

"It's not the same thing," Cody said. "I was kidnapped, and yeah, I got shot during that part of it. And I was scared. But then your friends found me and brought me out of that. I was scared again when I got so sick in the hospital, but you were there then and it was better. I'm better."

Greg met Cody's gaze, and then looked at Robert. "So I guess to answer your question, we're both okay."

Robert nodded slowly, and Greg, who'd never considered himself particularly insightful, realized something important.

Neither he *nor* Robert fully believed Cody. And neither one of them could do anything about that little thing.

* * * *

"That's probably the only pass you're going to get from me, Cody Harper," Rebecca said. As they stepped out onto the sidewalk, Rebecca turned and waved good-bye to Jillian. After a short discussion, they'd decided to walk the few blocks to *Lusty Appetites*.

Before leaving the clinic, Greg had tried to call his parents, but they were in Houston for the day. There was no answer at the twins' ranch, so he left a message. He did manage to track the triplets down—they were also in Houston—and he'd called Julia.

The three of them were headed over to visit the new mom and dads and babies right after lunch.

The men arranged themselves so that they flanked her, and that suited Rebecca just fine.

"What do you mean by that, Blue Eyes?" He held back when Greg scooped her hand in his. Rebecca reached for his hand, and waited the few seconds for him to relax.

She noticed when he spied another threesome on the opposite side of the street also walking hand-in-hand-in-hand.

"I mean, we're not lovers yet, so I allowed you some privacy in there with my brother the doctor. But you might as well know right now, once we cross that line, then we cross that line. In Lusty that means, most of the time, when you go in to see a doctor, so do your lovers."

"Is that a fact?"

"That is a fact. So get used to it."

Rebecca had been thinking long and hard about the situation of one Mr. Cody Harper. She'd never been a woman to shy away from a challenge, and he certainly was that. One of her friends from college, Nathan Gray, had joined the marines and gone off to war. When he'd returned for the last time some five years later, he'd been diagnosed with PTSD. The man's wife, Peggy, had pulled out all the stops to get him help—devoting herself to his care personally. They were also getting help from the Wounded Warrior Project.

Rebecca made a point of visiting them whenever she was in Dallas. They would spend time together, the three of them during the day. She and Peggy would sit up late at night sometimes, when she'd stay over with them. Mostly, she would just listen. She knew a little bit about the affliction, not just from those late-night chats, but from reading up on it and talking with some of the professionals connected to that very worthwhile organization that helped them out.

Cody wasn't a wounded warrior, per se—but he *had* been wounded. He'd been kidnapped, shot, and likely terrorized. She'd read of similar situations, of aid workers and journalists being subjected to those kinds of traumas. She'd read their accounts and knew that a popular tactic modern armed terrorists liked to use was to mess with their victims' minds.

One thing she knew beyond question was that before Cody could get better, he had to acknowledge he had a problem, and he had to talk about what had happened to him with someone he could trust.

She didn't think he'd done either one yet. Rebecca decided that since Greg was taking the role of tender lover in this relationship they were trying to put together, she'd be the one offering the tough love.

She didn't know, of course, if she loved Cody or not. It was too soon for that. But she loved Greg, and had for most of her life. Since he loved Cody, she'd perform loving acts for him—the kind outside of the bedroom as well as inside it—and see what happened.

Rebecca understood very well that love wasn't just a noun. It was a verb, too.

"Now that is a catchy name for a restaurant," Cody said.

"My cousin Kelsey owns it," Greg said. "From the few times I've eaten here, I can tell you, the food is damn good."

Lunch was served from eleven thirty until about four. Rebecca had become versed in the rhythm of the place because often, it was just as easy to eat here than to go back to the cabin and prepare a meal for herself.

Cooking for one really wasn't much fun.

One step inside the doors, and Rebecca's stomach growled.

"Hey, Greg! Welcome home!"

"About time you showed your face around here, stranger!"

"All hail the wanderer!"

"Even chickens come home to roost sometimes," Greg said in response to the greetings flying at him from practically every direction.

"Well, son of a bitch."

That voice had Greg spinning on his heels. Rebecca grinned when two rip-cord lean cowboys got to their feet and headed straight over.

"You sure haven't gotten any prettier," Chase Benedict said. "You need a scar like mine. Ain't nothing that attracts the ladies or the men like a good scar."

"Got one of each now, don't need no more." Greg returned Chase's hearty hug, and then gave one to Brian, too.

Then he reached out for Cody, and when that man looked to want to hang back, Greg just grabbed his hand and yanked him forward.

"This is Cody Harper. He's mine. And Becca you know, of course. She's ours."

Not yet, not really. She saw the slight flicker of doubt in Cody's eyes. And she knew in that moment, it wasn't just his reception by the family that Cody questioned.

It was where he fit in with her.

"Welcome to the family," Chase said. He gave Cody a hug which startled the man. Then Brian did, too, just as the door to the kitchen swung wide open.

Rebecca watched as Carrie Benedict came right up to Greg. Arms akimbo she gave him a good up-and-down look. Greg copied her pose and returned the favor.

"You're Greg, my last new big brother. I've been waiting a long time to meet you," Carrie said at last. "Funny, but you look like a *GQ* model, *not* an adventurer."

"You're Carrie, and my new baby sister. Funny, but you look like a punk rocker, *not* a chef."

"I guess that just goes to show y'all can't judge a person on appearances." Carrie grinned.

"Guess it does." Greg pulled her into his arms and gave her a huge hug, lifting her off her feet in the process. Carrie squealed, her husbands laughed, and just about everyone in *Lusty Appetites* grinned.

He set her down and slid his arm around Cody. "This is Cody. He's an amazing photojournalist, and a very hungry man. Do ya think we can fatten him up, some?"

"Hey, and ruin my slender figure?" Cody's natural penchant for humor came to the fore, and Rebecca knew he was fighting his discomfort.

Carrie smiled and easily gave Cody a hug. "I'm so pleased to meet you. I have your book. Completely compelling photographs. You tell a powerful story with your camera."

"Thank you." Genuine pleasure lit Cody's eyes. He looked around and Rebecca knew he was encountering smiles and nods.

Lusty tended to like to welcome family home with a very open heart.

"Y'all will be needin' a larger table," Emily Anne Bancroft said. "I've got one set up, right there in the front corner by the window."

Rebecca had been going to suggest that they sit by the windows, because next to the glass, with the downtown of Lusty right there, it almost seemed as if only three walls instead of four surrounded them.

She'd already noticed that Cody wasn't completely relaxed in enclosed spaces.

There was no question of having a table just for the three of them, and Rebecca watched how Cody dealt with being in the midst of what to him must seem like a huge crowd.

"Looks busy. I thought this was a small town." Cody sat down opposite Rebecca, leaving Greg to choose his seat. Rebecca grinned when he chose to sit next to Cody. Chase and Brian took their seats, and Carrie sat down, too.

Emily Anne made quick work of transferring the cowboys' drinks to this table.

"Boss lady said I can take a few," Carrie said.

"I'm going to have to go see Kelsey, too, before we leave," Greg said.

"Naw, she's going to come out once I go back. So, likely mom and the dads and everyone will pussyfoot around, but I won't do that. I'll just come right out and ask. You planning to stay around for more than a few days this time, Greg?"

Greg looked from her to her husbands. Chase raised both hands. "Hey, she's small, but she's mighty."

Greg shrugged, and if he was uncomfortable being put on the spot, he didn't show it. He cast one look at Cody, and then met Rebecca's eyes.

"Yeah, we're staying for more than a few days this time."

"Good. I'm not as old as you are, and not nearly as well traveled. But I've learned one thing since coming to Lusty. There really is no place like home."

Chapter 9

There really is no place like home.

Greg didn't know Carrie's story, not all of it. But he'd heard from Rick that she and her sister Chloe—soon to be married to his cousins Grant and Andrew Jessop—had been orphaned as the result of the tornadoes that swept through part of the South in 1998.

Trauma wears a hell of a lot of faces in this town.

Kelsey came out bearing a tray loaded with food before they'd even ordered. "Today's special is fried chicken, with a side of mashed 'n' gravy. But I didn't know if Cody liked mashed 'n' gravy so I've a plate of fries here, too."

"Hey, cousin." Greg had gotten up and given her a hug, and introduced her to Cody. She'd distributed the plates of food, and then taken the chair that Carrie had vacated.

"Man, my list of Texan keeps getting longer. 'Y'all,' 'all y'all,' and now 'mashed 'n' gravy.'" Cody sighed and Greg recognized the smart-ass in him coming out to play.

"Mashed 'n' gravy isn't Texan, it's mine." Kelsey grinned. "But otherwise, yeah, the learning curve is long and steep. I'm still a Northerner by most accounts as I've only been in Texas going on a dozen years. I was born and bred in Philadelphia."

"Hey, Philadelphia, I grew up in New York City. We're practically neighbors." He looked around as if checking to see if anyone was listening. "Do you mind if I call you if it gets to be too much? We can talk Yankees and Mets and Eagles and Penguins and how *real* dumplings are fat and fluffy, not long and thin, and other Northern stuff like that."

"Greg has my number," Kelsey said, and extended her hand so they could shake on the deal.

It was good to see Cody's natural gregariousness come out. It had to be a good sign. Maybe he was going to be all right. Maybe this whole PTSD thing the doctors back in Turkey talked to him about wasn't really manifesting after all.

Sure, he had nightmares, but who wouldn't after being kidnapped? Greg had to believe that if anything really horrible had happened to him, he'd open up about it. They were lovers, and they were in love. They'd come a long way in the weeks leading up to that damned trip to Syria—and a hell of a long way since.

That all had to count for something.

Kelsey had gone back to the kitchen and they were just tucking into some very good pecan pie when the door to the restaurant opened and another cousin came in—one that Greg hadn't seen much of in the last few years.

"Hey, Flyboy!"

Morgan Kendall came right over to their table, hand extended. They shook, of course, but family called for more so they shared man hugs with the requisite *very* sound backslaps.

Emily Anne came over to the table, a huge smile on her face. *Pretty little thing, and that smile is a winner*. He hoped she had a couple of good men waiting for her at home.

"Hey, Morgan, pie and coffee?"

"Please. And if Tamara asks, it was a very small piece of pie—even though I'm hoping it's not."

Morgan joined them, and Greg said, "Your wife is just an itty-bitty thing, if I recall. You scared of her?"

Morgan snorted. "You know damn well where the power rests in this family and it sure as hell isn't in the hands of the men."

"I thought, though, Tamara coming from out of town, you know, things might be different for y'all."

"They might have been if Mother and Kate hadn't 'bonded' so well with her first off." Then Morgan gave him a big smile, and Greg could see his cousin was a very satisfied man. "I wouldn't change a single thing about her, and neither would Henry. Swear to God."

"So how's the charter flight business?"

"We're building it, but it's a gradual thing."

"You're a pilot?" Cody asked.

"Indeed. So are my brother, Henry, and our wife. Henry and I just retired about a year ago from the Air Force. And Tamara—well, her uncle taught her how to fly as a way to channel her passive-aggressive tendencies that weren't overly passive."

"Morgan held the rank of Major," Rebecca said. "And it's rumored that he sometimes would go into stealth mode and join in some black ops kind of stuff while he was over in Afghanistan."

"Becca," Greg chided. "*Everyone* knows the Air Force doesn't do black ops."

"Right. I forgot. Sorry."

"So you served in the war?" Cody asked.

"I did, indeed."

"Thank you for your service. That takes guts. Real guts. We're lucky there are those brave enough to put it on the line for the rest of us," Cody said.

Morgan waved that off. "So does taking a camera to show the world what's happening *in* the world," Morgan said. "I don't imagine it's always easy to walk amongst the afflicted. Those stories have to be told. How do we change as a society unless we see the face of hunger, the ravages of natural disasters, or the devastation of the man-made disasters—like war? Whether you're there to serve, or to record those events for posterity, it's got to be tough."

A half hour later, they took their time walking back to Jeep. It was a pretty day, and Greg appreciated the warm temperatures without the high humidity of summer.

Cody seemed to be looking everywhere, and Greg tried to remember the last time he'd been someplace new in the same way that Cody was new, here.

And he realized that he had to reach all the way back to 2003 and the one trip to England he'd taken with Daniel. Only then, of course, there was no parade of family to welcome either man. Greg guessed he understood a little better why Daniel had been so disbelieving of the stories Greg had told about Lusty. It didn't matter that Greg had never lied to Daniel, or to anyone else, then, either. In hindsight Greg realized that Daniel's mistrust and disbelief had come from inside himself—because he, himself hadn't always been truthful.

"You have a lot of cousins, here," Cody said. "Any idea how many, exactly?"

"Of the town's residents, or actual numbers?" Greg asked.

"I was thinking the town's residents."

Becca laughed. "Most of them. Actually, this town is built on family land. Settled in the 1890s." She pointed toward the museum across the street. "Next time you come in to town, you need to stop in and have a look."

"Maybe I will."

They made quick work of grabbing a few groceries to take back to the cabin, and then he drove over to see his sister.

He'd only met her husbands once, and he'd forgotten how big the men were. Devon Wakefield answered the door, holding one of the babies in his arms. He welcomed them in, and nodded when he was introduced to Cody. "This one is Billy. Drew's holding Dee—that's what we're calling Darien. And mom has Madison. The ladies are in here."

Greg hadn't been around little babies in years, but he had to admit, his nephews and niece were incredibly beautiful children.

"I hope you're going to stay around for a while," Julia said. "Mom was talking about having a bit of a party, because so many of us are all in Lusty at the moment."

"We're here for a while," Greg said, "So don't worry about it. I needed a bit of a rest. I realized a few weeks ago that I've been on the go pretty much since I left college."

"He's mother-henning me," Cody said, "on account of the misadventure I fell into a few weeks ago back in Syria."

"Heard about that," Dev said. "Julia mother-hens us, too, sometimes. My advice is to take it while it's being offered. Nothing wrong with being pampered by the ones who love you."

Greg thought it was kind of an odd thing for a Navy Commander to say. But then, his wife did just have triplets.

Greg supposed a guy couldn't help but get a little soft as the result of such a huge, and humbling, event.

* * * *

The sun had begun to drop toward the horizon by the time they got into the Jeep and headed back to the cabin. All through the visit with the James-Wakefields, Rebecca had felt both Cody and Greg's gazes light on her, and then skitter away. Or they would each look at her a moment, and then wink.

She knew exactly what they were thinking, too. She hadn't forgotten the bargain she'd struck with the men—their silence with her brother in return for getting a good look at her tattoo.

Wouldn't they be disappointed if it turned out to be a butterfly on my shoulder?

She'd thought about it—about how and where she was going to perform "the big reveal," and she'd come up with the perfect plan. Rebecca had felt Cody's tension throughout the day—it had started as they'd entered the clinic and then built steadily as family had surrounded and intruded and pressed close. Funny thing was, that as his tension had increased so had the outward displays of his sense of humor.

The man had a good one, but she recognized armor when she saw it.

She'd insisted, for the ride back to the cabin after the stop at Julia's place, that the men should share the front seat of the Jeep. Maybe next time they'd take her Ford F150. It, at least, had a bench seat.

Cody had tried to argue with her but she'd just hopped in the backseat. She hoped that in time, he would be able to relax more around her. But for right now, it was Greg who formed his center, and his anchor.

Greg is the center for us both, and the pivot of this relationship we're trying to build, all three of us, together.

Rebecca never doubted even for a moment that they would be able to build a strong, and loving one. Her heart was already engaged with Greg—and warming very quickly to Cody.

"So." Rebecca looked out the window at the passing scenery. "Y'all kept your end of our bargain."

"Are you sure about that, Blue Eyes?" Cody's half snicker from the front seat made her want to sigh. Despite that she sensed his tension had lessened some, he still needed to let go, and she knew just the way to do that for him. For the moment, however, she could play into his one-liners.

"Oh, yeah. If you'd said anything to Robert about my crazy stalker chick problem, he'd have stormed out of that exam room and aimed right for me. At this moment I would likely be chained up in a private room of that club of his where no one would ever be able to get near me again. It's what bossy, arrogant Doms do."

"Well, now, that just fires my imagination all to hell," Greg said. "I've been to the kind of club Robert belongs to, and I know what kind of interesting…toys they have there to play with."

"Why doesn't that surprise me?" Rebecca shook her head. The things the men in her family were knowledgeable about—of which she remained blissfully clueless—were kinkier than she ever could have guessed.

"Why, lover, do you have a little latent Dom in you?" Cody sounded surprised by the prospect. Rebecca's curiosity was piqued. She waited to see how he'd answer.

"There really is nothing latent about the Dom in me, it's just controlled and mostly kept out of sight. Just like there's nothing necessarily latent about the sub in you, babe. But that is a topic for another day."

I guess Greg knows himself pretty well, too.

"Huh." Cody seemed to consider what his lover had just said. "You might be on to something there."

Greg reached over and stroked Cody's shoulder, sliding the caress down his arm and then clasping his hand.

Rebecca's body had been humming with arousal since those kisses earlier, both the ones she'd received and the one she'd watched. This tiny display of affection, as well as the visual images she'd imagined to augment them, simply added to that buzz.

Rebecca had taken only two lovers in her life. The most important one, her first, was in this car. And she was about to take her third, a man she really didn't know all that well at all. Hell, the truth was she really had just met him.

But she possessed really good instincts, and those instincts were telling her that while Cody Harper would never be a simple or easy man to love, he would be worth the effort. This sure as hell would be no one-night stand.

She and Cody shared a connection through their art—both photography and painting were visual mediums, and they'd already communicated on a level a lot of people couldn't imagine existed. Cody had been wounded, but refused to give in to that, refused, in fact, to see himself as a victim. That was both good and bad.

Most importantly, he loved and was loved by Greg Benedict.

She was all about what it was to love *that* man.

Rebecca couldn't deny that she'd been attracted to Cody at first sight. His kiss had taken her in and taken her down very nearly as sexily as Greg's did, and that was saying a lot because no other man's had even come close.

Greg caught her gaze in the rearview mirror. She saw the question in his eyes, and nodded.

"So, about our payoff." He said only that, leaving the degree of what would happen next completely up to her.

"It's been a pretty stressful day all around, what with you dragging us both where we needed to be but didn't want to go. After we put the supplies away, why don't we meet up in the master bath? I think that I'd love a long, hot soak in the Jacuzzi. And you know how perfect an ice breaker bubbling hot water can be. Don't you?"

Greg raised one eyebrow. "Won't it take time to get heated?"

Rebecca said, "Oh, did I neglect to mention that I took care of that little thing this morning?"

"You might have done," Greg said. He shot a look at Cody who met his eyes. Rebecca couldn't see the look they exchanged nor the expressions on their faces.

Then Cody said, "With, or without bathing suits, Blue Eyes?"

"You can wear one if your modesty demands it," Rebecca said, "but I'm just bringing my robe, and a smile."

"And the tattoo?"

How had she known that Greg's interest would be piqued by her having a tat? Rebecca guessed she knew him better than she thought she did.

"Darling, I can assure you, once I drop my robe, you won't be able to miss it."

Chapter 10

Sofia Torres Harris had been married nearly thirteen years, had two children, and worked as an accountant for a mid-sized financial services company in Austin, Texas.

It hadn't taken Connor long to find her. Melvin called her and arranged for this meeting, which she'd agreed to, albeit reluctantly. At the moment she looked extremely uncomfortable as she listened to him explain to her exactly why he and Connor were there. She sent a glance over his shoulder toward the door of her office, which stood open.

"We have no desire to embarrass you, Mrs. Harris. You should know that the statute of limitations has expired, so no charges can be filed, not against Mr. Baxter, nor against you for whatever role you may have played in his theft of the Rhodes sisters' inheritance. Neither of you can even be sued in a civil suit by the Rhodes sisters, either."

Sofia sighed. "I don't blame you for thinking I had something to do with what he did—with what Ralph Baxter did. But honestly, the only thing I was ever guilty of was being young and incredibly stupid."

"Why don't you tell us what happened?" Connor asked. "Our only goal here is to give those two young women some closure. Our finding Baxter, allowing them to confront him, will do that."

Mel and Connor had been in perfect agreement as they'd prepared for this interview. They wouldn't mention their suspicion that Baxter had murdered Neil Jackson. They'd wanted to make it as easy as possible for Ms. Torres—now Mrs. Harris—to tell them everything she could recall of that period in her life.

She might not feel as free to do so if she thought there might be a charge of accessory to murder in her future.

"I really didn't know what Ralph was doing, either before or after that horrible tornado. I'd landed the job with Rhodes and Baxter Real Estate right out of high school. I'd been interviewed by both gentlemen, and they'd both hired me—but it was Ralph Baxter who caught my eye, even if he was more than ten years older than I. Mr. Rhodes, he was a bit older and a nice man. He had pictures of his wife and daughters—he used to call them his girls—on the credenza behind his desk. Sometimes…sometimes I'd go into his office to give him the letters I'd typed for him, and he'd be just sitting there, staring at those pictures. A few times, Mrs. Rhodes came into the office—he acted as if a movie star had come into the room, his face just lit up so." She smiled, and Mel thought it was a shy smile. "After all these years, despite everything else that happened, *that's* my most vivid memory of that time of my life."

"We heard he was a man who truly loved his wife and daughters," Connor said.

"He was. Mr. Baxter—Ralph—for all that he was Donald's friend as well as partner, wasn't like him at all. He was single, for one thing, and always ready with a joke or a smile. With hindsight, I can tell you the man was a real salesman. And he certainly sold *me*—he had me believing that he was in love with me. I thought I'd found my Prince Charming."

She shook her head. "Now, I look back, and I can't *believe* I fell for him—for the lies he told me. I can't believe I was that stupid, but I was."

"How old were you at the time?" Mel asked. "Nineteen? Twenty?"

"I was nineteen, and yes, I was naïve even for my age."

"No one could blame you for believing the man, Mrs. Harris. From what else we've heard, he was what you might call a player. You believed he was in love with you because that was exactly what he wanted and needed you to believe. He set out to make you fall in love with him. It made it easier for him to use you."

"I know that now, but I still feel stupid when I look back on it. I realize now that he needed me to cover for him—I've learned since that he gambled a lot, but I don't think Mr. Rhodes knew about that. I swear to you, *I* had no idea that he owed so much money to the wrong people—after he disappeared, and after the bank sent the first late payment notice—the business had a mortgage on the building—a couple of men showed up, looking for him." She sighed. "I didn't know who they were. By then, I was beginning to understand that I'd been lied to, majorly. I was distraught. I thought, at first, that Ralph was just taking a few days away from work, away from town, on account of everything that happened. I thought he was grieving for his friends. But when he didn't come to the office, and I couldn't reach him by phone, I went to his apartment. I had a key. I found it *empty*. It even looked like it had been hastily vacated. I got scared and I called the police. I reported him missing, and I tried to convince myself that something horrible must have happened to him.

"But I knew. In my heart, I knew he'd simply left. And still, I didn't realize exactly what he'd done, not until those thugs showed up. And then, of course I got the foreclosure notice from the bank."

"Those thugs didn't hurt you, did they?" Connor's voice sounded quiet. Mel realized he was angry.

Likely, he was angry with Baxter for putting his young lover in such an untenable position.

"No. I guess they could see how upset I was. They believed me when I told them I had no idea where Ralph Baxter had gone. I thought they were going to give me a hard time—I remember being scared—and they probably would have, if a very handsome young police detective hadn't chosen that moment to come into the office."

For the first time since she'd begun to tell her story, Sophia Harris smiled. "Detective Michael Harris was following up on the missing persons report I'd filed. He'd come to tell me that, as far as they could tell, Ralph Baxter had left of his own volition. He also told me that they suspected he'd taken money he wasn't entitled to."

"Detective Harris—the man you eventually married?" Connor asked.

"Yes. So I could say something good came of that mess. I met Michael because of Ralph Baxter's perfidy." Sofia sighed. "He was—and is—my *real* Prince Charming."

"You packed up the office, then, and put everything into storage?" Mel asked.

"I did. I felt as if I'd somehow enabled Ralph to do what he had done. Even though I'd truly had no idea of the crimes he'd committed, I still felt partly responsible. I felt that paying that monthly storage charge was a just penance for what I'd done."

"Is there anything you can think of, anything else at all that Ralph Baxter was doing in the days after the death of the Rhodeses that seemed odd or unusual at the time?" Mel asked.

"I thought it was strange that he focused *so much* on work—before that tornado, Ralph wasn't what you'd call the industrious sort. Mr. Rhodes once remarked that Ralph had a way of charming the birds out of the trees, and that if anyone *could* sell ice to Eskimos it would be him. When it came to the real work that needed to be done, I knew it was Mr. Rhodes who did that. Mr. Baxter, he was the happy-go-lucky partner, the salesman."

"But in the days following the deaths of the Rhodeses, he seemed unusually busy?" Connor asked.

"Oh, yes. He was making lists of properties—rural properties that were for sale, all over the central and southern part of the state. This was something that I knew he'd been doing even before Mr. Rhodes died. But now, it seemed as if he'd become almost frantic in his quest. I remember thinking at the time that maybe he was submerging his grief in his work. In hindsight, I have no idea what he was doing, because after he disappeared, no client ever called or appeared wanting those lists."

Mel looked at Connor. That man raised one eyebrow. He wondered if Connor was thinking the same thing he was, that Baxter had been looking for a place to run to.

"It's a shame that we can't get our hands on those files you packed away back then," Connor said to the woman. "I think they'd have the information we need in them."

When Mrs. Harris looked like she was confused, Mel explained, "There might have been something there that would have helped us figure out where Baxter headed as soon as he 'went missing'—or where he is today."

Sofia Harris met his gaze then and stared at him for a long moment. He thought she came to a decision because she reached for a piece of paper. She scribbled something on the page, and then reached for her purse.

She handed him the paper, and a key.

"That's the address, and the unit number I rented. I think you're the reason I felt compelled to keep paying my penance all of these years. "

* * * *

I don't think I ever really thought about this *moment.*

Rebecca had had a goal, one that she'd had, really, for a lot longer than the few months since her brush with death in Seattle. She'd even had a plan—sort of—about how she would get herself and Greg and Cody—she'd known his name even before she'd left Seattle—into an intimate situation. But she'd not really given a great deal of thought to the moment when her plan would come to fruition—when she would take that one pivotal action that would be the start of *everything*.

She'd never given a thought to the moment when she would offer herself to them as a lover.

Rebecca walked into the master bath as far as she could without being seen by them, and stopped just before she stepped around the corner. Just another foot or two and she would be in full view of the two men she could hear talking quietly in the Jacuzzi. Fit into a corner, facing the windows that looked out over the plains of Central Texas, the spa tub was one of her favorite places here at the cabin.

She had one installed for her private use in the house she'd shared with her parents when she'd been eighteen. If she decided to move into her own house here in Lusty—always a possibility—she didn't have to worry. Most every house came equipped with a large master bedroom and adjoining luxurious bath.

That was a tradition that Grandma Kate once told her had originated with Sarah and Caleb and Joshua Benedict, seconded by Amanda and Adam and Warren Jessop-Kendall, and embraced by darn near every family since.

Even families that weren't ménage families had a big-ass tub in the master bath.

Some luxuries were of universal appeal.

You're stalling, Rebecca. What are you, chicken? You need to woman up here.

Her inner imp was always pushing her. One of these days she was going to grab the little bugger and kick it into next week.

Rebecca inhaled deeply, tried to settle her nerves, and stepped around the corner.

Somehow, the steam that rose off the bubbling froth carried the aroma of both men, their masculine scent triggering something feminine and feral deep within her. She inhaled deeply and felt her nipples tighten into hard buds. Moisture seeped out of her cunt.

"There you are," Greg said. "We were beginning to wonder if you'd gotten cold feet." He tilted his head to the side. "Bargains aside, you don't have to take this step yet, Becca, if you're not ready to."

"My feet *are* a bit chilly, but I expect they'll be warm, soon enough." She looked from a pair of avid aqua eyes to an equally interested pair of brown ones. Her own gaze flicked, for just a moment, on the white bandage that sat so casually on Cody's shoulder. Then she met each of their gazes once more. "I want this, for me. I need this, for *me*." She stepped closer so they would be able see her.

She wasn't going to stall any longer, but she did need to make a bit of an explanation first. "I got this tattoo for you." She met Greg's gaze. "I'd already decided that I needed to try, with you. Because after all these years, I'm still in love with you. The only possible obstacle was Cody." She met that man's gaze. "I didn't know if you and I would mesh, if my body would respond to you, or if yours would respond to mine."

"Blue Eyes, get your pretty little self into this tub and I'll show you how my body responds to you."

Rebecca smiled. Greg seemed very pleased with Cody's words—and with hers. He nodded to her. "I've never stopped loving you, either. I love Cody, but I love you, too. I don't know what this is going to be." He looked at her and then at Cody. "I *am* afraid of commitment, damn it. But I don't want to be that way anymore. So let's try this, let's see if we can make this work. If we can find the right rhythm, the right…"

"The right simpatico?" Rebecca asked.

"Yeah. The right simpatico. Now lose the robe, Becca."

Rebecca looked at the men. They'd ranged themselves in the corner, as far away from the steps in as they could get. She looked at those two steps on the outside leading up to the tub and thought of the visual effect the added elevation would give her. They'd get an eyeful of her tattoo, really up close and personal.

She walked toward them and then took the two steps so that they had to look up to meet her eyes—but not to see the tat.

Then she dropped her robe.

Both men's gazes swept her body and zeroed in on the tattoo. The bubbles churned, and the only other sound in the room was Greg's indrawn breath and Cody's low whistle.

"I think I finally understand that saying, 'a picture is worth a thousand words,'" Greg said.

"Nothing subtle there. For the record, though, Blue Eyes, you didn't need to paint directions to show the way. Your pussy's not very hard to find."

Rebecca raised one eyebrow and looked at Greg.

He smiled, gave her a nod, and turned to Cody. "Remember what Rebecca just said? She's obviously saying that since I seemed to have so much trouble finding it *again*, I needed an arrow to point me in the right direction."

Then he held out his hand to her. She stepped down into the tub and took his hand. The heat of the water slid up her legs to her hips, seducing her into releasing her own tension. The men made room for her between them, and that was the gesture she needed the most. When they each reached for one of her hands, she shivered in pleasure.

"Personally, I usually hate it when folks stand around and discuss what the artist *really* meant, exactly," Rebecca said. "But in this case, darling, you got it in one."

She hoped they thought her flushed face was from of the heat of the water, and not because she was totally naked between two men who were similarly clothed.

"So, Rebecca, do you come here often?" Cody met her gaze and raised his eyebrows twice in a mock leering gesture.

Rebecca burst out laughing. She didn't think either one of these men would ever let her get away with anything. They'd figured out how nervous she was, and that was Cody's way of letting her know it.

She thought that if they could each do that for the others—reach out to shore up flagging spirits, or call them on it when they tried to dissemble, then that would come damn close to being the perfect relationship.

Only time would really tell.

Cody lifted her hand to his lips and kissed it. He met her gaze, and then looked beyond her to his lover. In the next moment he reached for her and brought her to sit on his lap, sideways, so that she faced Greg. She helped him with the move the moment she realized what he wanted to do. She had to work at not wincing even as she worried about him hurting his wounded shoulder.

"We're not going to fuck you in this tub," Greg said.

"Instead, we're going to play." Cody traced a finger down from her throat to her right breast. He used it to circle her areola.

Her body responded immediately by pebbling that circular pink patch and contracting her nipple into a tight little button. A tingle of heat washed through her and she felt her pussy clench as if looking for a nice, big cock to grab hold of.

"God, you're responsive." Cody cupped her chin and gently brought her head around until she met his gaze. "And not very experienced, sexually, are you? Baby, have you ever had anal sex?"

Rebecca sighed. "No, but I understand what stepping into this tub—what proposing to join the two of you—means." Cody released her chin and she settled further into his lap and laid her head on his chest. The sensation of his hard cock pressing against her hip stirred her arousal, a light puff of air on the embers that had smoldered all afternoon. She swore she could hear the muted *swoosh* of those embers catching fire.

"And what does it mean, Becca?" Greg slid closer and lifted her legs onto his lap. He massaged her feet and she felt her bones begin to liquefy.

"It means that I need to be open to trying everything. I'm not naïve, although, no, I'm not very experienced, sexually." Her face colored slightly.

"I imagine the talks between you and Auntie Pam were a little more interesting than the coming-of-age talks young ladies elsewhere receive," Greg said.

"Mmm, and I've read the journals, too. Sarah's and Amanda's." She grinned then. "We think we invented it all, living in these modern and progressive times. But let me tell you, Sarah Benedict and Amanda Jessop-Kendall were ladies who took on two husbands each, more than a century ago." She sobered then, and met each of the men's gazes. "Amanda's husbands were lovers to each other first, as you well know. Like you and Greg are." Rebecca reached up and stroked Cody's chin. "Only in those days, they could have been arrested and hung for their loving each other."

"I think I'm definitely going to have to tour that museum." Cody stroked her chin again and she looked up at him. "But for now, I want to play. Kiss me, pretty Rebecca. Let me drink your fire."

Rebecca put away the rest of her questions, sat up a little, and set aside the worries she had about the man whose lap she covered. Cody Harper's hands were on her body, stroking her breast and her back while his eyes compelled her.

She saw need and hunger in his gaze, and maybe a little fear of rejection, too. Maybe this wouldn't be forever. Nothing in life carried a guarantee. But unless she tried, unless she was willing to take a chance, how would she know? Yes, this was risky. But the risk was far and away preferable to the heartache of yearning, and never trying.

So Rebecca lifted her arms, encircled his neck, and laid her lips on his. Warm and wet and wonderful, his mouth covered hers, his lips supple and questing as they caressed and then opened hers. His tongue stroked hers, a slow slide, a trembling, joyful glide that lured her deeper and then deeper still. The flavor that was Cody flooded her bloodstream and drenched her soul. His hand slid up to cup her head. He dislodged the clip she'd used to keep her hair up, and she didn't even care.

She liked the feel of his fingers combing through her tresses, then grabbing hold, as if he would keep her right there and never let her go.

Cody released her lips. She felt Greg move, and her head was turned, and he was there, his face so close. He wrapped them both in his arms and said, "It's hot as hell watching you two kiss. I need some of that."

His mouth mated with hers, his lips and tongue forceful in their possession of her. Surrounded by hot and hard male flesh as the spa tub surrounded her with hot, bubbling water, Rebecca surrendered. She let herself go, returning Greg's kiss with all the passion that had lain dormant in her for so very long.

Cody took her nipple into his mouth and suckled, and Rebecca moaned against Greg's lips as an electric current of arousal zinged from her breast to her clit.

"You're very responsive to us each, and to us both." Greg kissed her cheeks, her forehead, and then leaned in and kissed Cody.

Lying as she was between them, with them kissing over her, she felt the heat of their hardened cocks pressing against her, felt the way those impressive organs flexed as the men's lips locked with each other's and their tongues mated.

The look in Greg's eyes when he lifted his mouth from Cody's made her heart melt. Joy, such absolute joy wreathed his face. She didn't think she'd ever seen Greg look so happy.

"Lover, I like that look on you," Cody said. "I like it a lot."

"I had this dream once," Greg said. He kissed her lips chastely then did the same to Cody. "Hell, I've *always* had this dream, because to me paradise always meant loving two people—but I didn't know if I would be given the chance."

"It wasn't just the chance you doubted," Cody said.

Rebecca counted this a rare moment, for in this place and at this exact time, the two men seemed to have reversed the roles she'd already grown accustomed to seeing them occupy.

They're both of them wounded souls.

That realization was an "aha" moment for her. They both had healing left to do. Yes, Cody's wounds were fresher, and in a way, more immediate. But Greg had suffered, too—and likely still was.

Her personal revelation continued on, in a direction she hadn't expected. For wasn't she a wounded soul, also? Hadn't she lived without her heart's desire, without the sense of completeness she knew her parents, aunts, and uncles had found? Hadn't she feared that she would be forced to live her life, lonely and alone? Hadn't she practically resigned herself to that fate?

"No, not just that." Greg acknowledged his lover's point, but said nothing more. What he did was move so that now he was on Cody's left. The two men put their hands on her, arranged her on them so that she was mostly out of the water. She didn't feel at all cold because the heat of their bodies warmed hers, and the searing passion in their eyes, as they looked and touched, heated her soul.

"You have such a pretty little pussy," Greg said. "I thought so that first time, when you gave me your virginity. I didn't expect to see it bare." Greg ran his hand over her flesh. "But I like it."

They each traced their fingers over her mound, then down, to stroke her labia and tease her clit. "Mmm, there's…a new day spa in town." She could barely form the words because they made her so damn horny. She pushed her cunt closer to their roving fingers, and the men both chuckled and continued to tease her unmercifully.

"A new day spa, is it? So you'll be waxing on a regular basis?" Greg's tone conveyed his interest even as he kept his eyes where his fingers played.

"Maybe." Rebecca let her eyes drift shut as the amazing sensations washed over and through her. She licked her lips, and whimpered because their touch came close, so very close to where she needed it the most.

"What's the matter, Blue Eyes? Need something?"

She opened her eyes and Cody gave her his teasing grin, but this time all she felt was frustration. Did he think she wouldn't speak plainly? Oh, but she would. To get what she craved she would likely say anything, do anything. At the moment they held her down, spread open, her hands behind their backs, her legs held apart so that they could play at will. They both were out of reach of her hands and her mouth—unless she counted their shoulders. She just might possibly be able to lick—or bite—their shoulders.

So Rebecca returned his smile and prepared to drive them both crazy the only way she could at the moment—with words.

"Yes. I need something. I need a couple of things, actually. I need your cocks." She felt a twinge on either side of her hips and mentally fist-pumped the air. "I need your hot, hard cocks fucking me. I need you to fuck my cunt and fuck my mouth. I need to taste your flesh. I want to drink your cum."

"Vixen!" Greg reached around and pinched her left nipple, not too hard but hard enough she knew it was meant as a mild rebuke. "I seem to recall you like to call the shots and rush the play," Greg said.

"You know, lover, we ought to tie her down and drive her crazy. Take her *just* to the very edge and then stop." Cody used two fingers to stroke rapidly over her clit. Rebecca cried out as arousal surged, as she came close, so very close, to orgasm. "Over and over again," he finished. He lifted his fingers from her cunt and Rebecca couldn't hold back the sound of disappointment.

"Babe, you have a diabolical mind. I like that about you." Greg turned Rebecca's face toward him. "But we can do that another time. I want to watch her come, right now."

Greg grinned. He slid his hand down her body, brushed over her mound and slid his fingers between her labia. Slowly, oh so slowly, he thrust two fingers into her cunt.

"Sounds like a plan. Allow me to do my part in this effort," Cody said.

Rebecca thought they must have some sort of telepathic communication going between them because they moved, at once and together. She found herself splayed across Greg's lap, his fingers in her cunt, while Cody slid off the bench, put himself between her legs, and lowered his mouth to her pussy.

Chapter 11

"Oh, God!" Rebecca couldn't hold back the shivers of delight. Neither could she stop herself from pushing her cunt closer to Cody Harper's very talented mouth.

They held her in such a way that she couldn't really move to help herself, or to escape—not that she wanted to.

She'd never been held down and forced to take pleasure before. *Greg's right, I do try to rush it and control it.* Her thoughts scattered and her orgasm erupted.

Rebecca cried out as the waves of beautiful, endless bliss rolled through her, one on top of the next so that she couldn't think, and could barely breathe. The climax filled every inch of her so that there was nothing else, nothing left, but this.

Cody continued to stroke her clit with his tongue as her climax went on and on. As it began to ebb, he lapped lightly all around her slit. Finally, when she was reduced to the shivers of aftermath, he placed sweet kisses on the inside of her thighs.

Greg bent over and gave her a light kiss. Rebecca sighed. Greg eased her off his legs and into Cody's arms. He stayed where he was, kneeling on the floor of the tub and held her. Her body submerged now, she snuggled into him, laying her head on his shoulder as the water lapped and frothed around her.

"Do you have any idea how much I enjoyed that?" No teasing lit his tone. The words had come softly, as if he'd been nervous to jar the mood between them.

"Not possibly as much as I did," Rebecca said.

Cody chuckled. "I think you know better than that. Will you let me share it with you?"

Rebecca smiled. This proof of Cody's heart and his manners touched her. The man had a hard-on that felt like hot steel beneath her hip, and yet, he asked—he didn't push or demand. He would never really force her to do anything she didn't want to do.

She reached up and caressed his cheek. This close she couldn't help but smell her own juices on his face. Applying just the tiniest pressure, she turned his head so that his lips were very close, and she kissed him.

She'd never tasted this, never sampled herself on a lover's lips before. Musky, not unpleasant, it surprised her that Cody's kiss, coated with her own essence, aroused her so quickly.

The water swirled and she felt Greg come down into the water beside them. She weaned her lips from Cody and looked at him.

"You want to try that, too?" she asked.

He didn't wait for a second invitation, and as he laid his lips on Cody's, as his one hand rested on her head and the other on Cody's, she cherished this glimpse of Greg's heart.

He'd allowed the two of them to have something together, outside of himself. And she made a note to herself that for them, for the three of them, this would be key.

If this ménage was to work, if it was to grow and become what she hoped, in her heart, it would be, then they had to have not just time together, as a trio, but individual couple time as well—*all* the way around.

Greg ended his kiss with Cody, and then turned to her. She met his gaze and smiled, then licked her lips. Greg chuckled. He leaned in and kissed her, too, a gentle, questing kind of kiss that comforted as much as it aroused. "Why don't we move this party to the bed?" he asked.

"Yes, please. I'm beginning to prune."

Cody nodded. "So am I." He thrust his hip toward her, pressing his cock against her.

"Not in anyplace really important," she said.

Cody laughed, and pulled her into a brief, tight hug. "I like the way you prioritize." Then his look sobered, and he met Greg's eyes, and then hers again. "Do you know what I need?"

"What, sweetheart?" Greg asked.

"Two things. I need to sink balls deep into Rebecca."

He met her gaze and she reached up and stroked her hand over his face. "What else do you need?"

"For Greg to sink balls deep into me."

Rebecca had a flash, a moment of understanding that swept through her, touching her heart and mind, body and soul. "You need to feel anchored to us both."

Cody blinked, and Rebecca thought that maybe he hadn't understood the meaning of the craving that had him in its grip.

"You know what? I think I need that, too," Greg said.

Rebecca stretched up and kissed Cody, and then Greg. "Let's get out of this water."

Greg lifted her into his arms, and she would have protested, but the moment felt right to just give in. Cody practically raced out of the tub. He grabbed a couple of towels, laying one on the wooden bench so Greg could sit on it. They then set about to dry her, a lovely kind of pampering she'd never experienced before.

"I have regrets," Greg said. He seemed to be taking particular care with her, his touch with the terrycloth more than gentle. "About the last time."

"I think you kind of made that clear at the time. It's okay. We're past that, Greg." Rebecca didn't want to go anyplace mentally or emotionally that would pull her out of the lovely place she was in right then.

"No, baby. I already let those ones go. These are different regrets. I regret I didn't stay in that bed and awaken you slowly the next morning. I regret that I didn't take care of you, and cherish you the way a man should when he makes love to a woman for the first time. That goes double when the man takes his woman's virginity."

"You were surprised at the time that I *was* a virgin. I didn't tell you that you'd be the first, because I was afraid you'd turn away from me. I didn't take any time when you came home to find out what was bothering you—and I knew something was. So, darling? It's not all on you, and you're not the only one with regrets."

"Wait just one minute." Cody squatted down so that he was on eye level with them both.

Rebecca realized he'd quickly dried himself, and that his bandage, which had withstood the heat of the spa, had come off in the process.

Her heart clenched at the sight of the red, puckered flesh. She saw Greg looking there, too. She was closer so she leaned in and kissed the healing scar gently.

"I have something to say to you both on the topic of regrets and what came before." Cody shook his head and gave a bit of a self-depreciating laugh. "To us *all*, actually," he said. "We've all been through various forms of hell in our lives. But maybe, just maybe, we each had to travel the path that we did in order for us to wind up here, and now, and together. And if that's true—if *this* turns out to be our forever beginning—then I say, all that came before was worth it."

Rebecca couldn't have put into words exactly why, but she knew in her heart, right then and there, she fell in love with Cody Harper. How many men, she wondered, dealing with what she suspected he was dealing with, could turn away from their own demons to comfort others dealing with theirs?

"You're right," Greg said. "So let this *be* a beginning for us. I'm willing to risk the jump."

Rebecca found it hard to form words around the lump in her throat. "So am I."

Cody smiled, and the light of confidence shining in his eyes was as hard to miss as it was breathtaking to see.

"Come on, lovers," Cody said. "I need you. I need you both."

Rebecca kissed both men, but when she made to get up, Greg stood with her in his arms. So she looped her arms around his neck and said, "I need you both, too. Let's get this celebration started."

* * * *

Let's get this celebration started.

Trust Rebecca to say just the right words. If he had anything to do with it, then what they would find here in this bed—all of them—*would* be a celebration.

He hadn't pushed Cody for sex. It had been three weeks since he'd left the hospital, just barely a month since he'd been kidnapped.

And while they'd spent each night since Cody had been discharged in the same bed, there'd been no lovemaking.

So yeah, Greg was more than ready for some action. It didn't matter that his body was still damp from the tub. Greg didn't want to waste another minute. *Don't matter if I dry off or not. Things are going to get so hot the water will evaporate right off me.*

Cody made it to the bed ahead of him and whipped the comforter and top sheet clean off the large mattress.

"I think our man is a little anxious." Greg stopped at the edge of the bed and changed his hold on Rebecca. He let her slide down his body until her feet hit the floor.

"So am I," she said. Wrapping her arms around his neck, she pressed close. "Kiss me, please."

Greg combed his fingers through her midnight-black hair. He used his hold on her silky tresses to pull her head back so he could look into her eyes. Passion flared to life in those beautiful blues of hers. Not a baby blue, but a pure blue that sometimes—like now—appeared almost violet.

"Gladly." He laid his mouth on hers and drank. He'd never forgotten the flavor of her, despite the fact that years separated their last time from this time.

He used his tongue to taste every bit of her mouth, to dance with hers and stroke her into sweet arousal.

Her nipples poked his chest and he could smell the honey leaking from her body. His heart responded to that sexy scent, and his cock throbbed.

"Holy crap."

He'd heard the slide of a drawer, and knew Cody had taken a moment to think of protection. Greg's smile matched Rebecca's. She looked over her shoulder at Cody, who'd reached into the bedside table drawer and lifted out some of the items he'd found there.

"Do you think Cody's figured out yet why our town is called *Lusty*?" Rebecca asked.

"I think I get it," Cody said. He held up both hands—condoms and lube in the right, handcuffs and flail in the left.

Greg grinned. "Looks like we have just about everything we're going to need to have ourselves a very good time."

And then, because he was feeling playful and joyful and free, he picked his Becca up and tossed her onto the bed.

Her laughter ended on a sigh when both he and Cody dove for her at the same time. Greg came down on her left and Cody on her right.

"Ahh, finally. I'm the filling in a man sandwich."

"Yep. Better than peanut butter." Cody cupped her cheek and she turned onto her side to face him. He took her face in his hands and kissed her.

Arousal spiked, and Greg rejoiced that he could feel only the heat, only the fire and the burn of it at the sight of his two lovers loving each other. Needing to be a part of them, he ran his hand down Rebecca's body, and then down Cody's. Hunger wrapped in deep yearning compelled him, and he moved, making a place for himself between them, settling in at waist level to feast on them both.

He wrapped his hand around Cody's cock, so damn happy that he was hard and obviously horny. As he gave his man a few hard, masculine strokes, he buried his face in Rebecca's pussy and began to nuzzle and lick.

"Mmm." Rebecca's soft sounds came muzzled. Greg looked up and saw they were still locked at the lips, and that pleased him enormously.

He set out to drive them both wild. The flavor of Rebecca's cunt fed him a nectar he knew he'd always been missing. Hot and musky, sweeter than honey, Greg savored her even as the taste of her drew him higher and made him harder.

Need turned to frenzy. He took his lips and tongue from her, turned his head, and without taking a single moment to lick or tease, sucked Cody's cock into his mouth.

"Jesus!" Cody surged into his mouth, giving him two strong pumps. "Stop, or I'm gonna come."

"I'll get you hard again," Rebecca said. "Go ahead and come, baby. Give Greg a good drink."

Rebecca reached for Cody's head and dragged him in for another kiss. Greg closed his eyes and focused all his attention on loving Cody.

His cock tasted better than any other, but more, this act, this stroking and sucking and pleasuring satisfied him better than pleasuring any lover ever had, save Rebecca.

Images and emotions swirled through him and he set them all aside, closed them all out. He inhaled and drew in Cody's unique aroma, the scent of his scrotum and perspiration an aphrodisiac like no other. He swallowed and the flavor of the tiniest drops of pre-cum tasted like the most exotic appetizer.

When he'd drawn Cody's cock into his mouth the hint of Rebecca's cunt had still been on his tongue, and the combination of the two tingling on his taste buds damn near made him shoot his load.

Cody's moans of pleasure thrilled him, and he opened his eyes, just once more, to look up at his two lovers.

Rebecca's nipples had turned to tight little peaks. Her body, hot with her own arousal, pulsed her fragrance over him, and he knew beyond doubt that this act of joining with him to give Cody release thrilled her, too.

Greg needed to taste him, needed to swallow his cum and taste him as he hadn't done for weeks. Reaching up, he cupped Cody's balls and began to squeeze in a rhythm timed with his sucks.

Cody jerked, breaking his kiss with their woman and cried out as he began to come.

Greg sucked hard, swallowing the salty, pungent cream, sucking and sucking until he felt his lover begin to shake, until there was nothing left for him to swallow.

He slowly released his cock from his mouth and sighed. He rested his head on Rebecca's leg, and caressed Cody's hip with his own trembling hand.

"God in heaven, babe." Cody struggled for breath, his words softened by his effort to draw in air.

"Glad you liked it." Greg leaned forward to kiss Cody's stomach. Rebecca moved out from under him, but he didn't even get a moment to wonder where she was going.

She turned around, slithered down the bed, and grasped his cock—his painfully rigid cock—in her hand.

"Your turn," she said. She gave him the cheekiest smile he'd ever seen. "And something tells me this isn't going to take long."

Chapter 12

Her teachers had always told her she was a very quick study. Never had she more appreciated that trait in herself than right now.

She'd watched as Greg had sucked Cody's cock, and considered it an excellent crash course in how to do the job right—since he who gave also received.

Then she moved down, wrapped her hand around Greg's cock, and drew it into her mouth. Later she would take time to examine this amazing part of the male anatomy. She'd do a comparison study. The idea flitted across her mind to paint them both in oils—just their cocks—and see if they could tell whose was whose.

Thoughts splintered as the flavor of Greg seeped into her. She moved her head on him, up and down, as she used her tongue to stroke his shaft and her mouth to suction lightly. She tasted the salty drops of dew he gave her and found she hungered for more. She inhaled him, and found the scent of his body alluring and compelling.

She cupped his balls in her hand and marveled at the soft, yet hard weight of them as they seemed to become even hotter, and as it felt as if they drew up.

"God, *Rebecca*."

She hadn't needed his words to know she pleased him. She could feel it and she tasted it. She felt Cody move and when he slid down the bed and fastened his mouth on Greg's, her own arousal began to spiral.

Why did the sight of them touching, kissing, loving, turn her on so fast, and so much? She had no answers at the moment, and really didn't care. Only one thing mattered right now and that was making Greg come.

"God, yes!"

His cry heralded the first pulse of his ejaculation, and Rebecca swallowed and sucked even harder. Stream after stream nearly overwhelmed her, but she caught his rhythm. The flavor was more than she'd expected, dark and strong, and yet she wanted, needed more of it. Knowing she gave him this, she understood what Cody had said earlier.

The gift of completion really was its own reward.

"Holy hell." Greg struggled for breath the same as Cody had. Rebecca gave his softening cock a final little lick, and then let him go. Looking up, she met his gaze.

"Not bad for a first time, huh?"

Greg's eyes widened, and then he laughed. The sound was joyous and full of fun. "God, woman, you're full of surprises, aren't you?"

"She's a treasure," Cody agreed. "And do you know what?" He turned his gaze on her and she loved the steely look of purpose he wore. "You were right. I am hard again."

"Why, so you are, Mr. Harper. What do you suppose we should do about that?"

"You, young lady, are going to grab two of those condoms from the bedside table, and put one on each of us. And then you're going to lie on your back with your legs spread so I can fuck you."

"I don't know if you can call me 'young' lady since I do believe I am older than you by three years."

"It's not the years, honey," Cody said. "It's the mileage."

Greg moved then, turned over, and got on his knees. He reached over and gave Rebecca a not-so-gentle swat on the ass.

"Hey!" She reached behind to rub her bottom and tried to hide the tiny tremble that vibrated through her.

"That little shiver of pleasure is promising," Greg said. "Becca, suit us up, baby. And hand me that lube."

Rebecca couldn't control the quivers as she hurried to sheath her lovers. She wanted to feel Cody's cock inside her pussy. But more, she wanted him in her while Greg fucked him. She craved the dark and feral pleasures being offered, and craved to help give Cody what she knew he needed above all else.

Grounding. Connection. Being a part of their triad, melded, together, one.

She wouldn't think of his pain, except to seek to relieve it. She wouldn't think of his ordeal except to offer him a safe harbor inside her body.

These were thoughts she'd never had about Greg, and she'd loved him for years. This new love was different—edgier, maybe a little rawer.

She liked doing this, liked holding their cocks, stroking them, and then covering them with the latex. She liked the way they felt covered with that protection, the extra bit of silkiness over hard muscle that was already hot and silky.

"That's it!" Cody didn't wait for her to lie supine. With his hands on her shoulders, he practically lifted her then laid her flat.

He spread her legs with his own so that she was open to him. Then the touch of his hand on her pussy, the sensation of his fingers delving deep into her cunt, wrought a moan from her.

"You're dripping, Blue Eyes. I think you like what we're doing—to you and each other."

She saw the need in his eyes, but wouldn't give him the words, yet. Yes, he needed them, but she would wait until, when hearing them, he'd believe them.

He'd think she spoke only in the moment if she told him she loved him now. So instead, she put her emotions in her gaze and her smile, and asked, "What's not to like? Please. I need your cock inside my pussy."

She felt his tremors and knew he needed this, too. Yet he entered her gently, being careful as he pushed his hot, hard cock into her.

It had been a couple of years since she'd taken a man into her body. It wasn't painful, but the fit of his cock in her pussy was tight, and the sensation of being stretched a rare and exciting one.

"Damn, baby, you're tight." Cody withdrew and pushed in, then did it again, and again, and finally he was buried inside her to the hilt.

He rested his forehead on hers and she could feel him fighting for control.

"That looks so fucking hot." Greg was on his knees behind Cody.

Rebecca could feel his presence so very close, and when Cody lifted his head from hers, she opened her eyes.

Cody was looking over his shoulder, likely at Greg's cock. "So does that hot rod of yours, lover. I don't think either of us is going to last."

"Probably not—at least not this first time. There's no rule that says we can't nap and have each other again, later."

Rebecca didn't feel as if she was being left out of the conversation, exactly. But she did want to assert that she had been waiting for more than a few moments and wanted Cody to move in her.

So she did what any modern woman would do. She squeezed her pelvic floor muscles with all of her considerable strength in a slow, pussy-stroking-cock contraction.

"Good God Almighty." Cody snapped his attention back to her and she gave him what felt like a very smug smile. "That's some damn good muscle tone you have there, Rebecca. Do it again, please."

She was more than happy to oblige, and Cody returned the favor by thrusting into her pussy, his strokes long and deep.

She felt him shiver when Greg reached toward him. It didn't take a lot of thinking to know that man had just spread lube on Cody's anus.

"Stop." Greg's one word of command had Cody responding immediately, as he paused midstroke.

"Hey!"

"Patience, Rebecca. I thought it might be fun if we all came together. But Cody needs to hold still and hang onto his urge to come until I'm inside him."

"Do it!" Cody's two words sounded half command, half plea.

Rebecca giggled when Greg "tsked." "I guess I'm not the only impatient one around here," she said.

"None of us is patient. We're all too hungry for each other." Greg said those words between his teeth.

She watched him move and position himself behind Cody, as he put his hands on Cody's ass.

Cody flexed inside her and she met his gaze. Riveted on hers, it was as if he wanted to share this with her completely.

She could have sworn she felt Greg enter him, for his body shivered and his cock grew, giving a heavy pulse inside her cunt.

"Wait." He put his head on hers again, and struggled for breath.

Rebecca ran her hands over his head and down his shoulders. As he continued to work at corralling the sensations and the physical urges, she gave way to her emotional ones.

She sighed, and lifted her legs, wrapping them high on his hips, close, very close to Greg's hands.

When Cody raised his head and met her gaze, she knew passion had consumed him. "Okay, lover. Fuck me." He moved inside her pussy, thrusts that were deep and fast, yet controlled. He reached down and stroked her clit, and she whimpered because it felt so good.

Hanging on the edge, and hanging by a thread, Rebecca closed her eyes and tried to hold off her own climax.

"God, I can't wait." Greg's voice sounded tight. "You feel so damn good, Cody. And knowing you're fucking our woman..." He didn't say any more—likely couldn't say any more. He growled, and bare seconds later, so did Cody.

Then Cody pinched her clit, and Rebecca cried out. The explosion came as if out of nowhere, her arousal shooting up to full climax in an instant. Her pussy clutched and clenched, and she felt her own juices flowing out. Unable to hold anything back, she screamed as the electric thrills consumed her completely.

* * * *

Rebecca opened her eyes and blinked, trying to clear the sleep from them so she could see. On her stomach, her head on a pillow, she knew immediately where she was. She guessed she'd slept for a couple of hours, because the room was bathed in the shadows of dusk.

On either side of her came the sound of soft snoring. Heat from two male bodies cocooned her and she sighed as the reality of the afternoon washed over her.

When she'd begun to think about what it would mean to have a relationship with Greg Benedict—knowing that he was bisexual and in a relationship with Cody—she'd wondered how reality would measure to imagination.

Sure, thinking about it had aroused her. She'd been pretty certain that she would be at the very least okay with it all. But there'd been a few huge issues to ponder.

It had been nearly ten years since that one time—basically a one-night stand. She thought she was still in love with Greg. But what if she wasn't? What if all she was really in love with was the memory of a green girl's infatuation, of her first drink from the cup of Eros? What if that memory, that dream, had taken over and colored reality completely?

Waiting here this past month, first for the tattoo to heal but mostly trying to get up her nerve to go and find him, face him, those doubts had worried her.

It was probably the best way for everything to have happened—Robert's butting in and telling Greg he and his lover could use this cabin that was already in use. She'd had no time to shore up any defenses, and no time to think things through.

She'd come face-to-face with her past and her hopes for the future, and then she'd laid eyes on Cody Harper for the first time and knew she was lost.

Never mind the fear that they wouldn't get along. She'd never dared to hope she could love him so quickly or so surely.

She knew at this point that her love for him was new. Based on a common passion for art and a chemistry that spoke to her inner woman, there would be time for that love to grow and strengthen and mature.

She hoped.

"You're thinking pretty loud there, baby." Greg's voice, sleep-sexy, rippled down her back.

"I don't know how to turn the thoughts down. Sorry."

"You need Greg to give you a back rub. I can tell you, he gives damn good back rubs."

Cody's voice, equally husky, just increased the shiver factor. "He does, huh?"

"I can do that." Greg leaned over and kissed her shoulder. "Lie still. There's some moisturizer in the bathroom."

"Not going anywhere."

Cody chuckled. He reached over and turned on the small lamp on the bedside table.

"Damn, this is one big-ass bed."

"It's a bit larger than usual." Greg returned from the bathroom and climbed back onto the bed, and then onto her. "Because when they furnished this cabin, the Town Trust wanted to make sure there would be room enough for the couple of families that were *ménage à quatre*."

"*Ménage à quatre*?" Cody sounded puzzled.

"Aunt Samantha has three husbands who are brothers—triplets," Greg said. "Those would be my Uncles Charles, Taylor, and Preston. And, of course, my triplet brothers are married to Maggie."

"So multiple births run in that family, too?"

"Yes. The first Benedicts to settle in this area back in the 1890s—my great-great-grandfathers—were twins, Caleb and Joshua Benedict."

"The multiple births in the Jessop-Kendall branch of the family, before they split off again to Jessops and Kendalls, come from a couple of sources. Amanda Dupree, who married Adam Kendall and Warren Jessop, had twins in her family, and Warren did as well."

"And there you were, lover, not a womb mate in sight." Cody could have been saying that to either of them, but Rebecca knew he was talking to Greg.

"Hush. Now is not the time for delving into my psyche. I'm here to give our woman a back rub."

"I was hoping that after you did that, you'd fuck her. I'm feeling a little voyeuristic."

"Hey, don't I get a say in this plan of yours?" Rebecca figured there should be at least a token protest. The fact that it felt as if her cunt had just gushed with that suggestion would be her little secret.

Greg must have poured some lotion on his hands, for the scent of almonds filled the air. She heard him rubbing his hands together, probably to warm the cream.

Then he put his hands on her midback and moved them slowly up toward her shoulders. He leaned over her and said, "We can both smell your arousal, baby. But yeah, of course you get a say."

"Good."

"You get to say if you want me to take you from behind, or while you're flat on your back."

Rebecca sighed and giggled. The sensations of Greg's hands on her flesh felt fabulous, and his words tickled her sense of the ridiculous.

She lifted her head to look to her right, so she could see Cody. It had been his suggestion, but she needed to see he'd be okay with it.

"If this is going to work, there're going to have to be times when Greg and I are together, just the two of us. You'll want that, too, some one-on-one time—hopefully with both of us."

"Yes." She reached out her hand to him. He took her hand in his and brought it to his lips. "There's no doubt at all that I'll want one-on-one time with you."

"Good. I've changed my mind on being a voyeur. I'll do that another time. For right now I'm going to go and throw together a meal for us." He leaned forward and kissed her cheek. Then he stretched up and kissed Greg. "Have fun, kids."

He snagged his boxers and T-shirt from the dresser where he must have set them before getting into the spa earlier. Then he was gone, the sound of his bare feet hitting the stairs as he went down echoed faintly.

"Is he all right?"

Greg sighed. "I think he needs some time to process everything."

"Like the reality of family in Lusty as well as moving from having one lover to having two?"

Greg eased off her and lay beside her. She turned so she could lay her head on his shoulder.

"You're a pretty clever woman." He wrapped his arms around her and held her snugly. This was something she'd never guessed could feel so damn good. She liked being held by Greg Benedict.

Rebecca reached up and stroked his face. "You don't have to make love to me if you don't want to."

He moved faster than she would have believed possible. Laying her flat, he loomed over her and said, "Flat on your back it is, then." His smile sobered. "You've been a hunger in my blood, all these years. I wasn't going to allow myself to be with *anyone*, and then Cody broke down my resistance. But even then, I knew that to be complete, I needed you, too."

"You can have me. You could always have had me. You just needed to tell me that you wanted me. That you needed me."

"And you waited for me."

Rebecca thought to deny that, but she didn't want there to be any lies between them. So she opted for total honesty. "I didn't realize at first that I was doing that."

"Thank you for waiting for me." He looked off toward the door, where Cody had so recently disappeared. When he turned back and met her gaze again, he said, "Thank you for waiting for *us*."

"Love me, please."

"I will. I do." He lowered his lips to hers.

Rebecca let her eyes drift closed as she experienced the wonder of his kiss. His mouth moved on hers, a graceful slow dance kind of sliding, warm and wet. She loved his taste, loved the way his mouth sucked on hers just a little. His tongue met hers and here their dance turned to a hot and steamy salsa.

Rebecca's heart swelled with joy to finally, *finally* be here, beneath him, naked and needy. Sighs and subtle sounds—moans, hums, and a slightly hissed breath serenaded and seduced.

Hands caressed and cupped, fingers gently flitted, teasing and testing and treasuring.

She wrapped herself around him and let her fires burn, no thought to rush, no need to control. As Greg kissed his way down her body, she arched so as to make his reach easier. He tasted her everywhere, his lips and tongue languid at first, burning a trail of passion across her flesh.

"More." She sighed her need, not worried that he would use that need, that aching vulnerability against her. When he urged, she rolled over, and he kissed and licked a line from her neck to the dimple above her ass.

Whimpering, she tried to urge him to do more than just kiss, and he chuckled, his laughter warm and wet against the flesh of her bottom.

He moved up and to the side and she knew he snagged a tiny packet of protection. Her heart raced as she heard the sound of the tear, and then the glide of the latex over his swollen cock.

He turned her once more. Her back hit the mattress and her hands reached for him, need spawning a sense of urgency.

Now, hurry, now. She needed him to rush, because she knew what it was to have, and then lose.

He seemed to sense the emotion behind her rush, and he kissed her. Slow and deep, long and languid, his mouth and tongue consumed her.

He moved and his cock slid into her in one solid and powerful thrust. "You're mine. You're ours. I'll never be without you again."

Rebecca clasped him, arms and legs, and moved her hips against his. She relished the friction of his cock moving inside her, of his groin rubbing against her clit. She shivered as the arousal spiraled up and up. Faster, deeper, his movements lost their finesse. He, too, seemed desperate to take and give and hold.

Perspiration drenched her and gathered between their bodies as they raced together toward their climax.

"*Rebecca.*" He thrust hard and held himself deep. She felt his cock pulse, felt the heat of his seed in the condom and came with him. Shivering, quivering, crying his name, she came and came and came and wished it would never, ever end.

Chapter 13

Why in the name of all that's holy did I agree to this?

"No, you may not turn tail and run." Greg had moved closer and put his hand on Cody's back, a physical way to underline the words he'd just said.

"You said a *small* family gathering at the restaurant," Cody said. "I was picturing a table for ten, tops."

Above the buffet was a sign that read "Welcome home Greg and Cody." Cody was still trying to take that in, and the fact that the *entire* restaurant was the scene of this event.

Greg had the nerve to laugh at him. "Trust me, there are a lot more Benedicts, Jessops, and Kendalls in the family than there are here tonight. And I don't believe I've even mentioned the Parkers, the Joneses, and the Parker-Joneses."

At least the venue—*Lusty Appetites*—was a little familiar. In the week he'd been in the vicinity of Lusty, they'd eaten here a few times. And come to think of it, most of the faces he could see—people gathered around in small groups, chatting, smiling, and laughing were somewhat familiar, too. To quell his nerves, he began to put names to faces—something he usually did very well. He recognized Greg's brothers, the twins, Chase and Brian, and their new wife Carrie. He'd met Carrie's sister Chloe, and her two huge fiancés, Grant and Andrew, who were also Rebecca's brothers. He'd met Rick, Trevor, and Kevin, his lover's triplet brothers, and their lovely wife Maggie. Cody had felt more than a little sympathy for his man when he'd seen how well each set of brothers interacted—with each other and with their wives.

He'd bet that the bite of loneliness Greg had lived with all the years of his youth simply from the way he'd been born had been the major factor that had kept him roaming all these years.

Cody returned his attention to naming all the people present. Of course, he knew the sheriff and his brother the lawyer—Adam and Jake—their spitfire wife Ginny, her son, the pistol—Benny, and a couple of new young ones, and Rebecca's other two brothers, the Drs. Jessop and their wife Jillian.

He hadn't yet met *any* of the older generation, though. He'd been told, just after they stepped into the place to a round of applause, that Greg's parents, his aunts and uncles, Rebecca's parents, *and* Grandma Kate would be attending tonight.

The current generation was all well and good, but it was with the older set—people of the same generation as his own parents or older—where there might be the problem of, and the potential for, shit hitting the fan.

At least it had always been so in Cody's experience.

"Do I *have* to meet your grandmother? Really? I mean, I agreed I should meet your parents." There was no way that Cody could figure to get out of *that* one, and when Greg asked to meet his, he was just going to have to tell him the truth. "But your grandmother?" Cody had vivid memories of his own grandmother. She'd been stuffy and starchy and miserable as hell. The woman had never smiled that he could recall.

She'd certainly been no friend to his older brother, Gene, when he'd needed her to be one the most. She'd sided with his parents, and condemned Gene to a three-month-long hell.

Greg rubbed his back, pulling him out of the dark and ugly past. "It's going to be fine, sweetheart. Aren't you the man who went intrepidly into some of the worst disaster areas on the face of the planet to snap a few pictures? Trust me, you've got this thing covered."

Cody almost answered that that had been *before* the debacle in Syria. Of course he was still nervous, thinking of future assignments, of resuming the life he led before he'd been kidnapped. He hadn't even been able to bring himself to pick up his camera. He told himself that was all only normal. It had barely been a month and a half since the incident. He was just *now* physically healed. Anyone would be leery of returning to one of the world's hot spots after what he'd been through.

He didn't need counseling and he sure as hell didn't need a fucking *shrink*. All he really needed was time. And if he wanted the time—like a mini sabbatical—then right here with his two smoking hot lovers seemed to be as good a place as any to take that time.

For the most part, the three of them stayed on their own at the cabin. They ventured into town for meals occasionally, and once more for Robert Jessop to look at his shoulder—this time after that doctor had consulted the full medical records which had arrived, via e-mail, from the hospital in Turkey.

He looked at Greg. A good, sound, logical answer eluded him. So he said, "That's different."

"God, Harper, you're such a *guy*," Greg laughed.

Cody burst out laughing, too. "Yeah, I guess I am that."

"I love my grandmother more than I love any other member of my family, and that's saying a lot because I love them all." Greg had bent close to say that. "It means a lot to me that my family wanted to welcome us—*you and me*—home this way. And it will mean a lot to me for you to meet Grandma Kate."

"Well, hell, Benedict. Put it like that, why don't you?"

Rebecca joined them, carrying three glasses of sweet tea. Cody reached out to help her, and her smile of thanks warmed him all the way to his toes.

"Come on, let's grab a place to sit. Anyone wants to say hi to the wandering gypsies, *they* can wander over to us," Rebecca said. "Nothing worse than standing here all centered out and everything."

Man, he was beginning to really love this woman. It seemed to him that she just got him, so easily and naturally. "That sounds like a plan," he said. "I won't feel quite so on display that way."

"We're used to having parties here," Rebecca said. "Most often, we've had engagement parties or just lately, baby debuts. Of course for bigger events, we use the community center."

"See?" Greg gave him a light cuff on the shoulder. "It *could* have been an even bigger party."

Cody nodded. "I've noticed a fair number of little ones in attendance." He nodded over to the corner where Greg's sister, Julia, and her two husbands each had a babe in their arms, next to another cousin, also married to two men, who had one baby. It took him a moment to recall that they were the Alvarez-Kendalls.

They're a bisexual ménage, just like us. He still felt the shock of looking at them as they'd come in tonight, and recognizing that fact. He'd paid attention, of course. Despite the assurances he'd received from Greg and Rebecca, it had surprised him some the warmth and affection with which the Alvarez-Kendalls had been welcomed.

The restaurant's owner—Cousin Kelsey—was there with a baby girl on her hip—cute little thing. Then, of course, were Greg's cousins whom he'd just met today—Josh and Alex—and their wife Penelope who had almost the same rich shade of black hair his Rebecca had. It was too soon to know whether their daughter Ellie would have black hair, or not.

Cody had to admit the inclusion of the babies was different from any kind of function he'd ever heard of, or attended, growing up.

"There you are! Oh, I'm so glad you're all here!"

Greg practically leapt to his feet at the sound of the soft voice. Cody stood as well and turned around to see the woman who inspired such a look of affection on his man's face.

She wasn't very tall and looked fragile as hell, but the grin on her face invited a smile right back.

Rebecca's painting certainly did this woman justice.

"Grandma." Greg lifted the woman clean off her feet, and she laughed! He set her down gently, and then kept his arm around her.

"Grandma Kate, this Cody Harper. Cody, my grandmother, Kate Benedict."

"How do you do, Mrs. Benedict?" Cody nodded, not sure if he should try to shake her hand or not.

"It's Grandma Kate to you. I'm so pleased to meet you, Mr. Harper."

"Just Cody, ma'am."

"Cody, then." And she resolved his dilemma by taking his right hand in both of hers. "I have to tell you I have been captivated by your pictures. I'd seen some of them in a few of the news magazines. But I have your book, too, and oh my, what an eye you have! You have a talent for showing us the reality of what some people endure—while also showing us they're just like us at heart. That is a phenomenal talent."

Cody was floored. In all his life, not a single member of his family had ever even said to him, "well done." Well, except for his brother, Gene. And even that had been tepid, because the years stretched between them and the gulf that separated them was a direct result of the cruelty of his parents.

He'd only been twelve at the time, but he remembered, and couldn't blame his brother for his hesitancy.

"Thank you, Mrs…Grandma Kate."

"You're welcome." The older woman let her gaze drift around the room. "This must be overwhelming for you, Cody. So many boisterous, *nosy* people in one fairly small place!"

Cody couldn't help but laugh as Grandma Kate took a seat. He and Greg both sat back down.

How did the woman know exactly what he'd been thinking before she came up, including the fact that he felt completely out of his element?

"It's been a bit of a culture shock," he admitted.

"I'm sure. Now, I was wondering if you'd had the opportunity yet to make it over to our museum?"

"No. I'll be honest with you. I've kind of put it off."

"Well now, if you're not interested in seeing the story of this family—and there's nothing wrong with that—you might, perhaps, be interested to see some of the earliest works of Jeremy Parker Jones."

The name was familiar to Cody, of course, for he'd studied the history of photography as an emerging medium in America. Jeremy Parker Jones was one of the pioneers of photography…and had moved, in the middle of his life, from Virginia to Texas.

"Wait a minute…" He closed his eyes, then began to recite, "Benedicts, Kendalls, Jessops, Parkers, Joneses, and Parker-Joneses." He opened his eyes and stared at Grandma Kate. "Jeremy Jones was a member of this family?"

"You have a lot in common with him, I think. I never met him, of course. He'd already passed on when I came to live here in 1942. But I knew some of his children. This family, of course, treasures his creations as a furniture maker, as much as his photographic work—the museum is full of the latter. As to the furniture, he was the one who designed the unique bedroom sets to be found all over Lusty. One of his descendants—his great-great-grandson, Carmichael Jones—still owns the furniture business, though he tends to produce only custom pieces specially ordered."

Cody looked at Greg. "I *have* to go to that museum."

"We'll take care of that tomorrow," Greg said.

Kate Benedict reached over and patted Cody's hand. "Life sometimes hands us a damned hornet's nest for us to navigate through, sometimes beginning with the family we're born into. We do our best and get stung a whole hell of a lot. This town—these people—can be the best medicine, if you just let them be. I should know. They certainly were for me."

She gave him a wide smile. "Now, I hope you'll excuse me. There are so many babies here for me to hold!"

Cody got to his feet. "I'm very glad to have met you, Grandma Kate."

"I'm glad to know you, too, Cody Harper. I'll see you later. Enjoy the night."

"Yes, ma'am. I will." Cody watched the spry, elderly woman walk off, watched the way the faces of folks simply lit right up the moment they saw her.

I have got to photograph that woman. He thought of how and where, of the angles and the lighting and even of the medium. But he wouldn't think any more about the enormity of that desire, the first strong urge to return to his craft. Nor would he think about the revelations that seemed to be going off inside him like Fourth of July firecrackers. No, he wouldn't think about them until later.

* * * *

Tonight's the night.

Rebecca had watched as Cody interacted, first with Grandma Kate, and then with the other members of the family. As Greg's parents, and then her own had come to be introduced to Cody and then to say hello to her and Greg, she'd seen the emotions—uncertainty, fear, curiosity, wonder—and finally that last one. *Envy.*

Cody Harper was many things, but an open book sure wasn't one of them. During the day he could be an intriguing companion, a challenging competitor in checkers or chess, and an insightful conversationalist.

In the late afternoon or early evening, he became a passionate and consummate lover. He could cook better than she could—praise the Lord—and even picked up after himself, and after Greg, too.

But when the clock struck twelve and it was time for bed, Cody Harper turned into an obstinate, irritating man.

He wouldn't let her spend the night in the same bed with him.

Poor Greg had been forced to choose between them, and that simply had to end. After that first night, when Greg had come to her bed and then lain awake most of the night, listening for Cody's cries because the man could not sleep through the night without having nightmares, she'd insisted Greg sleep across the hall with Cody each night.

She'd thought to give it a week, and now the time had come for her to take the bull by the horns—pun intended—and have a come-to-Jesus moment with the man.

With both men, in fact.

Cody was clearly suffering from nightmares, and Greg was just as determined to pamper him through them.

Nothing wrong with pampering, every living jack one of us needs it from time to time. But there had to come a time where the pampering was replaced with some tough love.

She couldn't make Cody talk about what he'd been through—and tonight she had her first clue that what had happened to him in Syria was only a *part* of the story. She was, however, convinced the longer he went without talking, the more damaging to his soul his silence would become.

Tonight, he'd had a few revelations about family, Lusty style. She and Greg had laid themselves bare already—literally and figuratively—for this man so he'd been able to get to know them. Now it was time for Mr. Harper to toss his clothes to the wind and drag his baggage out of the closet.

They would never be able to move forward if something didn't begin to give, and give soon.

Tonight, Rebecca thought, was as good a time as any to begin what she thought might be a long, painful process. She thought about letting Greg in on what she had in mind, but decided against it. This was her play to become an equal partner in this relationship—in this family. Whether either of the men involved realized it or not, they were a family already. They could stay a family and reach astounding heights of intimacy and happiness, together. Or they could be a family destined to splinter and break apart under stress.

Rebecca really didn't know which of the two endings was fated to be hers, but the fear that it would be the latter and not the former really, really scared her stomach.

In a way she couldn't explain or justify, Rebecca Jessop knew that these two men were it for her. If they couldn't work this out, she knew that after their end came, she would spend the rest of her life alone, lonely, and would very likely die broken-hearted.

Artists. We're all so fucking melodramatic.

True enough. But Rebecca knew to her core that melodramatic or not, that last part had been gospel.

She turned away from the window and approached the two men. Sitting side by side before the fire, they each nursed a half glass of brandy, and had fallen silent.

She approached them from behind, bent slightly over the love seat, and slid her arms around Cody's neck.

"Do you know what I want right now?"

She licked the shell of his ear and ran her hands up and down his chest so as to give the man a clue. She could see his erection pressing against his pants.

"I can guess, Blue Eyes. But it's getting late." He ran his hands over hers. "Isn't it almost your bedtime?"

Rebecca beat down the spurt of temper that wanted to erupt. "Let me tell you what I want, then. I want us, all three, naked in that hot tub upstairs. Then I want us, all three, naked in that Lusty-sized bed that's up there, making very hot and passionate love to each other. And then I want us, all three, to snuggle down in that bed, together, and go to sleep."

"Rebecca…" Greg started to intervene. She whipped her head to her left and shot him a look he should have no trouble interpreting.

Greg snapped his mouth shut.

"Baby, that's sweet. But I'm tired." Cody sounded almost sad, and that more than anything spurred her on.

"Me, too, baby. I'm tired of being treated like the token cunt in this bromance y'all have going on here. I'm good enough to fuck, but not good enough to be an equal partner? Is that it?"

"Becca!" Greg's shock was genuine, and so, too, was Cody's if the way his body had just jerked was any measure.

"No, of course not!" Cody grasped her hands and lifted them from around his neck. Then he was facing her, kneeling on the love seat, meeting her gaze.

"How could you ever *think* such a thing? I've never treated you with anything but the utmost respect and tenderness. Damn it, Rebecca, that accusation *hurt!*"

"So does knowing I'm worthy of being fucked, but not worthy of spending the night with you."

"You don't understand, honey. It has nothing to do with you."

"You're right, I don't understand. Explain it to me, please. Explain to me how you could possibly be thinking that we've got a shot at being a *forever* thing when you won't even let me share your bed at night."

"Honey…" Cody looked really perplexed, and that was a really good sign. It meant that what he'd been doing—excluding her—hadn't been calculated, so much as it had been instinctive.

He inhaled deeply and turned toward Greg. When that man said nothing, Cody sighed. He met her gaze again. "Honey, I don't sleep really solid at night, lately. I…I have nightmares."

"Wow, news flash. Cody, I *know* you have nightmares. I've known since the first night you spent here. I hear them, every single night."

"I'm sorry. Damn it, why didn't you say something?" He ran a hand through his hair. "The last thing I want to do is wake you every night because of my pathetic dreams."

"Oh, Cody! How can you be so smart, and so *stupid* at the same time?" she asked.

"What the hell do you mean by that?" He'd gone from pleading to angry in a heartbeat.

Now we're getting somewhere. "It doesn't matter that you wake me in the night. What matters is, it hurts me knowing you have those nightmares. It hurts me knowing you don't want me near when you do. Don't close me out, damn it. *Let me in.*"

"I'm not trying to close you out. I'm trying to *protect* you. You don't understand. You don't know, how could you possibly know? You've grown up in this fucking Shangri-la, this oasis of love and support, and you have no idea that—" Cody stopped and Rebecca knew he'd begun to say something he'd never intended to say.

She tilted her head to the side, met his gaze, and said, "And I have no idea that some people grow up without real love, or real support. Is that what you were going to say? Or that, maybe, I don't understand that *you've* grown up without those things? Baby, I'd already figured that one out."

"You don't know what you're talking about."

"I do know what I'm talking about. I know pain when I see it. Do you think you can protect me from that? I don't want or need to be *protected*, Cody." It was, Rebecca knew, time to play her ace. She reached out, caressed his face and laid her trump card—and her heart, on the table.

"I don't want or need to be protected, Cody. I want, I need, for you to accept my love. I love you, Cody Harper. And I need you to be all right with that. I need you to let me love you, and I need you to love me back."

Chapter 14

They'd foregone the tub in favor of the bed in the master bedroom.

Rebecca looked over at Greg as he finished lighting the candles that she'd set out earlier. "You want to help me undress this hunk?"

"Oh, absolutely."

Cody blushed, which Rebecca thought was sweet as hell. "Cut it out, you two. 'Hunk,' *right*. I'm a skinny runt compared to some of the men I've seen in this town."

"That's true," Greg said.

"You *do* have a point." Rebecca went up on her tiptoes and kissed him lightly. "Yeah, blond hair and brown eyes, swimmer's lithe physique, you're a skinny one, all right." Then she began to open the buttons of his shirt. "Thing is, you happen to be perfect. For me."

"Yeah, for me, too." Greg pressed up behind Cody, and when Rebecca finished opening his shirt, Greg took it off him. He pressed a kiss to the back of Cody's shoulder, and that man closed his eyes and shivered. His nipples puckered and his blush traveled down his neck.

"Go on with you." Cody sounded embarrassed.

It hadn't taken long for Rebecca to realize one thing Cody Harper did not have was an inflated ego. Oh, he was authoritative when it came to his own art, or discussing photography in general. But the man had no real ego at all. Just the opposite in fact, and she wondered how much of that was innate and how much could be laid at the feet of his parents. She hoped she'd be able to get him to open up about whatever had happened in his youth to wound him so. In the meantime, she had something she wanted to do now that ought to make him feel pretty damn good.

"It's true. Maybe you need a demonstration."

"Oh yeah? Just what do you have in mind, Blue Eyes?"

Rebecca didn't answer, at least not in words. Instead, she unbuttoned Cody's jeans, put her hands inside the waistband, and ensured his cock wouldn't get caught. Then she pushed the jeans and his briefs down, off his hips until they hit the floor.

She followed them down.

Kneeling before him, she took a moment to look at his cock. Now this part of him definitely was *not* skinny. Hard like it was now, with purple-blue veins pulsing along the length, she thought it a marvelous, wonderful thing. His cockhead, slightly purple, circumcised, glistened with a tiny drop of pre-cum that actually made her mouth water. She took a moment and nuzzled him, right at the very spot where his cock emerged from the nest of hair surrounding it. He smelled good, different from Greg, but still good.

Maybe the day will come when I'll be able to tell them apart, blindfolded. That was a happy thought.

"Jesus Christ, woman. You're driving me crazy!"

"That's the plan, lover. I really like your cock by the way." She used her nose to brush against his balls and the bottom of his penis.

Cody's response was a strangled kind of wordless sound that she had no trouble understanding.

"She's being a little minx, isn't she?" Greg sounded amused as he directed his comment to their lover.

Rebecca looked up and smiled at Greg, resting his chin on Cody's shoulder and looking down at her. She liked that look in his eyes, a look of happiness and love and peace.

"You *say* you like it," Cody said. He looked down at her, his gaze fierce. "But talk is cheap. What I need is a little demonstration here, instead of just words—show, not just tell."

Rebecca grinned, then used her tongue to give him a nice long lick from balls to tip. She let her tongue swirl out and lap up that tiny drop of viscose syrup he had there waiting for her.

"God, you are *so* going to get a spanking." Cody's words sounded aggrieved, but his tone sure didn't. He combed his fingers through her hair, pulled her closer, and said, "Suck my cock, woman. *Now*!"

Rebecca was nothing if not obedient—well, when she wanted to be, at any rate. At the moment what she wanted to do was suck Cody's cock. She didn't just want to taste him, she wanted to pleasure him. She wanted to surround him with as much love and affection and good feelings as she possibly could. No, she could never make up to him the lack he'd grown up with. But she could damn well guarantee that he wouldn't ever feel unloved or unwanted or threatened again.

Cody jerked and she grinned because she knew that Greg had just reached down and begun playing with his ass. She closed her mouth over Cody's cock and took him as deep as she could. Sliding her tongue up and down his shaft, she treated him to tiny little sucks that she hoped would get him hot and horny, fast.

She loved the flavor of him, a deeply musky salty combination that her taste buds recognized as Cody. The sensation of having his cock in her mouth, of having her lips stretched wide to accommodate him combined with that flavor, sent "fuck me" signals to her cunt. She'd been mildly interested when she dropped his pants. Now, she was hot and aroused.

She moved her head up and down, and used her hands to help—one wrapped around his cock so she could pump him as she sucked, and the other to gently cup his scrotum.

She squeezed his sac rhythmically, amazed at how that soft, fragile-feeling part of him got hotter and seemed to draw upward, readying, she knew, to release his sperm.

"God, woman, you have such a fantastic mouth! I'm close, baby."

She felt him trembling, and her heart sang for giving him this. His cock gave her little tiny drops of nectar, but she wanted more.

She wanted it all.

She stretched her hand out so that the fingers cupping his balls could also stroke upward toward his anus.

Greg's fingers found hers and caressed, and she felt fully there, completely a part of them for the first time.

"Oh, God, *yes*, I'm coming!"

Rebecca hadn't needed his words. She'd known. She sucked on his cock, long, strong draws that effectively pulled the seed right out of him. His cries of victory signaled she'd brought him higher, and as he kept shooting into her mouth, she continued to suck and swallow until she did indeed have it all.

Rebecca sensed as much as felt Greg's arm come around Cody to keep him upright. She tapered her ministrations, until she finally released him. Unwilling for this moment, this intimate, loving moment to be over, she placed little kisses on his hip and inner thigh.

He reached down and stroked her head, the gentlest of touches that communicated so much.

"I love you, Rebecca. Seriously. I didn't ever dream I'd be lucky enough to love and be loved by one person in this life, let alone two."

Rebecca stood up, laid her head on his chest and wrapped her arms around both him and Greg.

"Cody Harper, you *deserve* to be loved. You deserve every good thing that can come your way."

"What she said." Greg's other arm caressed her side.

"Maybe the day will come when I can really believe that."

"It will." Rebecca stepped back. There was only one thing to do now, and that was get this most fragile of her lovers into bed. She began to peel her clothes off. "Come on, babe. I need you to hold me."

"You should need me to do a hell of a lot more than that." He brought her close, pressing his flesh against hers. His cock began to harden and she liked her chances for round two.

"That was a gift, darling. Something I needed to give you."

Cody kissed her, a sweet, tender kind of a kiss. “All right. Climb in, and we’ll snuggle.”

Rebecca waited until Cody snuggled up to her left side, and then she giggled as she rolled over him, so that he was on her right.

Greg had stripped, and he got into the bed on the other side. Cody was in the middle, which was where she wanted him—where Greg wanted him, too, apparently.

“How come I get to be the filling?” Cody didn’t sound terribly disappointed with this turn of events.

“Because you’re the one we’re focused on right now,” Greg said.

“Gosh I feel all special.”

“You know, lover, Rebecca isn’t the only one who can be spanked.”

“Promises, promises.”

“Robert and David and Jillian belong to a club.” Rebecca sighed as she snuggled into Cody. All this talk of spankings was getting her wet. “It’s in Houston. Now, if there’s one club in that city, there’s got to be another one, right?”

Cody snickered. “What’s the matter, Blue Eyes? Afraid to do a scene, all naked in front of the docs? They’re docs, you know. I’m sure they’ve seen naked women before.”

“Hell, they’re Doms,” Greg said. “I’m sure they’ve seen naked subs before, of both genders.”

Rebecca shivered. “I’d just as soon not encounter them at all there, if it’s all the same to you.” She sighed again. “Okay, let’s forget I even mentioned it, all right? I’ve changed my mind. Maybe we could just play here. Sometime.”

“You craving a little D/s action, baby?” Greg asked.

“Y’all get talking about spankings and my pussy gets wet. Wouldn’t hurt to experiment.”

“Speaking of experiments.” Cody moved fast, so fast she didn’t even see it coming. The next thing she knew, she was sprawled on top of him, and Greg was on his knees, stroking his hand over her ass.

"We want to fuck you here," he said as he moved his fingers back and forth over her anus. "So we're going to start to get you ready for that right now."

"Hand me a condom, lover, and then hold her up for a moment."

Rebecca didn't really like being talked about as if she wasn't there—usually. It continually amazed her that what she *usually* didn't care for worked very well when it came to these two men and sex.

The sound of a drawer opening and closing was followed by the sensation of a square packet being tucked into her hand.

"Put this on him while I lift you up, Becca."

Rebecca shivered because Greg's voice had taken on a quality she'd never heard in him before.

He lifted her, and she was able to open the packet and smooth the condom over Cody's now very hard cock.

"Something tells me you've been to that club of Robbie's," she said.

Greg nuzzled her ear. "*The Lyon's Den*? Nope, never been there. But darlin', there are BDSM clubs all over the world, and there really isn't much I haven't tried."

Oh, God. That smacked of a promise and a threat all at the same time.

"Take his cock inside that hot little cunt of yours."

Rebecca reached down and centered Cody's cock at the opening of her pussy. She slid down onto him, and moaned with the pleasure of being filled.

"Down."

She didn't get a moment to think because between them, the men moved her so that her head lay on Cody's chest, and her ass was in the air.

"Oh!" Her gasp of surprise was met with smug male laughter. Greg's fingers, covered in lube, worked back and forth over her anus. "That feels incredible."

"Glad to hear it. Keep us posted, Becca."

Keep them posted? Before she could open her mouth to ask what he meant, he began to press his finger against her anal opening.

Strange and burning, the intrusion also added to her arousal. Rebecca angled her head so she could see Greg. The expression on his face kicked her heart rate up a notch. *Impassioned* looked damn good on him.

Cody's hands stroked over her back.

"I still remember the first time I had my anus stretched by a lover," he whispered. "I remember the burn, and the thrill, and the discovery that there seemed to be thousands of tiny nerve endings surrounding that tiny little hole, just waiting to send pleasure to my cock."

"Oh, God." Greg had breached the opening, and she felt that burn and that stretch and yes, those tiny little nerve endings.

"How does it feel to have my finger in your ass, honey?"

"I…mmm. It's good. Burning…but good."

"Cody?"

"Her nipples have turned rock hard and her cunt is squeezing my cock, drowning me in her juices."

"Good. This may not take long at all, then."

Greg eased his finger out of her, but before she could protest, he was back. More lube, she thought.

And then she felt the burning, hotter than before, and the stretching, greater than before, and she realized he'd added a second finger to the first.

"Okay?"

Rebecca couldn't manage a word. The sound that emerged from her throat must have told Greg what he wanted to know, because he began to move his fingers in and out, and, it felt like, swirl them around.

"Fuck her if you can, lover. Slowly. I'm just barely holding on here."

"Squeeze me, Blue Eyes. Let me feel your cunt milk me."

Rebecca already felt fuller than full with Cody's cock in her pussy. Cody grasped her hips and began to thrust in her, a short, fast kind of thrusting that managed to strum her clit. She clenched on him, and on the fingers in her ass, and shivered with the sensory overload.

She heard Cody's heart pounding louder and faster and that beat seemed to echo the arousal pulsing through her.

Greg moved, his body leaning forward. The drawer beside her opened again, and she saw a flash, a silver streak just at the edge of her vision.

Tear. Glide. *Oh, God.*

Greg moved again, angled closer, and eased his fingers out of her. "Take me, Becca. I need to feel your ass around my cock. I need to feel Cody's cock in your cunt."

"Oh! *Oh, Greg*!" She went from bereft to burning, from burning to pain in a heartbeat. She felt Greg's hands on her ass, spreading her cheeks. He leaned over her, pressed firmly, and grunted as his cockhead entered her, as it slid in past her sphincter. Then he pushed and she felt his cock slide all the way in until his balls bounced on the bottom of her cunt.

"Hold on. Just give me a moment. God, yes. *Becca*." Greg trembled, and she heard him struggling for breath.

"Fuck me. Oh, God, I need you both to fuck me. I can't…it's too…" She ended on a whimper, unable to get her mind or her mouth to work. She'd never been so full, never felt so on the edge between pleasure and pain before.

"God, Greg, her cunt is so tight and I feel you fucking her. It's like you're fucking us both at the same time."

"Yeah, lover, I can feel your cock, too—your cock surrounded by our woman's cunt. *Fucking wonderful*."

"Move. Do it. Oh, God, please, I need to come." Rebecca didn't care if she had to beg. She'd never been so hot, never been so aroused, and at the same time, she'd never felt more helpless to do anything about it.

"Okay, Becca. We'll do you. Hang on, baby."

They moved in her, tiny in and out, back and forth movements in her pussy and in her ass that made sure she had at least one cock to the hilt in her the entire time. Friction added to the shivery excitement, and Rebecca wondered how she could possibly survive this pleasure.

"Yeah, like that, fuck, this is beyond hot." Cody kept one hand on her head, holding her down, and she knew, she *knew*, he was meeting Greg's gaze. "Rebecca, you're so hot, so tight. Squeeze me again, Blue Eyes. Make me come inside you."

"So close," Greg panted. "Let's just do it. Let's just grab it."

Rebecca tried to flex her inner muscles, but felt so surrounded, so full and on fire, she barely managed a flinch.

Suddenly inside her it felt as if their cocks really connected, as if they battered the same spot, and she cried out as her rapture exploded out of her.

"Fuck, yeah!"

Her orgasm took over the milking, the clenching, and as wave after wave of the purest bliss assailed her, she felt the men's cocks twitch, heard their shouts and knew that they'd followed her over the cliff.

Free falling, no net, Rebecca cried as everything inside her screamed in jubilation.

Chapter 15

He didn't care for her properly after, the way he should have that first time. He wouldn't make that same mistake again, *this* time.

Greg came back to the bed from the bathroom, warm, damp cloth in hand. Carefully he cleaned the lube from her, and when she moaned, he gentled his touch.

"Are you okay there, Becca?" He bent down and kissed her ass and stroked his hand over her.

I should have been more patient and taken a couple of days to prepare her better first.

"Dead. Heaven." The words came muffled against her pillow. He met Cody's gaze and they both grinned like fools.

Cody leaned over her and kissed her shoulder. "No, beautiful Blue Eyes, you're not dead. Couldn't speak if you were dead."

"'Kay." She sighed

Greg made quick work of taking the linens back to the bathroom, so he could return to the bed.

He understood why it was Rebecca had wanted Cody to sleep in the middle, especially this first night when they were in the same bed. She thought to surround their man so that when the night horrors came—and they would come, no matter Cody's assurances that they wouldn't—their man would be cocooned in their caring.

Greg loved Rebecca for that, alone. And he'd been with her one-hundred percent in that strategy. But one look in Cody's eyes and he knew they were going to be the macho men snuggling in the little woman.

Tonight, at least.

So he wouldn't worry about Cody so much, tonight. Instead, he'd sleep with his Becca beside him and trust her to look after their man.

She sighed and lifted her head, and tried to see over him to get a look, he figured, at the clock.

"What time is it?" she asked. She turned over so she was lying on her back, and yawned.

"Time for you to go to sleep, baby." He moved in closer on her right side and grinned when Cody moved in closer on her left. Cody nodded, and Greg reached for Rebecca, and turned her so that he could snuggle her close. She laid her head on his shoulder and Cody moved in to spoon her.

Cody's arm came around her, but his hand rested on Greg. Greg put his arm around Rebecca, but his hand rested on Cody.

Connected. Together. This was what he'd always wanted, and always been afraid he could never have. *We're only beginning.*

"Now who's thinking too loud?" Rebecca said.

"Me. This feels so damn *right*. I'm almost afraid to believe it." Greg sighed. He was worried about Cody, and worried that Rebecca wouldn't really be interested in the long haul.

He was worried, period, and he hated being worried. That was one of the reasons he'd avoided commitment for so long. He'd *worried* that he would never been able to get beyond the worry to the living.

That and the fact that he had so much to do, and most of what he wanted and needed to do with his life wasn't here in Lusty. Hell, a lot of it wasn't even here in the States. Cody traveled with him, for the most part, and was able to do his thing wherever they went.

When Cody had gotten that offer from his publisher to accompany that asshole Drummond Pierce to Syria, of course Greg had gone with him.

Supporting each other in their careers was what people who loved each other did. Greg let that thought echo for a second time in his mind. It was what people who loved each other did.

Daniel really did a number on me, and I'm only now just realizing how much of a one.

"Instead of worrying about it, talk to us." Rebecca's breath puffed against his chest with her words.

"It's not ready to come out yet."

"What is it with men and their need to keep secrets? In my experience—from growing up in a family with four brothers and being way outnumbered, period, by so many male cousins—those secrets tend to be tiny little pockets of self-doubting poison."

"It's because we're just poor, dumb bastards," Cody said. "Always thinking with the wrong head."

"Well, *duh*." Rebecca jiggled the bed with her laughter.

Greg found himself smiling.

"I was thinking about Daniel and the way we really were, together."

"And what conclusions did you draw?" Rebecca ran her hand down his chest.

And then he felt his two lovers join hands on him.

"It was all about *Daniel*. Our relationship. He was a doctor—a surgeon—and yes, he spent a lot of time doing charity work. But as I look back, I don't think his actions were motivated by any great sense of love of humanity, or need to do good. It was about his ego."

When neither of his lovers commented, he went on, expressing in words what he'd barely allowed himself to think in the past.

But the words were right there, ready to be said so he knew they'd been brewing, and he'd been thinking subconsciously about it all these years.

"Our fight that Christmas? It was because we were going to be taking the time to fly to England, and visit his family, and I was just to be his 'assistant,' some American he met in Jakarta and had befriended. His family didn't know he was gay—and yeah, who am I to talk when I didn't ever openly tell anyone here that I liked men just as much as I liked women?"

"You would never have brought a lover home and asked that lover to live a lie like that," Cody said.

"Not in a million years," Rebecca agreed.

He felt her pause and then she asked, "Didn't he want to come here, to meet your family, too?"

"Hell, no. I started to tell him about Lusty. He thought we were all a bunch of *amoral philistines*. His exact words." To this day Greg could hear the dismissive tone in Daniel's voice.

"That's not how love speaks, sweetheart," Cody said. "It sounds to me as if Daniel had his own issues and hang-ups, and was using you, and your perceived inadequacies, to deflect them, and his own." Cody inhaled. "Hell, he was using you, period."

Greg didn't imagine the anger in Cody's voice. But it did surprise him, because his lover was generally a very "live and let live" kind of guy.

"Judgmental prig," Cody said. "Had he never heard that saying about people living in glass houses? I hate people who judge others based on who they are, especially when they're so imperfect themselves. What the fuck? Why can't people love others for who they are instead of trying to mash them into some image that makes *them* look and smell good?"

"Who mashed you?" Rebecca asked.

Cody nearly pulled his hand back, but she caught him, and Greg laid his on top, so that they were joined, perhaps only symbolically at this moment, but joined nonetheless.

The silence stretched, and Greg fought the urge to prod him. Finally, he felt Cody relax, and then heard him sigh.

"Not me. Gene."

"Your older brother?" Rebecca didn't know as much about Cody, Greg realized, as he himself did. But she knew a little, and maybe, Greg thought, she was the perfect one to handle this. He sensed he was about to learn things he'd never known, and so almost held his breath, waiting for Cody to answer her.

"Yeah. Older than me by six years." Cody sighed again. "It's kind of funny, and kind of weird that we're both of us—Gene and I—bisexual. I'd just begun to know that about myself when I was eleven. Gene was seventeen, and already giving our parents fits. You know, normal teenage growing pains."

"Went through some of those myself," Rebecca said.

"Not like Gene. Mom and dad came home one night from being out at the club—they were all about the club. Hell, they were all about *image,* period. Tony Tribeca address, summer house in the Hamptons, the whole fucking nine yards."

Rebecca didn't turn around. Greg guessed she must have figured that Cody felt safer talking to her back. But she did begin to stroke his arm, a silent signal that she was with him. Greg squeezed his hand in encouragement.

"Anyway they came home all liquored up—they were all about the booze, too. Checked on me on their way to bed—don't get all sappy thinking, aw, that's sweet. They never came in, pulled a blanket up or kissed my forehead. They were checking to see that I was in bed and my room was spotless. Their habit. Anyway, Gene had had his buddy, Norman, over earlier in the evening. I didn't keep track of them, really. Gene was supposedly babysitting me, but I was pretty self-sufficient. Anyway, the next thing I know, there's screaming and Dad is beating the hell out of poor Norman. Who'd been asleep, naked, in bed with Gene, who was also naked."

"That's horrible! I hope the police charged him."

"Charge Douglas Harper with anything? No, Blue Eyes. Dad slipped the proper folks some cash and it all went away. So did Norman, and so, the next day did Gene." Cody shivered. "They had him committed to a mental hospital."

"They *what*?"

The outrage in Rebecca's voice matched Greg's emotions completely.

"Oh, yeah. Homosexuality is a sickness, didn't you know? A mental illness. Anyone who's gay or bisexual needs to be *cured*."

"Oh my God! What happened?"

Cody sighed. "It didn't take Gene long, maybe a couple of months, but he escaped. He got in touch with me before he took off, out of the area. It was five years before he got word to me that he was on the West Coast. Mom and Dad never mentioned him again, but they made me start going to a shrink—you know, just in case the 'homosexuality' thing was contagious—although they never actually came out and admitted that."

He met Greg's gaze, and must have found comfort there, because he seemed to relax even more. "I was a pretty smart little bugger even then. Had the shrink convinced that I was genuinely one-hundred percent hetero."

"And when you came of age, you left?"

"Yeah. I'd been banking my allowances, which were generous as long as I kept producing those As and met their highest standards—looking good and smelling good, and all the rest of that bullshit. I felt like a fucking traitor to my brother, but we'd talked on the phone a couple of times, and he thought I was being smarter than he had been. He never gave me grief over the act."

"That's why you were nervous tonight. Christ, sweetheart, if I'd known, I wouldn't have sprung so many new relatives on you all at once."

"I was nervous, yeah. But everyone was great. Still having trouble wrapping my head around this place you live in. Man, with acceptance like that, why'd you ever leave?"

Greg said the first thing that came to mind. "Because I was stupid."

* * * *

Rebecca came awake immediately, and before she even fully processed what was happening, she reached for Cody.

"Shhh. It's all right. We're here."

"No…no…please don't….oh, God, please don't pull the trigger…*please*!"

Rebecca's heart broke at the small, frightened sounds of Cody's terror. She snuggled into him, wrapped her arms around him, and stroked his back.

His shaking jarred her, but that didn't matter. She crooned to him as she continued to use her hands and her heart to comfort him. She felt him come awake, come aware, and for one moment he stiffened in her arms. But then he held on. He held on tight and Rebecca sent up a prayer of thanks.

"Sorry."

"Hey! Didn't you ever see that old movie? I quote, 'Love means you never have to say you're sorry.'" And because there was enough light for him to see, she batted her eyelashes at him.

Cody laughed, as she hoped he would. "You're a nut. Did you know that?"

"You tell me how I could grow up practically drowning in a sea of testosterone and not be a bit nutty." She met his gaze then reached up and stroked his face. "Do you want to talk about it?"

"I don't remember it, really. I never do."

Rebecca didn't know if she bought that one-hundred percent, but she decided to let it slide. She couldn't, after all, make him be ready to talk about his nightmares or his nightmare experience in Syria.

So instead of pressing, she asked, "Are you all right?"

"Yeah, but I'm drenched in sweat."

"So let's shower." She turned her head to look at Greg, who she knew was awake. Propped up on his right arm, he smiled at her.

"Y'all get started. I'll be right there."

"It's not right, you guys letting me wake you up and disturb your sleep this way."

"Sure it is. Maybe, sometime down the road, it'll be my turn." Rebecca climbed over Cody and began to pull him from the bed. "You've both mentioned the chance of forever. Well, forever implies that at some point I'll be pregnant. You gonna bitch at me if I wake you in the middle of the night?"

"Do you want that?" Cody asked the question softly, and Rebecca wondered at her instincts, that she would say such a thing at such a time. "Do you want to have children?"

"Yes. But not just any children. I want yours and I want Greg's. Someday, if we get all the kinks sorted out and decide together that's what we want to do."

"I'm pretty fucked up. You sure you want to take a chance, spreading my DNA to a new generation?"

Oh, Cody, what are we going to do to make things better for you? "I'm very sure. And, babe, you're not as fucked up as you think you are."

She led him into the bathroom, right over to the large shower. She turned the water on full, then set to work washing him. Only a few minutes passed and Greg joined them. They made quick work of getting clean. Once outside the shower enclosure, she and Greg both worked on drying Cody.

"I'm not an invalid," he groused.

"Guy gets a couple of love slaves and he bitches about it," Greg said. "What are ya gonna do?"

"Dunno," Rebecca said. "Sure beats the livin' hell outta me."

Cody laughed. "Okay, I get it. I'll stop bitching. Seriously." He cupped Rebecca's face. "I'm sorry. Having nightmares makes me bitchy."

"There's that word again." She stretched up and kissed him gently. "No apologies."

In just a few moments they all climbed back into bed. Greg had changed the sheets, because Cody really had been drenched in sweat.

This time, Rebecca had her way and sandwiched Cody in the middle. Greg hauled the man into his arms, and she happily spooned him. She leaned over and kissed Greg lightly, then laid another soft buss on Cody's cheek.

She snuggled down, amazed when the sensation of dropping off came so quickly.

* * * *

Rebecca blinked, and tried to focus on her surroundings. She could smell bacon, and coffee, and her stomach rumbled.

"He really likes cooking breakfast first thing in the morning," Greg said softly.

She felt herself being drawn into his arms. She wrapped herself around him, but for once, it wasn't the arousal he always stirred within her taking center stage in her heart or in her thoughts.

She knew it was just the two of them in the bed, and in the room. Still, she whispered, "What are we going to do to help him?"

"I don't know, baby." Greg sounded as sad, and as bewildered, as she felt. "I do know we can't ask him to seek professional help. Not now."

He meant not after hearing about what happened to him in his childhood. "No, we can't. I guess all we can do is stay close. Watch over him. Maybe after a while, when he feels more secure, the nightmares will become less frequent."

"Maybe." Greg's agreement didn't make her feel any better, because she heard the same doubt in his voice that she felt in her heart.

"I haven't pushed him at all," Greg said. "I maybe should have. You did last night, a little, and it was the right thing to do."

"You were there. You went through the terror of not knowing what was happening to him. It must have put you right back to 2004, to the horror of those days."

"It did. I thought it was happening all over again. Then, when my friends told me that they'd found him, and were bringing him across the border into Turkey, all I wanted to do was take care of him."

She heard the catch in Greg's voice, and held him tighter. "He was sick."

"They thought he might die from the infection." He didn't say anything more for a long moment. Rebecca waited. "Then, he got better. When he was discharged from the hospital, I decided that I needed to bring him here. It was safe here, and here, he could finish healing."

"He is healing, darling. And he will get over this. We just have to be there, let him see how we're there for him. And maybe prod him a little here and there if we think it'll work."

"Okay, that sounds like a plan. Rebecca." He tilted her chin up and placed a gentle kiss on her lips. "I'm really glad you love him, too."

"So am I." Her stomach growled again. "Let's go downstairs and see what our man has prepared for us, shall we?"

"Yeah, with Cody you don't want to wait too long once you smell the bounty."

"What, does he threaten to feed it all to the dog?" Her Aunt Heather, Tracy's mom, always used to do that. The fact that *those* Jessops didn't have a dog never diminished the threat.

Greg chuckled, clearly recalling the memory. "No, it's worse, much worse. He'll eat all the bacon and just give you a saucer of drippins to dip your toast in."

"Cody has a cruel streak, does he?"

"It only comes out when food is involved," Greg said.

"In that case, we better get a move on." Rebecca tossed aside the blankets and thought, for a moment, of just going downstairs, naked.

At the last minute she changed her mind, and copped a pair of panties and one of Cody's shirts—the thing practically hung to her knees—instead.

She thanked herself just a few minutes later when Adam Kendall came to the door.

Chapter 16

Daddy used to say that a person should always be willing to try new experiences.

Naomi smirked at the thought, because she had a pretty good idea of the kinds of new "experiences" her daddy had in mind, and they weren't none of them to do with anything except fucking.

She should know. She was one of his "new experiences." Before he'd had her sent to that boarding school.

Naomi pushed the thoughts of the past away. It was useless to dwell on those things anyway. Her memories should be dead and buried—as dead and buried as her parents.

The bus pulled into the station, and she got off, adjusted her hat, and looked around while she waited for the driver to open the luggage compartment. Naomi shook her head as she realized the place didn't really look all that different from the ones she'd been through during the last week or so. She guessed that these facilities looked the same all over the country.

Not that she'd been all over the country, exactly, but she watched a lot of television, and some things were pretty hard to fake.

See, daddy, I'm having a new experience. I'm in Texas! Naomi had never been to Texas before, but she'd watched reruns of Dallas all the time. She felt confident that she spoke the language, and would be able to fit right in.

Trusty backpack in hand, she stepped out of the facility and onto the sidewalk and checked the street signs. She'd studied the map of Waco for the last hour on the bus. It had taken her several days to come this far, and she was exhausted. She'd traveled as unobtrusively as she could, all the way from Seattle. She hadn't taken a plane or train—both of which would have been much faster modes of transportation. Faster, and the first places the authorities would check for her, probably.

Naomi watched police and PI shows, and she was way too smart for that.

She figured it might just be possible for the cops in Seattle to have tracked her to her original apartment. That would be unfortunate, but since she'd been smart enough to take everything she'd needed from there when she'd fled to her temporary home, including her new "identity," it didn't really matter. She never had to go back to that apartment, and had left the house she'd been staying in after it way ahead of the police coming anywhere near her.

On the off chance that they knew who she was, she'd made a crucial decision and had decided that the time had come to officially change her identity.

Naomi Lake had ceased to exist the moment she got on the bus in Seattle.

She'd guessed that if they were looking for her, they'd check out the airport and the train station. She doubted it would occur to them to stake out the *bus* station. Who the hell fled town and the cops in this day and age by hopping on a bus?

Now that she'd arrived in Texas she could afford to take a couple of days to rest, and plan. It was only a few blocks, really, from where she was, at the corner of Eighth and Mary, over to the Hilton on University Parks Drive. It was a nice day, and the walk would do her good.

She'd traveled cheap the whole trip, but this was where things changed. This was where *she* would really change. As she walked, she put herself into character. She'd paid for her fake driver's license and social security card early last year, even before she'd met Brady Alexander.

Planning. One never knows when one would have to have a brand-new start. She'd followed her father's tenet on being prepared, and for once, she thought, the old bastard's voice in her head had proven useful.

Naomi had wished for a new start many times in her life. Now she was taking one, but she had to do one teeny tiny little thing first. There remained only one loose thread to tie off, and then she'd be free—free to live the way she'd always longed to live. She'd be free to finally meet her destiny!

She just had to get rid of that faithless whore, Rebecca Jessop, first.

Once that was done, her life could truly begin anew. As she walked along Mary Street, she reminded herself that she wasn't *Naomi* anymore. Naomi had been a pathetic loser, a mousy mouse of a woman who'd never really fit in anywhere. She had a new name, and a whole a new identity now. She'd make it a triple blessing, and give herself a new personality, too.

She was now Caroline Jeffries, from Sacramento, California. She'd taken her mother's maiden name, and wasn't that rich?

After she'd gotten the fake ID—which had cost her a damn fortune—she'd applied for and obtained a credit card in that name, and had used it sparingly, always paying the bill on time. She'd been rewarded, of course, for her good management of the account with a higher spending limit. Now she had lots of money to play with, enough that she'd be able to back up her new image with a few choice accessories.

She'd be sleek and new, right here in Texas. She'd get herself a new boyfriend before the month was out. Just see if she didn't! She'd aim for a rich one this time, because momma had always said it was just as easy to fall in love with a rich man as it was a poor one.

She knew there were rich oil men all over this state, just waiting for the right woman. She was bound and determined to be someone's right woman.

She would check into the Hilton, rest for a day or so. She'd eat well and go for a swim in the pool and sleep well. Then she'd rent a car and take a drive westward.

Caroline Jeffries would make her way to that tiny little dot on the map and have a look around. She'd done some research online and hadn't been able to find out much about the place at all. There was the mention of the Sheriff's Department, but not much else. *Probably not much more than a crossroads there, if that. Maybe a gas station and a greasy spoon diner. It shouldn't be hard to find the woman.*

Rebecca Jessop was an artist, the kind of woman, her momma would say, that decent folk steered clear of. If there was much of a town there, in that Lusty, why then probably there'd be places to pick up the latest gossip. *Funny name for a town. Probably a family name.* She'd see how it went but she wouldn't be the least surprised to discover that the good folks of Lusty considered that woman to be the scourge of their community! Who wanted an amoral artist in their midst? Decent folk certainly wouldn't.

Caroline knew all about decent folk, as her momma had pounded into her time and time again that she was to grow up and be decent folk.

Not the same kind of pounding daddy gave me that's for sure.

No, it shouldn't be too hard to find Rebecca Jessop at all. She'd never even know Naomi—oops, *Caroline*—was coming for her. She would never know what the hell had hit her.

It's what you deserve for stealing my man, you faithless whore.

* * * *

"Does the law always come a-calling this early in the morning?" Cody asked.

Greg had gone to the door to let Adam in. Rebecca turned and gave him a smile. "You'll have to get used to it. Adam and Matt are cousins, and we were all kind of close, growing up. On top of being family, they're friends, and they both take their jobs seriously. Adam especially sees it as his sworn duty to protect *everyone* in town, which was why he was giving me such a hard time when we went to his office and told him about the crazy stalker chick."

Adam came into the kitchen and nodded at everyone. "Good, you're up," he said.

Rebecca knew he'd spoken to her. "Just barely up, but not awake enough yet."

Adam skewered Cody with a direct stare. "Hell, man, give that woman some coffee, quick. None of us are safe until you do."

Cody chuckled, and she was reminded that he'd already had a thing or two to say about her morning caffeine-deprived grumpiness.

"I'm on it. Would you like a cup, too, sheriff?"

Adam put his hands on his hips and raised one eyebrow. "Yes, please. When do you think you can learn to call me Adam?"

Cody shrugged. "I'll work on it."

"Fair enough." Then he turned his attention toward the stove, and Greg and Rebecca traded a look. Adam looked like a starving man eyeing manna from heaven.

"Would you like some breakfast, too, Adam?" Rebecca asked.

"I shouldn't. Looks like Cody's cooked for the two of you. That granola and yogurt Ginny gave me this morning was actually pretty good. I'm getting used to it."

Rebecca giggled.

Greg said, "Does our sweet Ginny have you on a diet, there, Adam?"

"Yeah, me and Jake both. She's worried about our cholesterol levels. I tried to get your brother to tell her I'm healthy as a horse." Adam pointed at Rebecca.

"Oh, Robert would just have chortled and told you that a heart-healthy diet was a good thing, and good for you while he agreed as to the state of your health." The look on Adam's face told her she was right on the money.

"Did he add, 'for a man your age'?" Greg asked.

"Yeah, the rotten bastard. And Ginny was right there, too!"

Greg said, "I think Tamara has Morgan and Henry on a diet, too."

"She does," Rebecca said. "You know what that means."

Adam sighed. "Yeah, it means I don't even get a break at Sunday dinner. I *knew* Mother had to be behind this."

Cody laughed. "You're breaking my heart, Adam. Man *cannot* live on yogurt and granola alone. Come, sit down and have some breakfast. I actually made more than I should have, because my mind wandered while I was cooking."

It didn't take the sheriff long to make a decision. "Thanks, I appreciate it. Only…"

"Not a word to Ginny, I promise." Rebecca said. "You want me to pinky swear, like we used to when we were kids?"

"Naw, I trust you."

While they'd been jabbering, Greg had set another place at the table and Cody had poured out the coffee. Soon, they were all sitting and eating.

Cody had fried the side bacon so crisp it melted in her mouth. Rebecca only allowed herself one sausage patty, enjoying the bite of the spicy pork. Gus, at the grocery in Lusty, had a fine hand at making sausage.

She wasn't as disciplined when it came to Cody's French toast. She didn't know what all he put in the dipping batter, but it was the best French toast she'd ever eaten.

They didn't speak for a several long minutes except to compliment Cody on the food and make appreciative sounds.

"Good thing you can cook," Adam said to Cody. "This guy, here, can microwave a mean Lean Cuisine. But that's about the extent of it."

Cody nodded. "Yeah, I know. Greg's idea of cooking dinner is to pick up the phone and order in."

"Hey, it works, and there're no pots and pans to scrub up afterward." Then he frowned. "Of course, there's no place to do that here at the cabin."

"Pizza Palace in Gatesville delivers to Lusty, and it's pricey, but they take plastic." Adam grinned.

"Good to know," Greg said.

"I can cook, but not as well as Cody," Rebecca said. Then she shrugged. "It's never particularly bothered me that I didn't excel at the traditional female tasks." She figured her gift was her art, so that was what she'd developed. "It was always kind of depressing cooking for one, so I never tried to get really good at it. But I *can* cook."

Adam nodded. "Yeah, I remember what that's like, cooking for one." Then he smiled in such a way that Rebecca knew he was, these days, a very contented man, despite the recent diet.

He set aside his plate and sat back to take a sip from his coffee.

"I'm going to guess it wasn't a sudden need for my man's cooking or our conversational brilliance that brings you out here this morning, cousin," Greg said.

"It's not, though I consider both a really great bonus." He looked at Cody. "Thanks for the meal. It was very good."

"You're welcome."

"Actually, there're a couple of matters I need to discuss with y'all." Adam took another sip of his coffee. "After you came in the other day, I reached out to Detective Dwyer of the Seattle PD. He assured me the investigation into the attempt on your life was ongoing and in fact, they were expecting a break in the case shortly. He called back last night."

Adam pulled his smart phone out of his pocket and worked it for a moment. Then he held it toward her and asked, "Is this the woman you've reported as having been following you?"

Rebecca would never forget that strange-looking woman. Blond hair, brown eyes, she looked like a plain Jane, but Rebecca had seen the insanity in the woman's eyes. "Yes, that's crazy stalker chick."

"Her name is Naomi Lake. Until three years ago, Ms. Lake was a guest of the state of Washington, in one of its restricted mental illness facilities."

"What did she do to end up there?"

Rebecca knew she didn't imagine the slight edge in Cody's voice. Fortunately, Adam didn't notice it—or if he did, decided to ignore it.

"She murdered her parents when she was fourteen years old." Adam focused on her picture for a moment, then diddled with the phone again, obviously bringing up some notes. "The defense in the case stated that her father had sexually abused her for years, and that her mother had been complicity silent and physically abusive. There wasn't a great deal of evidence, but the psychiatrist that the state called in to examine Naomi confirmed that she had many of the symptoms of longtime sexual and physical abuse."

"I feel sorry for her." Rebecca shook her head. "Something like that can ruin you forever. No wonder she's crazy."

"Naomi apparently refused treatment for the first year of her incarceration and then gave in, and three years ago she was released—three of the four psychiatrists on the institution's panel were convinced she was cured. The fourth was not."

"Let me guess," Greg said. "The lone holdout was a woman."

Adam raised one eyebrow. "How'd you know?"

"Just a hunch. Rebecca, you said that Brady told you he'd dated crazy stalker chick just once, and yet she seemed to have some sort of obsession with him?"

"Yes. He was very forthcoming about the entire situation—even *after* I told him there was no way I could go out with him. I'd already decided to track you down and get in your face."

Greg grinned. "My very own private stalker chick." He put his hand over his heart. "I'm touched. Not as touched as you are—in the head, that is—but still."

"Jerk face. You're going to be 'touched' if you keep it up. By my fist."

Cody looked at Adam. “This could go on for a bit. They tend to slip into some kind of juvenile sniping mode every once in a while.”

Adam nodded. “Nothing ever changes. You should have seen them when they *were* kids. Talk about oil and water.”

“Hey, we’re older and wiser now,” Greg said. “So now it looks like the female shrink was right, because the cops in Seattle think Naomi Lake killed Brady?”

Adam leaned forward. “And two more men before him, they think, now that they’re tracing her background. One in Portland, Oregon, and the other in Tacoma—she’s averaging one obsession a year. And it’s worse. They also think she killed the girlfriend of the man in Oregon.”

“See, I *knew* she was crazy.” Rebecca slapped the table for emphasis. She had known it when she’d looked into the woman’s eyes. Rebecca shivered. Greg saw, of course, and reached over for her hand. Cody grasped the other one, and she felt better.

“Yeah. Anyway, that’s not the worse news. The *worse* news is they found her apartment—not too difficult—*and* her bolt hole.”

“Bolt hole?”

“According to witness reports, Naomi was last seen at her home just over a month ago. A neighbor said she looked frantic, didn’t respond to his hail. She had a small bag, like a knapsack, slung over her shoulder. Police gained entry to her place, and more importantly to her electronics. They pointed to another place, a home whose owners were on an extended vacation and had hired a security company to monitor it.”

“Pretty clever.”

“She’s clever and not quite sane. A dangerous combination.” Adam inhaled deeply and met Rebecca’s gaze. “So here’s the *worst* news. They missed her by, they think, a few days, but they found all the research she’d been doing, before and after Brady’s death. Research on you—and Lusty. And she’s gone. Vanished. They have no idea where she is, but they have a pretty good idea where she's headed."

"She's headed here," Cody said. "She's obsessed, and she's coming for Rebecca."

"Odds are," Adam agreed.

Rebecca sat back. "This cabin isn't on any map, or even *listed* anywhere," Rebecca said. "She won't find me here."

"No," Adam said, "she'll head to Lusty."

"You'll be ready for her." Rebecca said.

"Hell, yes, we'll be ready for her. From the information Dwyer has dug up on the woman, we can take a guess on what her strategy is going to be."

"I hope the men in town can resist what appear to be her 'fatal' charms," Cody said.

He looked really worried about it, so Rebecca rubbed the back of his hand with her thumb.

Then, something she'd said a few moments before seemed to come back to him. "What do you mean, this place isn't listed?" Cody asked.

"It's kind of a family safety thing," Greg said. "Benedicts, Kendalls, and Jessops have always been targets because of our wealth, so when we decided to have a place to get away from it all we ensured this cabin wasn't listed anywhere and doesn't even show up on Everywhere Earth satellite photos."

Cody gave a low whistle. "You have this location scrubbed? Now *that's* what I call influence."

"What was the other thing?" Rebecca had been watching Adam, and he'd been sort of keeping an eye on Cody. When she asked that he met her gaze. "You said you had a couple of things to talk to us about."

"The other thing is about Cody."

"You come to arrest me for something?"

"Hell, no." Adam sighed. He looked off to the distance for a moment and Rebecca knew he was choosing his words carefully. She felt Cody tense, and stroked the back of his hand with her thumb again. "One of the things that the head of security for Benedict Oil and Minerals does is to keep his ear to the web, as it were. He has alerts out for the mention of anyone in the families, with regard to anything, anywhere, online."

"Sort of like an Everywhere alert," Cody said, naming the world's largest Internet search engine.

"Exactly," Adam nodded. "Any news item, any…well, any *anything*, he finds out about it and if he deems it significant, he reports it to the Town Trust."

"Okay," Cody said. "But what does that have to do with me?"

Adam raised one eyebrow and looked at Greg. Greg leaned forward so he could meet Cody's gaze, and said, "That sign that hung at the party last week that said 'Welcome home Greg and Cody' wasn't just a decoration, boyfriend. Even if we don't *stay* here, even if we carry on with our nomadic ways, Lusty has claimed you, so Lusty is your home, now. Your name would have been added to the names being monitored. You're family."

"What's happened?" Rebecca asked. Personally, she really didn't like all the pussyfooting around both Greg and Adam were doing.

"Does the name Drummond Pierce mean anything to you?" Adam asked.

"Asshole." Greg practically spat that.

Adam quirked one eyebrow.

Cody shook his head and said, "Yes, he was the former ANN news anchor I went to Syria with. He's got a book deal with my publisher, who asked me to go along and get some photographs for the book he's writing. Why?"

Adam looked at Greg. "Why'd you call him an asshole?"

"He and Cody were kidnapped together, but somehow that asshole managed to free himself and then fled. He didn't even *try* to get Cody out of that mess. Then, when he made it back to Turkey, he didn't even wait around to see if Cody got out, too. He acted as if Cody was already dead, which terrified me *and* pissed me off. Fucking asshole was on a fucking plane to New York before anyone could say the words, 'news cycle.'"

"Well, fuck, the guy *is* an asshole." Adam sat for a moment, and Rebecca could almost see the wheels turning. "I don't like that. And y'all won't like this, either. Pierce gave an interview on Morning People on ANN—and he claimed that you, Cody, are mentally unstable. He said that you had been under psychiatric care as a child, and that you're, in his words, 'sadly delusional, likely even schizophrenic.' He was playing it up as if anything you said couldn't be trusted."

Greg's eyes widened in anger. He surged to his feet. "What the fuck! That fucking little cockroach. I'm going to fucking kill that bastard!"

"I win ten bucks from Jake," Adam said. "I told him you'd threaten to kill the little pissant. Jake thought you'd just want to fuck the guy over in the press."

Cody looked from Adam to Greg. Then he met Rebecca's gaze. "It doesn't sound as if anyone here believes Pierce's claims."

"Why the hell would they?" Greg demanded.

"Of course they don't, darling. You're ours, and that's that. And by 'ours,' I mean ours, and Lusty's."

Cody shook his head. Rebecca thought the look of wonder on his face was something. "Well, I *did* see a psychiatrist when I was twelve."

Adam waved his hand. "Irrelevant. Pierce's claims, though, do beg the question."

Cody sat forward. "Yeah. What the hell is he up to? There has to be a reason for him to try and discredit me. What's in it for him, doing that? I know he didn't like that the publisher wanted me in on his little project."

Adam nodded. “That’s the question, isn’t it?” He looked at Greg, then back at Cody. “It’s up to you, of course, to say yes or no, but the Town Trust is ready to look into that little thing, on your behalf. Pierce won’t know it’s you asking questions, but he’ll sure as hell know that *someone* is. Someone with a hell of a lot of clout.” Adam rubbed his hands together. “If he’s up to no good—which I believe he is—that ought to scare the shit out of him.”

Greg met Rebecca’s gaze. She nodded. “I say let’s do it. I don’t like anyone trying to screw with my man.”

“Neither do I,” Greg said.

The look on Cody’s face was priceless. Rebecca thought they were really making headway with him, because doubt was being supplanted by joy. “Okay. Who do I have to talk to in order to authorize this?”

“That part’s easy,” Adam said. “You talk to me.”

Chapter 17

Greg had absolute trust and faith in his cousin, Jake Kendall, and that man's determination as the manager of the Town Trust to protect the good people of Lusty. He knew that it wouldn't take long for him and whatever investigators he had on retainer to get to the bottom of whatever the hell it was Pierce was up to.

But he had his own resources, and flat-out hated waiting for other people to do something when he could be doing something himself.

He looked up from his computer and watched the two people he loved. They were all three of them in the great room of the cabin, each of them occupied, Greg thought, by aspects of their particular passions.

To his right, Rebecca had already slipped into that special place she found whenever she picked up a paintbrush—or a piece of charcoal. The portrait she was painting of Grandma Kate was nearly finished, and damned if he didn't think it was the best portrait she'd ever created.

To his right, Cody was working on his cameras, cleaning them, inspecting them the way he would do before going out and submerging himself in his work. He also did that if he was troubled, or thinking over a problem.

Maybe he'll take them and go outside, take a few shots. God, I hope so. He mentally shook his head. He wasn't going to worry about the fact that Cody hadn't taken a single photograph since coming back from Syria.

He'd pick up his cameras again, shoot again. When he was ready.

And Greg was pulling strings and online, looking for information, determined to take care of his lover.

He had a suspicion about Drummond Pierce, but he hadn't wanted to say anything until he was absolutely sure. Sometimes, he had a sixth sense about certain people. When he'd taken an instant dislike to Pierce, he chalked it up to the fact that he could tell the man hadn't wanted Cody in on his book deal. One would almost think that Pierce was being made to pay Cody out of his own advance, which according to one publishing news website had been substantial. The fact was that Cody's being signed for the book by the publisher didn't diminish Pierce's potential income one whit. In fact, Greg was positive that the inclusion of photographs by Cody Harper would have just the opposite effect—likely the book sales would soar from the photos, alone. But then, Pierce wouldn't be alone in the spotlight.

"Maybe that's it."

"Maybe what's it?" Cody asked.

Greg tossed a glance at Rebecca, but she seemed to be completely oblivious to them. He turned his attention back to Cody but kept his voice down. "Maybe he's trying to ruin your reputation because he wants the publisher to cancel the contract you signed. He doesn't seem the kind who wants to share the spotlight."

"I can tell you he's not. He's also got a rep for being a real PITA." Cody shook his head and put his focus back on the camera he was working on. "Remember Smitty, that kid who came with us? The one on the plane sitting with Pierce?"

"Fuck, I forgot about him." Greg had forgotten everything, practically, in the hours and then days following Cody's kidnapping. "He was a nervous-looking fellow who jumped anytime anyone said anything to him."

"Pierce's personal assistant. I chatted with him for a while the day before we headed into Syria. He was looking for another job. Couldn't stand his boss."

"Hmm." Greg made a note to try and see if Smitty the personal assistant would be willing to tell tales out of school. In his estimation, close staff always knew where the skeletons were buried.

"I figured you wouldn't be able to leave *any* of it alone," Cody said. He grinned when he looked up from his camera. "You're digging into Pierce, doing what you can to 'take care' of me. And I did see you put another handgun in the other bedside table in the bedroom, and I do note that the rifle is still beside the back door."

Greg shrugged. "Hey, I think our woman was right. Lake is a crazy stalker chick. We should be ready for her, even though there is no way I can imagine that she can find this cabin."

"And you're one-hundred percent positive that no one in town would fall for her, um, 'fatal charms'?"

"It's Lusty," Greg said. "Trust me when I tell you that by now, everyone will be on the lookout for her." Greg ran a hand through his hair. His thoughts kept circling on Pierce. "I just can't imagine why this dipshit is doing what he's doing." Greg sat back from his computer. "It's almost the kind of thing you'd do to get even with someone, only you didn't do anything in the first place to provoke his actions."

"Huh."

Greg looked over at Rebecca. "Huh?"

"Sometimes when I'm just tidying up a painting, like I am this one right now, my mind wanders. I listen to what's going on around me, and I don't necessarily think about what's being said, and I may look as if I'm not tuned in, but my brain is working nonetheless."

"Becca, darling, neither of us would *ever* accuse you of not having a good, working brain."

She flashed him that fast smile that he'd fallen in love with years before. "Anyway, y'all were chatting and my mind sort of gathered in what you were saying and what y'all said before. And I was wondering…what was this Pierce person like when he spoke to you?"

Since she put her brush down and turned to face him, Greg knew she was talking to him.

"When, baby?"

She looked over at Cody, then back at him. "When he arrived safe and sound in Turkey. I take it *he* hadn't been wounded?"

"No. Hell, he hardly looked worse for wear."

"Didn't he talk to you when you got in his face?"

"What makes you think Greg got in his face?"

Rebecca shrugged. "He loves you. The two of you went into Syria and he came back without you. I know damn well Greg would have been in his face."

Greg exhaled. He hadn't really wanted to share with Cody the hell he'd gone through during those days. Cody had had enough to deal with. But now he met Cody's gaze, and although Rebecca had asked, he directed his answer to Cody. "That's when I started to fear the worst. Because Pierce said he hadn't seen you after the two of you had been taken, but he acted…he acted like he believed you were dead."

"Which he more or less backed up with action when he got out of the country," Rebecca said. "Remember how your publisher released a statement just coming short of declaring you a casualty of the chaos over there?"

"Drummond Pierce would have told them that when he got back to New York," Greg said. "But I have no idea why he would do that."

Rebecca looked at the painting she'd just finished. "I do all right. I've had some showings, and I've even got a couple of wealthy patrons—people who believe I'm going to be famous in time. But you know what?"

"What?" Greg wasn't sure where she was going, but he could see Cody begin to slowly sit up straighter and focus on her.

"If crazy stalker chick kills my ass dead, my work is going to be worth a fucking fortune, instantly."

Greg felt as if he'd just been shot. He looked from Rebecca, to Cody—whose eyes had widened in shock, too.

"But I'm not dead," Cody said slowly.

"No, you're not, darling. I bet Mr. Pierce isn't very happy about that fact either. But I wonder, is he also scared? Because the only thing he thinks he gains by smearing you…" Rebecca let the sentence hang.

"He thinks he's discrediting me. As if he's afraid of what I might say? What the hell could I say?" And then, Cody said, "Well, fuck! I might say the fucking coward ran away, saving his own ass, and purposefully left me behind—believing I would be killed."

"That asshole!" Greg said. It was the only thing any of them had come up with so far that made any sense. But as the idea settled in, Greg wondered if maybe there could be one other reason for Pierce's ploy. And he wondered if there was a way he could find out.

* * * *

"Well, we never did think this was going to be easy."

Melvin grunted as they stepped out into the sunshine of a San Antonio midday afternoon. He'd come to appreciate Connor Talbot's dry wit and sense of humor in the weeks they'd been working together.

It feels like I've known the man forever. Mel couldn't say he'd ever had an experience quite like it. Sometimes he knew what Connor was thinking just from looking at his face. The only thing weirder than that was the fact that Connor could sometimes read his thoughts, too.

If he was the sort to believe in such things, he'd swear they'd been brothers in a previous life.

"I had no idea the list of properties would be so large," Melvin said, "or that it would cover so many counties."

"Me neither. But this feels right. I think that bastard didn't do what you or I would do—make tracks either for another part of the country altogether, or hell, head overseas. I think he hunkered down right here in Texas. I think it was something he'd been planning to do long before the Rhodeses died. When we find him—and we *will* find him—I'll bet you he's within a day's drive of where he started out from in Austin."

"I won't take that bet because I think you're right." Melvin eyed the folder in his hands. "In the meantime we have more than two hundred and fifty properties, in five different counties, to look into. And with limited resources online—because we're talking up to sixteen years ago when he began his search—it's going to be slow going."

"Maybe we should recruit some help," Connor said.

"I say we head over to the River Walk and grab some lunch first," Mel said. "We can discuss our options over food."

In Melvin's experience, timing was everything, and every once in a while fate stepped in just when he least expected it but when he needed it to the most.

"See that, Kemp? They let *anybody* into San Antonio these days, even ex-cops!"

"It *is* a free country, Ace."

Mel turned around at the familiar-sounding voices. The two men facing him grinned. Mel extended his hand to greet them both. "Well, hell. Second largest city in the state, what are the odds?" Then he turned to Connor. "This is Ace Webster and Kemp Whittier, old friends—they're also investigators, from over near Divine. Gentlemen, meet Connor Talbot. Connor's my new business partner."

"Ex-military?" Ace asked as he shook Connor's hand.

Connor nodded. "Yes, Army Rangers. What gave me away?"

"Kemp and I are crack investigators," Ace said.

Mel grinned. "No offense, pal, but you do carry that look," he said. "Sort of like a sign that reads, 'Don't mess with me.'"

"Shit, Richardson," Kemp said, "you carry that same look, and you were only ever a cop, near as I recall."

"I guess it's all the same thing, just a different army and theater of operations," Connor said.

"You have a point," Kemp said.

"Did I hear you mention lunch?" Ace asked. "We were just headed for some ourselves. Why don't you join us? Our treat?"

"Thanks, don't mind if we do." Mel grinned. "We can tussle over the check later."

"Odds are about even," Kemp said.

That was true enough. Maybe they'd toss a coin over it.

They chose the Lone Star Café San Antonio River, one of Mel's favorite places from when he lived in town. They perused the menu, ordered food and beer, and sat back to await their meals.

"I heard congratulations are in order," Mel said. "I hear y'all got married."

Ace and Kemp exchanged a look. Mel figured they were surprised that he knew they'd married the same woman. Ace said, "Thanks, Mel. We're very happy Summer chose us."

"You both look very happy," Mel said. When Connor nodded, he said, "Actually, we've been considering walking the same path, ourselves."

"Is that a fact?" Kemp asked.

Mel recalled that between the two men, Kemp tended to keep his own counsel the most. Today he seemed downright loquacious compared to times past.

"I hear you had a bit of help from some friends of ours in the fall," Mel said, "over in Lusty."

"We did. Sheriff Adam Kendall and his men came through for us in a pinch," Ace said. "Didn't know you knew folks in Lusty, Richardson."

"Their Town Trust is one of my best clients," Mel said. "And as a matter of fact, Caleb Benedict was my training partner when I joined the Rangers."

Ace and Kemp were in the same business—investigation and security. Hell, if he wanted a couple more sets of eyes and brains, he *couldn't* do much better than to elicit their help. "Actually, it's a case for the Trust that brought us here today."

The waiter brought their beer, and Mel told Ace and Kemp about Ralph Baxter. One thing he recalled vividly about these two men who'd grown up as brothers—they got as pissed off over flagrant injustices done to innocents as any two men Mel had ever met.

"I hate bastards like that," Ace said. "And the fact that those two orphans fell through the cracks so badly, that just makes me even madder."

Mel nodded. "You know how it is. Sometimes shit does happen, and if there's no one there to take up for the innocents—" He didn't finish the sentence because there really was no need.

The waiter arrived carrying a tray loaded down with a whole lot of great-smelling comfort food. Mel had ordered a smoked pulled pork sandwich with fries. Connor and Kemp both got the Texas Two Pound burgers, and Ace had ordered the brisket sandwich.

They each took a few moments to tuck into their meals. Normally Mel would have added ketchup for his fries, but he'd asked for—and received—a little extra of their homemade barbeque sauce on the side.

His first bite was pure heaven, and brought back memories of his time here in this city.

"So what do you have so far in your search for this Baxter?" Ace asked.

"Not as much as we'd like," Connor said. "Mostly due to the time factor, and also because the business records for Rhodes and Baxter Real Estate weren't ever digitalized."

"And we're finding out that in some jurisdictions, back land transfers haven't been digitalized, either." Mel shrugged.

"In a couple of counties it's like they just entered everyone who's on the tax rolls as of activation date and left it at that." Connor sounded particularly offended, and it was all Mel could do not to smile.

Ace nodded. "So you have a list of properties that may or may not be the current home of your quarry."

"An extensive list. It means checking each one out, individually. And then, if we find him, that's still not proof of anything," Mel said. "When we find him, that's when the real work begins."

"If he did murder his accomplice, as you suspect, there's not much hope of you finding any evidence of that. Is there?" Kemp shrugged. "Like you said, it's been years."

"Your gut telling you something, Richardson?" Ace asked. Then to Kemp he said, "The man used to get these feelings when he was a cop working the city streets, here. His gut was downright uncanny, sometimes."

Mel laughed. "Just cop instincts, Ace, nothing supernatural." He sat back. He'd pretty much inhaled his lunch. He picked up his bottle of beer. There weren't more than a couple mouthfuls left. The waiter arrived, took his plate and offered him a refill on the brew.

Mel shook his head. "Just coffee, please." He had a few hours' drive ahead of him and didn't want to take any chances.

"Your cop instincts are telling you what?" Ace asked.

"First, that he's closer than we think he is, and has been all these years. And, second, that if we find him, with a little more work, we'll find evidence of his crimes."

"The bad guys don't always play smart," Kemp agreed.

"Underneath it all, I think Baxter is basically just an addict whose disease got the better of him. Only, instead of drugs, that disease was gambling. I think he stayed close because he always had it in his mind to stash himself somewhere, wait for the heat to cool off, then, after enough time had passed he could reemerge, as if nothing had happened." Mel looked off for a moment, and then he said, "The death of his partner, and being the executor of his estate, was a temptation too juicy to pass up. But it meant he was now hiding from the law, not just a local Austin loan shark. And years of living in limbo has likely taken its toll on him. I'm not sure what we'll find when we locate the man. But I'm thinking it might not be pretty."

Ace nodded. "You could be right. Do you have any parcels of land on your list in either Tarkett or Divine County?"

Mel nodded. "We do, yes. There're several."

Ace and Kemp exchanged a look. When Kemp nodded, Ace said, "Shoot us the details. We'd be glad to dig around for you."

"Thanks, we appreciate it." Mel sat back as the waiter brought his coffee. "It'll be good to have a couple more pairs of eyes on this."

Half an hour later they were in Connor's car headed back to Waco when Mel's cell phone rang.

"Richardson, here. Hey, Kendall. We were just thinking of swinging by and giving you an update." He listened for a moment then said, "Sure, you can run something else past us. We should be there in about three hours."

He hung up and looked over at Connor.

"They do keep us busy, don't they?" he asked. "What is it now?"

Mel looked at him. "Something that might be right up your alley."

"Well now you've got me curious." Then he grinned. "But hey, maybe we'll be in town long enough to have dinner."

"Or take someone *to* dinner, if she's not on duty," Mel said.

"I think I like that idea better."

"Yeah, so do I."

Chapter 18

"We were going to do this the day after the party," Cody said. "And then we let ourselves get sidetracked." Cody gave her a sly look and then winked.

We certainly did let ourselves get distracted. A part of her wished they were still back at the cabin, just the three of them, immersed in each other.

He beat her move to open the door to the museum, and she grinned at him. Last night, Cody had slept through the night without a nightmare. Rebecca was sincerely hoping he'd be able to eventually sleep through every night.

"Do we start without him?" Cody asked. He followed her inside and stopped in his tracks, immediately captivated by the first photograph that greeted all visitors to the Lusty Historical Museum.

In the large photograph that had clearly been digitally remastered and enlarged, six people seemed to look right at him, eyes vibrant, lips almost twitching to smile outright.

"These are the first of us," Rebecca said. She pointed to each person as she named them. "This is Sarah Carmichael Benedict, and her husbands Caleb and Joshua. Her cousin, Amanda, who married Adam Kendall and Warren Jessop."

He looked at the plaque that sited the date, and the photographer, Jeremy Parker Jones.

"It's a classic pose of the day, and yet different."

"What does your photographer's eye see?" Rebecca asked. She wondered how akin their individual art actually was.

"You can see the pride and the love radiating from them all. The men are very proprietary toward their women. Sarah's smile rivals the Mona Lisa's. You just know that she's...content." He paused. "Amanda looks like she's a real firecracker. She'd have to be, married to two men who are also lovers. Incredible."

Rebecca didn't know if he meant the photo or the situation. She led him into the museum, proper. "I've always loved this picture," she said. "This tells me so much about who Sarah, Caleb, and Joshua were as people."

Cody leaned in and read the small brass plaque. "Who were the Mendezes?" He no sooner asked that than his eyes widened and he answered his own question. "Their *staff*?"

"Sarah thought of them as members of the family. Family lore is that when Jose and Maria became too old to work, Sarah insisted they remain in their small house, which had always been their home. The Mendez children and grandchildren, for the most part, remained in Lusty, too, and over the years, there were marriages between them and the rest of the family."

"I don't see any pictures of the others with staff," he said.

"Amanda, Warren, and Adam didn't have any staff. Sarah likely wouldn't have had any, either, but they were here when she came—when she inherited the house. She couldn't let them go, because this was their home."

"Ah, yes, the blackguard who'd married her for her inheritance," Cody said. "Greg told me the story on our drive here from Dallas. I was beyond tired, but some of it soaked in."

Rebecca grinned. "We're very proud of our history here in Lusty, because six people decided to follow their hearts—and then made it possible for their descendants to do the same, if they chose to."

As they continued on, Rebecca heard the sound of a door closing. She grinned, and looked at her watch. Four minutes. Of course, her Aunt Anna would have known they were there as soon as the door opened. Morgan and Peter had installed new state-of-the-art surveillance equipment, so that her aunt could see anyone who came into the museum.

"Hello, hello," Anna Jessop came around the corner, a big smile on her face.

"Wow, Mrs. Santa Claus!" Cody said softly.

Rebecca laughed and hugged her aunt. Cody's words were familiar ones, as practically everyone who met Anna Jessop remarked on the similarity. "Aunt Anna, this is—"

"Oh, you don't have to tell me who this is. I am so sorry I missed that welcome-home party. I was a little under the weather, and Jackson and Craig had me tucked into bed and sipping chicken soup in a thrice." She smiled. "I'm so pleased to finally meet you, Mr. Harper."

Rebecca wanted to laugh. Her aunt had made another conquest, if the smile on Cody's face was any indication.

"It's just Cody, ma'am," he said. "I'm very pleased to meet you."

"Oh, none of that ma'am stuff. I'm just Aunt Anna—well, to everyone but my own children. I don't have any grandchildren as yet," she sighed. "I *do* wish someone would do something about that. The triplets are still in California, writing their screenplays, and both Ed and Warren seem married to their careers. Not that being EMTs isn't a very important calling." Aunt Anna sighed. "Nancy, of course, is busy in DC working to take care of our environment. She was home at Christmas, and I don't believe she's of a mind to have any children, *ever*." Aunt Anna shook her head, and then she gave them a smile. "Ah, well. Each of us has to choose our own way, don't we? That's what this town is all about—being free to choose to live—and love—however we will."

Cody tilted his head to one side as he regarded her. "That's what I'm discovering, Aunt Anna. You realize that makes Lusty, Texas, a very unique place."

"I've been thinking about that," Anna Jessop said. "Do you know what? I reckon there are other places, too, in this world where folks feel safe and special. It's too grand an ideal not to have been pursued at some point or other—and successfully, too—in other places."

Cody said, "God, I hope so. I'd like to think so."

Aunt Anna smiled, and patted his hand. "Then think so, Cody. No one can stop you. Now"—she turned and spread her hands—"enjoy our museum, and the artifacts and photographs—although most of those are older than even I am. It's been a good long while since anyone's perused our town with a camera, and the talent, to tell our story."

Rebecca watched Cody as he followed Aunt Anna's progress back to her office. After a long moment, he said, "I almost feel as if meeting her has been a life-changing experience."

Rebecca slid her arm around Cody's and leaned close. "Peter says that Aunt Anna is a secret weapon the Pentagon would be wise to latch onto."

"He has a point."

She chuckled and led him around the perimeter of the main room. Then came that moment she always liked, when whoever was touring the place for the first time saw what the family called the Fourth of July photograph. That large side yard at the Big House was still used for the family's picnic in the summer. But on this occasion, the Benedicts and Jessop-Kendalls had two guests, who'd arrived for a week's visit.

"Now I *am* impressed. I recognize the two gentlemen, too, because when you delve into the history of photography, you see pictures of them," Cody said. "Mostly because they were quite famous at the time when photography was starting to become a more common art form."

"They're listed on the plaque as family friends," Rebecca said, "but it kind of goes deeper than that. Lore is that Bat Masterson played a key role in helping Caleb and Joshua protect Sarah from the man Maddox had sent to kill her. And, of course, since the first Adam

Kendall was a Texas Ranger, there was a time or two those more famous erstwhile lawmen were at his side."

"I would love to hear the whole of the family saga. You know, I bet it would sell well. Has anyone ever thought to write all that down?"

Rebecca smiled. "Sarah and Amanda wrote journals, as did Joshua and Warren. They're only for family members to read." Rebecca frowned. "Let me clarify that. The women in the family read the ladies' journals, and the men read the men's."

"Kind of sexist," Cody said. She knew he was teasing.

"It really is, but it's also family tradition. Who can argue with that?"

Cody stopped at one display case and looked down at the contents. "That looks like a real gold coin."

"It is." She didn't say anything more, just let him read the carefully worded explanation of the contents.

"These belonged to the Jessop-Kendalls." He looked up at her. "Your great-great grandmother named her knife, 'Pocahontas'?"

Rebecca grinned. "She did. Came in handy a time or two, during the adventure she and her men went on."

"An adventure that has something to do with that gold coin. Do you know what I've just figured out?"

"What?"

"There's as much of your family story *not* told here, as there is revealed."

"I knew you had brains as well as beauty," Greg said.

Rebecca hadn't heard the door open, but she smiled when Greg joined them. He put an arm on each of their shoulders, standing between them and looking down at the collection under glass.

"You're just sayin' that because you want to get into my pants. I've heard how you Texan boys work," Cody said.

Rebecca laughed. That was the most lighthearted thing Cody had ever said.

"Well then, you can't feign shock when I do," Greg said. "So, what do you think of our collection so far?"

"Pretty impressive. This is likely the largest collection of photographs by Jeremy Jones anywhere." Cody nodded. "I find his work, and the way he shows the emotions of his subjects to be absolutely captivating. Seriously, man. This stuff is fabulous."

"We think so, too," Greg said.

Rebecca turned to her men. "I'm starving."

"What a coincidence. We've been invited to have lunch with Grandma, at the Big House. You okay with that?"

Greg had addressed his question to Cody, who nodded. "Yeah. I think I'm starting to get used to your family."

As they headed out, Cody stopped at one more photograph. This one was a little more modern than the others he'd viewed, and not, of course, taken by Jeremy Jones.

This photograph showed a woman in military uniform, standing on the porch of a large house, her arms folded, as she talked to a group of men who were sitting with their attention riveted on her.

Cody used a single finger to lightly tap on the image of the woman. "I have a feeling your grandmother was as much of a firecracker in her day as Amanda Jessop-Kendall was," he said.

Rebecca grinned. "*Was*?"

"Don't let Grandma Kate's age or her sweet smile fool you," Greg said. "She is for *sure* no one's little old lady."

Cody nodded. He looked from Rebecca to Greg. "I'll make sure to remember that."

* * * *

"I never really moved beyond being competent as a cook," Grandma Kate said. "My boys would tell you that their fathers were both far better in the kitchen than I ever was."

"That doesn't appear to be a regret for you," Cody said.

"It's not. We, each of us, have our different talents, don't we? I was never one to think that just because a person was born female, that they had to automatically follow a *set* pattern—much to my own mother's disappointment." Kate smiled at Cody. "And, too, I think, because I came of age just before the war, and because it really *was* an age of so many new things, and so many changes, that I dared to reject the common expectations put upon me."

"It can be a terrible thing to be a child who has to live under the weight of parental expectations," Cody said.

"Yes, I do believe it is." Grandma Kate patted Cody's hand. "At least *I* found it to be so."

Greg sat back and enjoyed the way his grandmother interacted with his lover. *The woman has a talent for reaching people.* For the first time—likely because he'd been so recently reminded by that photograph of the woman Kate Wesley Benedict had been when she'd arrived in Lusty—he realized that talent must have made her one hell of a good nurse administrator for the Convalescent Home.

Rebecca and Aunt Bernice came back into the dining room, pushing a tea cart loaded down with a coffeepot and what looked like pecan pie.

"I was hoping there'd be pie," Greg said.

"Darling, I did remember your sweet tooth," Bernice said. "I don't know whose in the family is worse—yours or Henry's."

Greg grinned. "I heard Henry is addicted to Tracy's cream puffs and éclairs."

Kate said, "I can't blame him there. Our Tracy is a *wonderful* pastry chef."

"Tell me, please, that I'm in time for dessert." Jake Kendall came into the dining room, his ever-present briefcase in hand, and a large smile on his face.

Greg laughed outright, and Cody shook his head. Rebecca said, "Why don't you and Adam tell Ginny that y'all don't want to be on that diet?"

Jake made a point, Greg noticed, of kissing Grandma Kate, and then Bernice. He said, "I love your pecan pie, Auntie." Then he sat down beside Kate, and thanked Bernice when she served him a generous slice of the dessert.

"I'll confess this sin to her when I get home tonight— even *before* dinner. Mostly, though, I guess we don't tell her because we don't want to hurt her feelings. She's spent a lot of time looking up recipes that are low fat, and low carbohydrates, and high protein."

Rebecca shook her head. "Low fat and low carbohydrates? What's left?"

"Water," Greg said, and laughed because Jake had said the same thing at the same time.

"Seriously, I've barely cheated on this diet she has us on, and really, I do feel as if I have a bit more energy than I did. Adam feels the same way, although he doesn't crave the sweets the way I do."

"No," Cody said. "His weakness is bacon and breakfast sausage."

Jake's grin was quick. "He told us about that breakfast y'all fed him the other day." He took a moment to savor a forkful of pie. "That is *so* good."

"Thank you." Bernice resumed her seat and fixed herself a cup of coffee.

"Did you bring the papers I asked for, Jake?" Kate asked.

"I did, of course." He set his fork down and bent to his case. He handed a file folder to Kate.

"Aside from the fact that I wanted to enjoy your company for lunch," she said, "I had something I wanted to discuss with you."

Greg knew she was talking to him. "What, Grandma?"

"Some years ago, your grandfathers and I set up a special foundation, and endowed it with most of our personal money. We named it for our late daughter—*Maria's Quest*."

"Good God. I've heard of that foundation!" Greg blinked. "Hell, I've worked with people from that foundation! I didn't know that was yours!"

"It's not something I publicize, of course. That's not the point, is it?"

Greg thought of all the places he'd been, all the causes he'd taken up over the years. *Maria's Quest* had been busy in just as many areas, funding projects to help to build schools, enable villages to become self-supporting—Greg couldn't name all the ways he'd heard of that foundation helping others. Often, he'd found himself working alongside people working for that agency. He'd always been impressed not only by the scope of the work the charity managed to sponsor, but by the caliber of people devoted to its goals.

And to think that it had been his own grandparents who were behind it! Then he thought of the question she'd just asked. He didn't think it was necessarily a rhetorical question.

"No," he said. "That's not the point at all."

Kate nodded. "I've appointed different people, in different places, to administer portions of the foundation. I think it's beneficial to have someone with boots on the ground, and who knows what's needed. Of course, I've been keeping an eye on it, all these years, with Jake's help."

"Your foundation does good work, Grandma Kate," Cody said. "It makes a difference in the world." He looked at Greg and said, "I can't think of anything more important than making the world better, even if only in small ways."

"Thank you, Cody. I think so, too." Grandma Kate took a moment to enjoy a sip of coffee. "The thing is, I think what's needed now is a fresh approach. Younger hands on the reins, as it were. The foundation needs someone at the helm who's willing and able to travel, to see the needs of others, firsthand. Someone who's already done a fair amount of humanitarian work in places where the hours are long and the labor hard. We can't solve all the problems of the world. But we can do our part. Gregory, I've long thought that of all of my grandchildren, you would be the perfect person to oversee *Maria's Quest*."

"*Me*?"

"Who better?" Grandma Kate spread her hands as if telling him a self-evident truth. "You have a powerful curiosity about this world, and you're already involved in so many, varied projects. I know there've been more than a few times when you've pitched in, helping our staff. Now, I won't misrepresent the job to you. This position would require you to spend some time off and on during the year, doing administrative work. There's an office in Waco, and a staff of thirty there who do most of the paperwork now. But you'd still be able to travel, still be able to be 'hands on,' which I think would be only a benefit—for the foundation, and for you."

"I don't know what to say." All these years he'd said he would never settle down, and he'd meant it. But settling down in his mind was staying in one place all the time and doing the same thing for the rest of his life.

You thought you'd never get married, too, but you've changed your mind on that one. Only because there'd only been one woman in his heart, and he'd convinced himself he didn't deserve to get married, to be happy.

Because of Daniel.

"I don't expect you to answer me right away. Take as long as you need to think about it, and to discuss it with Cody and Rebecca. And, sweetheart?"

His grandmother waited until he looked up and met her gaze. "No is a perfectly acceptable answer. You know I mean that."

He could say no, and his grandmother would never treat him any different than she ever had. Her love didn't depend on conditions. Her love—like the love of his parents, and all his family—was completely unconditional.

Why didn't I ever acknowledge that to myself before now?

When she handed him the folder Jake had given her, he automatically took it. "This should answer any questions you have. In the meantime, I'm here if you want to talk about it further."

He looked at Cody, and then Rebecca. This wasn't a decision he could make on his own. He met his grandmother's eyes. "We'll talk about it. I'll let you know."

"Take your time, sweetheart. There's no rush."

Except, really there was. Greg felt as if he'd been living in limbo all of his life. Maybe this offer was the very thing that would help him change all that—if, indeed, after all these years, change was even possible.

Chapter 19

Lusty was a small town, not a crossroads, and turned out to be bigger than she'd guessed. That surprised Caroline because she'd found practically nothing online when she'd done her research. *Shouldn't a place this big at least have been represented by a bigger dot on the map and a few websites on the Internet?*

She'd found her way here, eventually, after about two and a half hours driving around, complete with a couple of side trips. She'd found Crawford, Texas, and wasn't that a hoot? But she'd taken a wrong turn to get there, so she'd doubled back once she had.

There'd been a bit of a garage sale in one of the small communities. A couple of neighbors had all sorts of things out on tables, offering them up for whoever had the price to pay. There'd been a pair of men tending the tables, and the smell of beer had surrounded them both.

Caroline laughed out loud thinking about her little role playing, earlier. She'd looked over their goods, and put on a disappointed face. *They didn't even know that I was playing them.*

"What's the matter, sweet thing? Don't see what you're looking for?"

"I was just hoping there'd be a gun. I thought I was brave enough to travel all on my own, but a couple of times I was sure someone was following me! The woman at the hotel said I should get myself a gun. But I don't know where to look. I was hoping that my finding you here was a sign from God."

"Well, now. You wait right here. I can fix you right up."

He'd told her what sort of gun it was, of course, but she couldn't remember. She'd been glad to fork over the two hundred dollars for the thing, and for a box of ammunition. He'd shown her how to use it, too. And she'd made sure the clip was full.

She didn't need any more lessons, or any practice. How hard can it be? She'd watched folks on TV fire guns all the time. They took the safety off, they aimed, and they squeezed the trigger.

It had been a bigger jolt than she'd imagined, even though that smelly man had held his hand under hers to help, but she knew she'd manage just fine, when the time came.

Best of all, they would never be able to trace the bullet or the gun to her!

Caroline slid her glance for just a moment to her purse that sat so primly on the front seat beside her. The gun was right there, and no one even knew!

The cops would never guess it was her, because she'd never used a gun before.

She'd used a baseball bat on her parents and she'd hit Brady with a car. She rubbed her head, and tried to think. There had been another couple of faithless bastards, too. What had she used on them? Well, whatever it was, they'd deserved it.

She let the disturbing thoughts go as she entered Lusty. Caroline drove slowly through the small town, her gaze sliding from left to right as she traveled along Main Street. There were other streets that branched off of Main, too, with names like Elm and Oak and Masterson. She turned right down one of the streets at random, surprised when she could see at least three blocks of houses stretched out before her. She turned right again. All of the houses appeared to be well kept, with tidy yards. Many had fairly new cars or—more often—pickup trucks parked in their driveways.

The homes were all made of brick, and she didn't see a one that needed painting, or fixing up.

There has to be money here.

"Maybe I'll find me a boyfriend right here in Lusty." She pulled her car to the curb for a moment, a sudden idea seizing her. Rather than hope someone in town would willingly tell her—in a gossipy, "just between us girls" kind of way—where that slut artist could be found, maybe she could just ask for Directory Assistance.

The car she'd rented came complete with a built in GPS device, and the rental agent—a nice young man but definitely not the kind she was looking for—had shown her all the spiffy features that this car, and the device, had to offer.

One of the things the device could do was surf the web.

She went to a telephone directory site and put in the information required. It took her a few moments for the information she wanted to download, but then, finally, the screen pinged, as a list scrolled onto the screen.

Caroline blinked at the list of names and phone numbers. "There sure are a lot of Jessops in this town." There was *one* R. Jessop, but that one was a doctor. "Well, that didn't pan out. I can't very well phone each one and ask if they're the boyfriend-thieving whore I'm looking for. Hmm." And, with that many folks who had to be related to her, likely referring to her as a slut or a whore when she inquired wouldn't be a good idea, either.

"Maybe I can pretend to be a friend—no, an *acquaintance*. Yes! Just like I did with that old desk sergeant at the police station in Seattle. 'Becky said if I'm ever in Lusty I should look her up.' That sounds good. But where? Where shall I ask?" She pulled her car away from the curb, and made one more right turn to bring her back to Main Street. There was a traffic light, which turned red for her. She let her eyes scan what she could see of Main Street. Would she try the *Lusty Glow Day Spa* for her fishing expedition, or the restaurant, *Lusty Appetites*? Which one would have the most gossip-friendly women? The light turned green, but there was no one behind her. She sat there, thinking, deciding. The light turned red again, and she knew she'd have to move, as soon as it went green.

"Restaurant first. Then, if I strike out, I'll head to the spa. Somebody's *bound* to know Ms. Rebecca, the famous artiste."

Decision made, Caroline prepared to turn right when the light changed. A pickup truck drove past and Caroline focused on the people riding in it. *My God, that's her!*

And wasn't it just like a whore to be sitting between *two* handsome men?

The light turned green, but instead of turning right, as she'd been going to, she turned left. There wasn't much traffic, so Caroline held back, kept her speed down, but kept that pickup truck in her sights.

Fate was shining on her, and it would be only a matter of time before she finished what she'd started back in Seattle.

Caroline smiled as she followed Rebecca Jessop right out of town.

* * * *

Rebecca looked over her shoulder. Greg hadn't moved from the love seat in the great room. He appeared to be reading every bit of information that had been in the thick folder Grandma Kate had given him.

She turned back to the counter, where she was peeling potatoes. Cody looked up from the stove.

"Our boyfriend's been pretty quiet since we left your grandmother's," he said.

"Yeah, I was just thinking the same thing." They'd tried, each of them, on the ride back to the cabin to get Greg to tell them how he felt about the offer. What did he think about it? But he'd demurred, saying that he needed to read everything in the file, first, and think about it some before he discussed it with them.

As if the decision was only his to make.

Rebecca wished she knew what was going on in Greg's head, but she honestly didn't have a clue. She hadn't spent that much time with him over the past few years—or, in fact, as much as Cody had.

"What do you think he's thinking?" she asked him.

"The truth? I have no idea. Greg can be pretty emotionally distant, sometimes. Daniel really messed up his head *and* his self-esteem. Maybe someday he'll see that what he had with Doctor Montrose was, in essence, an abusive relationship. Maybe *then* he'll be able to fully forgive himself for something that really didn't need forgiving. A man treated me the way he treated Greg? I'd have walked, too, and a hell of a lot sooner than Greg did."

"But he told you about him."

"Oh, no, Blue Eyes. He only told me about Daniel in the most general and impersonal of terms. That they were together, they'd had a fight, and he'd left him in Jakarta and come home. The guilt was there, it didn't need expressing. A blind man could see it. He's blamed himself, all these years, for Daniel's death. If he hadn't fought with him, they would have been in England when the Tsunami struck.

"The real lowdown on their relationship I got from some people I met in Haiti who'd known the two of them back then." Cody shook his head. "Daniel had major issues with his sexuality, and from what I have come to believe, from all I learned, he was a complete narcissist." Cody turned his attention to the roast he was braising in the large sauce pan. "Greg has been more open since we came here, but still, sometimes getting him to open up about the stuff that's bothering him is worse than pulling fucking teeth."

Rebecca had stopped peeling potatoes, because she really couldn't believe what Cody had just said. "Um, pot? Meet kettle."

Cody met her gaze and she read the confusion in his eyes. Then he blinked, and it was as if a shutter came down. *Talk about emotional distance.*

"Totally different set of circumstances. I'd talk *if* there was anything to talk about. It's just nightmares, Rebecca, and they've been easing up some. If they bother you that much, I can sleep in the bedroom downstairs."

He thought they were easing up because he hadn't had one *last* night? One night? Rebecca could have argued with him that she was pretty sure he'd had a couple of flashbacks during his waking hours, too. But she didn't.

Instead, she said, "They only *bother* me because they hurt you, Cody. It pains me horribly to see you suffer with those nightmares. I told you that."

His expression cleared and he stepped close and placed a soft kiss on her lips. "Thank you for that, Blue Eyes. But I'll be fine, really. I just need a bit of time to finish getting over the incident."

How had she ended up in love with *two* men who were both experts at avoidance? She closed her eyes for a moment as she tried to get her growing temper under control. Why was she the only one who could see that if they kept on this way, they were headed for a disaster of mammoth proportions?

Rebecca wondered how the hell to get them *all* as naked, emotionally, with each other as they seemed to love to get physically. If they couldn't do that, if they couldn't be completely open and honest with each other when they were alone, the three of them, together, then what hope did they have for finding their very own happy ending?

Each of her men claimed they wanted forever. Well, damn it, forever took *work*. It took being open and honest and not closing out the people you were supposedly in love with!

Rebecca knew if she didn't step away for a few minutes, she was going to explode. Her temper had been brewing since leaving Grandma Kate's. She needed to scream or kick a tree, or…or something. The potatoes were ready, and she set them beside the stove so Cody could see them and put them into the pot with the roast beef, when he was ready for them. She rinsed her hands at the sink, and wondered that she could feel as if she was in a bubble, insulated, on the outside while it felt as if everything was boiling over on the inside.

"I think I'm going to go and stretch my legs."

Cody must have retreated behind his own thoughts, because he only made a bit of a grunting, noncommittal kind of sound to acknowledge her statement.

Sundown was still a good couple hours away, and the temperature had held all afternoon in the high seventies. She didn't need a jacket, or her purse, or anything, really, except time alone and space to think.

She pulled the door closed gently behind her and inhaled deeply. She hadn't stopped appreciating how good the drier Texas air smelled compared with the air on the West Coast. Seattle had been so very different in so many ways. A good city, to be sure, in a good state. This, however, was Texas, and Texas was in her soul. Texas was home and formed every single definition of normal that she knew.

She needed, more than anything right now, to breathe this good Texas air and get her unusually volatile emotions under control. She needed to walk and walk and walk so that her legs tired and her brain had a chance to think.

There had to be a way to get those two men to see the sweet light of reason. There had to be a way to wake them up to the reality of the dangers inherent in holding back and refusing to face the issues between them.

Maybe if she power walked, the answer would come to her.

* * * *

Connor expected to step into a sleepy kind of western sheriff's office, with Adam Kendall sitting with his boots on his desk, playing checkers with his brother Jake while the deputy sat dozing in his chair.

Instead, he stepped into chaos.

"What do you mean, she's not in the cabin? How could she not be in the cabin and how the *hell* do you not know where she is?" Jake

Kendall's voice couldn't hold any more anger as he held his cell phone to his ear and listened to the response.

"Captain Cornell, is your trooper still at the car? Damn! Okay, how long will it take him to get back there?" Adam held the phone to his ear with his left hand and waved them into the office with his right hand.

"Jasper, we need you here, now. We're heading out to the cabin. We have a situation." Matt Benedict also held a cell phone to his ear. Standing by his desk, he looked as if he was yearning to run.

"Grab a couple of rifles and go find her, now!" Jake Kendall said. "What's happened? I'll tell you what's happened. That crazy stalker chick is there, do you hear me? They found her car *right* at the entrance to the private lane, and we have no idea how long it's been there. Yeah, I thought that would light a fire under your—" He pulled the phone away from his ear. "Fucking cousin hung up on me." And then he grinned, but it wasn't really a nice grin at all.

Jake Kendall resembled a wolf with a really mean-looking snarl on his face and a bloodlust building in his soul.

"The driver of that car is suspected in four homicides in Washington State, and she's stalking one of *my* people—Rebecca Jessop. That lane leads to a private home that's on Benedict land. If your man follows the tire tracks, he'll get there. No, sorry, the gate is operated electronically, only. There's no emergency bypass. We're on our way now. Won't take us more than ten minutes to get there." Adam hung up his phone and reached for his hat.

"There fucking *will* be an emergency bypass," Jake said. "I'll get right on that little thing. As soon as we make sure Rebecca is okay and that crazy stalker chick is in custody."

Adam nodded. "Okay, let's ride." He looked at Connor and Melvin. "Y'all want to come along?"

"Absolutely," Mel said. "We're both armed."

"Good." Adam headed out the door.

He and Mel got into the backseat of Kendall's cruiser, and Connor buckled up as the sheriff stepped on it and peeled away from the curb. He put his siren on and barreled through the red light.

"I take it this isn't why you wanted to meet with us, Jake." Mel shot Connor a glance.

"No, that's another matter we'll get into later."

"How about you bring us up to speed with this situation?" Connor asked.

"A woman named Naomi Lake had been stalking our cousin, artist Rebecca Jessop, in Seattle," Adam said. "The cops there nearly grabbed her but she got away from them. They knew she was headed here. More thorough examination of the electronics she left behind gave them a huge break. She'd gotten a credit card under a different name, and had been making payments on it via online banking, out of her regular checking account."

"Not smart," Connor said.

"No, she crossed her fake I.D with her real one. We'd no sooner gotten a call from the Seattle PD with that alias—Caroline Jeffries—then we also got a call from the Texas State Police. They wanted to let us know a car had been left, keys in the ignition, on a road leading into Lusty. They were concerned that the tourist was lost or injured and were giving us a heads-up. They'd checked, you see, and the car came back as a rental."

"And when you called the rental company, the name on the rental contract was Caroline Jeffries."

"Yeah. So I had Jake call Rebecca's cell phone, but she didn't answer. So he called Greg's cell to alert him and Cody to keep Rebecca inside and to lock the doors—"

"Only to discover she wasn't inside the cabin at all."

"No, she'd apparently gone for a walk—and as near as Cody could recall, she's been gone for more than twenty minutes," Jake said.

"Is Rebecca armed?" Mel asked.

"Jake?" Adam asked.

"I don't think so."

"Of course not," Adam sighed, disgust dripping from his words. "This is turning into *another* cluster fuck."

Because Mel had told him all about the recent happenings in Lusty, Connor understood very well where Adam's exasperation was coming from.

"How far out are we?" Connor asked.

"Not five minutes from the private lane. And *I* can open the fucking gate, as I have a gate control. We'll drive in, and if that woman is walking along the path, swear to God, I'll be tempted to just run her down."

"Whether she is or isn't, we'll be ready to roll out." Connor pulled his weapon from its holster and checked it, same as he always did before an op. Military or civilian, the rules of engagement were basically the same. Then he took off his seat belt.

"Good." Adam met his gaze in the rearview mirror. "Once we get onto the track, I'll roll the windows down."

"For air?" Jake asked.

"No," Connor said. "So we can hear gunfire, if there is any."

"Fuck. I think I'm the only one in this vehicle not armed," Jake said.

"I'll pop the trunk when we stop," Adam said. "You can grab the rifle."

"Just get us there, brother, and I'll tackle her with my bare hands if I have to."

Connor resisted the urge to grin. He had no doubt, despite those words, that Jake Kendall would not make a tricky situation worse by going off half-cocked. Beside him, his partner was equally prepared, gun drawn. He met Mel's gaze and nodded once.

This would be the first time they'd stepped into potential danger together, and it was good to know Mel was doing the same thing he was—getting into the zone, mentally, ready for whatever happened next.

The cruiser slowed only long enough to wait for the gate to the private lane to swing open when Adam flipped the switch. Connor took in the site of the parked Buick—the rental car—and the State Trooper's vehicle just now arriving on scene. That car pulled in behind Matt's cruiser which was following them, and then they were bouncing over rough terrain as they headed south.

Not two minutes later the sound of gunfire came through the open windows.

Chapter 20

"What's happened?"

Greg met Cody's gaze and saw in his eyes the same dread there that surged through his blood. "That crazy stalker bitch found us. Jake says she's here, on the property—just out there somewhere."

"*Fuck.*" Cody headed toward the door, but Greg grabbed him, turned him around.

"Scoop up that rifle. I'll go grab the other one at the back door."

"No, you take this one. I don't know *how* to fire a gun." Cody shrugged.

"Seriously?" Then Greg shook his head. He *knew* not everyone knew how to use a rifle. Learning how to aim, shoot, and properly care for a weapon was one of the things he'd learned growing up, something he'd never really thought about.

But not everyone in the country did the same.

He cleared his mind of useless, trivial thoughts. His Becca was in danger. He had to move, *now*.

"Sorry, no sweat. Let's go."

They didn't close the door behind them. Greg simply stepped out into the late afternoon sun. "Becca!" He shouted her name and waited a beat, but heard nothing in return. The ground was hard and dry, which meant she'd left no footprints. He had no trail to follow.

"She walks when she's pissed," he said. "Fuck, I didn't even realize she *was* pissed." He scanned the area, looking for her. "My fault? Becca!"

He realized he'd been uncommunicative once they left Grandma Kate's. He'd fallen back on an old habit, and withdrawn. He could see the opportunity in what he'd just been offered, but he could see the trap in it, too, and he'd pulled back and hunkered down, emotionally.

When the fuck am I going to grow up? He knew that habit he had of pulling back was off-putting. Cody had told him so more than once.

If anything happens to her I'm never going to forgive myself.

"We both have a role in her anger," Cody said. "Does she know this area well? Does she have a favorite, private thinking spot?"

Greg stopped. "Yes, she knows the area, and no, no private spot that I know of. But despite knowing the area, she wouldn't have just gone off in any direction. I think she'd have followed the car path. She has a crappy sense of direction. She'd figure there'd be less chance of her getting lost if she followed the lane."

"If she wasn't too mad at us to think of that."

"She'd never be too mad to ignore basic safety." Then Greg sighed. "Except she did, because she went out *unarmed*."

"She's got quite a head start," Cody said. "How fast would she be walking? Maybe we could run and catch up with her?"

"No. She speed walks. Get in the truck, I'll go grab the keys. And my phone."

"Good plan. Let's hurry, lover, and find her."

Greg didn't have to be nudged twice. He ran into the house, grabbed the keys off the hook, scooped up his phone, and was pushing speed dial as he got into the F150 cab behind the steering wheel.

"Jake, where are you?" He hit speaker and set the phone down on the console.

"We're just about to turn onto the lane."

"Okay we're headed toward you. We'll keep our eyes peeled. Let's leave this line open."

"I'm all for that."

Greg decided she must have followed the track, and steered the truck in that direction. Cody rolled down his window, and Greg followed suit.

He drove slowly, giving them time to scan both sides of the lane, just in case she had veered off.

There were, he knew, a few large boulders here and there where a person could perch and think, if they had a mind to.

She'd left the cabin about twenty or so minutes ahead of them. If she'd power walked, as he knew she sometimes did, she could have quite a lead on them. This private lane spanned twelve miles from cabin to county road. But it wasn't flat, not by a long shot, and it was too fucking rough to drive fast on.

Ahead, the land rose subtly and then dropped just as gradually several times—the uneven ground just one of the characteristics of being on the edge of the Hill Country.

"I think I'm going to spank her for scaring me this way," Greg said. He kept his voice down, hoping his cousin on the other end of the phone couldn't hear him.

"I'd like a piece of that," Cody said.

Greg smirked. "We both know where it would head, then."

"That's good for me, too."

A snort sounded from the phone and Greg realized Jake had heard him just fine. *To hell with it. It's not like he doesn't understand these things.*

They continued on, the truck bouncing more than a little as they slowly made their way toward the entrance to the lane. He steered the truck down one slightly steep slope that had rutted somewhat—the one they usually drove around in order to avoid the ruts. He slowed the truck's speed just a little and cursed the bounce when his head hit the roof of the cab.

His gaze flicked to the dash clock. They'd been driving nearly five minutes and he figured they were nearly, but not quite, a couple of miles from the cabin.

"Fuck there she is! Jesus Christ, she's got a gun!" Jake's shout put fear in Greg's heart.

From up ahead and from the cell phone, the sound of gunfire exploded in the afternoon calm, and Greg's heart caught in his throat. One shot, then two more. And just bare seconds later, three more explosions followed by the rapid report of at least two other guns getting off a series of quick shots.

"No! No! Don't kill me! Please, oh God, please, don't kill me!" Cody threw himself to the floor of the cab, his hands over his head as he shrieked in terror.

"We got her! That crazy bitch is down! Get here, Greg!" The cell phone clicked and he knew Jake had hung up.

Greg slowed the truck as he reached down toward Cody. His lover lay curled up on the floor of the truck, trembling. His sobs broke Greg's heart.

Greg kept his attention split between the rocky path he was driving and Cody.

He dropped his hand onto Cody's head and stroked him gently. He didn't know if Rebecca was okay or not, but he had to have faith that the others—who had reached her—had the situation in hand. He burned with the urgency to hold her in his arms, but *this* lover needed him, too. "It's all right, Cody. You're safe, sweetheart. Come back to me, now. Come back to me. We have to go to our woman. Rebecca needs us." He felt his man tense under his hand, and then felt him give a shuddering sigh.

"Oh, God, Greg. What have I done?"

"No, it's fine. They have her. Come on, now. It's fine. Let's go to Becca."

Cody nodded, straightened slowly, and shoved himself onto the passenger seat.

He was still shaking and looked pale as a ghost, but he was all right.

At least he was, for now.

* * * *

Rebecca had slipped into her power-walk mode and had let her steps carry her where they would. She loved the cabin, always had. She supposed that eventually, though—probably sooner rather than later—they'd have to find a house in town to suit the three of them. Something they could come back to occasionally. Or maybe they could build a new house on one of the many parcels of land available to be leased.

Either/or, they couldn't stay in the cabin indefinitely. Others in the family would want to be making use of the cabin soon. And they'd want their own place for when they were in Lusty.

Rebecca set off, not really thinking about where she was going. After several minutes, she realized she was following the path toward the road. She shrugged. *Less chance of my getting lost that way.*

She liked the cabin and even cherished the quiet, country setting, but nature girl she was not. She wasn't ashamed to admit that she had a horrible sense of direction. Better to just stick to the path. Better to just celebrate what she was good at and not worry about the rest of it.

She was good at taking the images in her head and putting them on canvas. She'd never been the kind of artist who needed to set up in front of a vista in order to reproduce it in oils. Her visions went from her head to her sketchbook, and then to her brush.

She was good at traveling, and liked to wander, liked to see the world. She liked to light here and there, stay for a while, get to know a place. Then she usually would be on her way again. She returned home to Lusty a couple of times a year.

Rebecca wondered if Greg and Cody understood she wasn't anchored to any one particular place, that she had no qualms about traveling the globe with them. Yes, she'd like a base to come back to. Lusty would always be home and she would always need to return to her roots here in this small Central Texas town. But she could paint wherever she was.

She didn't care where on God's green earth they ended up, as long as they ended up there *together*. She didn't much care where they traveled to, as long as they traveled *together*. Didn't they understand that? Greg could take Kate's offer or leave it. It didn't matter to her what he did, as long as he was happy. She didn't care where they were, as long as they were *together* and happy.

And together to her meant not just occupying the same space. It meant being honest and open and laying all their emotional cards on the table.

Rebecca's step faltered. "Well, hell's bells, maybe I should *tell* them all of that. Maybe instead of getting all pissy-eyed and letting my inner imp throw a hissy fit, I should just tell them!" She wanted everyone to get emotionally naked, maybe she'd better be the first one to shuck those particular clothes.

"Becca!"

She stopped at the faint sound of her name being called and looked behind her, a little surprised when she couldn't see the cabin anymore. Turning back to the direction she'd been going, she couldn't see the fence line either. She was standing on one of the many small hillocks that dotted the path from cabin to road.

Perspiration dotted her skin and she labored a little for breath. She guessed she'd been making tracks for nearly a half hour. She was probably about a good two or maybe three miles from the cabin.

She supposed she should turn around and head back. She'd been enjoying the walk, but someone—it sounded like Greg—had just called her name. Her voice wasn't strong enough to carry against the small breeze that had sprung up from the southwest. She should head back. She didn't want to worry them.

It occurred to her just then that she'd left the safety of those four walls and those two delicious men *without* the loaded .22 that she'd been keeping by the front door since she'd come to the cabin a few weeks before.

She ran a hand through her hair and wondered where she'd left her brain. "Geez, Rebecca, talk about stupid things to do!"

"Hey, you talk to yourself, too. Isn't that *weird*? Do you hear voices, too, just like I do?"

The woman stood perhaps thirty-five feet away, and had been headed in her direction, and had likely just stepped over the rise. She was breathing heavily as if the trek had really taken a toll on her. Rebecca took a step backward, because even though she'd never heard her voice before, and even though her hair was dark, and not blonde, she knew who the woman was.

"No, don't do that. Don't walk away from me. I really need to talk to you. It's important!" And then the woman lifted her right arm from behind her back and pointed a very nasty-looking gun at her.

Rebecca found her mind suddenly clear and sharp. The gun looked like a Glock, and the woman was holding it one-handed.

Nobody who knows what they're doing fires a Glock one-handed. That's what they do on television, and it's just not realistic.

Fight or flight was a basic human instinct, a feral response to sudden danger. Rebecca didn't think, she just turned and ran. Legs already sore from walking protested, but Rebecca didn't care about that. She just dug deeper and ran as if her life depended on it—because, most assuredly, it did.

The sound of a gunshot and a ping on a rock to her left just made her dig deeper. Two more shots rang out, and she could have sworn she felt the heat of a bullet sail past within an inch of her face.

"Come back here, whore! Damn it, *stand still*. I have to kill you!"

Crazy bitch. Fucking crazy bitch. The thought was the only one in her head as she charged toward a small thicket of trees. If she could get to the trees, she might be able to grab a rock off the ground and bash that crazy fucking bitch's brains out.

Three more shots rang out. And then she heard return fire and a startled cry.

"Rebecca!" Jake's voice cut through her terror, and she stopped, slipping to her knees on the grass and dirt as the strength left her legs and the sound of his pounding footsteps neared.

He was there in an instant, his hands on her shoulders as he squatted in front of her. "Are you all right? Have you been shot?"

"I'm good. Winded, but good."

"Hey." Adam joined them a minute or so later, and when he held a hand out, she let him pull her to her feet.

She looked up at her lawman cousin and said, "Didn't I tell you she was a *crazy* stalker chick?"

"You did, indeed." He hauled her into his arms for a fierce hug.

The sound of pitiful weeping reached her. She pulled away from Adam and looked in the direction of the sobs. Naomi Lake was sitting on the ground, her head bowed low as she cried. Her left hand clutched her right arm and Rebecca could see blood seeping through her fingers.

Matt Benedict stood over her, as did a man she recognized as a state trooper. Two other men hung back—civilians, and vaguely familiar to her.

"Connor nailed her in the arm, which made her drop the gun." Adam said. "He gets a gold star for not killing her."

"You wouldn't have killed her either, Adam," Jake said.

The grunting sound Adam made was eloquently noncommittal, Rebecca thought.

"Becca!"

Greg's voice pulled her gaze to him. He and Cody had driven up, and were out of the truck in a heartbeat, running toward her. Cody looked a little worse for wear, and Greg's gaze moved between her and their man.

She'd never been so happy to see two men in all her life. She ran for them, not even excusing herself from her cousins first.

Then they had their arms around her and she *knew* she was safe. She was shaking, but thought maybe she wasn't the only one. She didn't know how long they all stood there, the three of them, but they didn't speak and, she thought, for this moment, no words were necessary.

The sound of voices and another car finally got through to her. She turned around to look at what was happening. Another state police cruiser had pulled up, and there was another cop on the scene. One of the troopers was wrapping something around Naomi's arm while Adam spoke to another of the troopers, gesturing toward them, and then ahead—toward the cabin. That trooper nodded, and he and Adam got behind the wheels of their respective cruisers. Jake climbed into Adam's car and the other two men, who Rebecca had recognized as investigators who sometimes worked for the Town Trust, got into Matthew's car.

Naomi was being led to the second cruiser, her hands handcuffed in front of her, likely in deference to her wound.

Adam pulled to a stop. "Let's all head back to the cabin. The state police are handling this, and the trooper behind me will want to take your statement."

"Okay. It'll just take me a moment to turn the truck around," Greg said.

Rebecca busied herself, a few minutes later, rushing about the kitchen, starting a pot of coffee and hauling out some cookies for everyone.

Greg had directed Cody to one of the kitchen chairs and then moments later set a half glass of Jack Daniel's in front of him. She watched out of the corner of her eye as Cody lifted the glass. His tremors, and the ashen look to him when she'd first set eyes on him, told her something had happened.

By the time she'd finished playing hostess, she'd figured it out—or thought she had.

She knew from all her research that loud sounds could trigger PTSD episodes. Likely the sound of the gunfire had done that very thing to Cody.

Sitting next to him, she reached for his hand, and when he seemed reluctant to give it to her, she simply took it.

A heartbeat later he laced his fingers with hers and held on tight.

"I'll send you the background on this situation, Trooper Brant," Adam said. "Rebecca came into my office some time ago to bring me up to speed on a situation she'd found herself in back in Seattle."

As Adam recounted the facts, and his interactions with Detective Dwyer of the SPD, Rebecca was able to calm down from her scare. When she shivered, Cody lifted his glass of Jack and placed it against her lips.

She sipped lightly and then grinned at him.

His grin in return wasn't one of his brightest.

"Miss Jessop, can you tell us what happened this afternoon?" Trooper Brant asked.

The state trooper had his smartphone out and recorded her words. She didn't go into details about the anger that had pushed her out the door. That had nothing to do with crazy stalker chick. So she gave the details as best as she could, ignoring the many different male curses when she spoke of turning away from Naomi Lake and running like hell.

"Why did you do such a reckless thing?" Trooper Brant asked.

Ah, the cursers are now snickering. She said, "Because I could see it was a Glock she had. I've fired a Glock. Those suckers kick back, and hard. I'm pretty experienced with both handguns and rifles. If I was going to fire a Glock at someone and hope to hit them, I'd use a two-handed grip."

She saw horror on most of the male faces, and fascination on one. That one was the man who'd shot Naomi Lake. Rebecca shrugged. "I ran like hell, and sure enough, her shots went other than where she thought she was aiming." No need to tell them just how *close* a couple of them had come to her. That would be like throwing kerosene on a wildfire—and despite recent behavior, Rebecca Jessop was neither stupid nor a pyromaniac.

Trooper Brant turned off his phone. "That should be enough for now. I'll notify Sheriff Kendall when you can come in to his office to meet with us there. We'll have you sign your statement at that time, and answer any follow-up questions we may have for you."

"Okay, thank you."

Matt got to his feet. "I'm going to head back. I'll show Trooper Brant the way back to the county road."

Rebecca got up to hug her cousin, who kissed her forehead. "I'll think about whether or not I'll call your brother on the way back to town," he said.

"Traitor." Rebecca said that with a pout, but Matt just laughed in her face. She returned to her seat as the two men went out the door.

She lifted her cup and took a sip of her coffee. Her nerves were slowly smoothing out.

"That was good thinking on your part," Connor Talbot said. "Although I'm sure none of the men in this room who are either your family or your lovers would agree with that assessment."

"Oh, it could have been much worse, believe me," Adam said. There was a slight, though definite sneer on his face. "She might have run *toward* the crazy stalker chick, thinking to disarm her by using some kung fu–type karate kick."

"I thought about it for a split second," Rebecca admitted. "Didn't like my odds. I figured she was a crappy shot, in which case the more distance between us, the better for me."

"Jesus. Okay, that spanking is definitely a go." Greg hadn't spoken that loudly, but everyone in the room heard him.

Rebecca was grateful, as her cheeks burned with heat, for the small blessing that everyone in the room chose to ignore his comment.

"Since we're here," Jake said, "why don't we fill Mel and Connor in on the reason I'd asked to meet with them in the first place?"

Rebecca raised one eyebrow, and then looked at her men. Cody appeared as confused as she. Greg said, "Good idea."

Jake turned to Connor Talbot. "Do you have any contacts among people, officially or unofficially, in Turkey, near Bab Al-Salameh?"

Connor crossed his right leg over his left. "That's an odd question, out of the blue. May I ask why you want to know?"

"Cody, here, is an internationally renowned photographer," Jake said. "About a month ago, he accompanied Drummond Pierce, a newsman who used to be with ANN, into Syria. Pierce has a book deal, and the publisher hired Cody to take photos for the project. Pierce went off and 'secretly' arranged meetings with his contacts, with a view to setting up interviews with rebel leaders in Syria. Then he announced he was ready, and he and Cody set off. Shortly after entering that chaos-riddled country, their car was ambushed, and the two men taken hostage. Pierce managed to escape, and find his way back to Turkey, practically overnight. He was on the next flight to New York, not even waiting to see if his photographer would be freed, or not.

"Fortunately, Greg had done some humanitarian aid work in Syria, helping out some of the rebel factions. They returned his kindness buy carrying out a manhunt. The long and the short of it is, Cody was rescued and brought to safety in Turkey six days after his capture."

"He was wounded, and nearly died from infection because the bastards who took him had shot him and failed to offer medical aid." Greg's words let everyone know how pissed he was about that. "Cody's publisher released a statement saying they believed Cody had been killed, *just* before he was brought to safety," Greg said. "And just recently, Drummond Pierce has been giving interviews where he's been telling anyone who will listen that Cody is unbalanced, mentally ill, schizophrenic, and basically a man whose word *cannot* be believed."

Connor looked from Greg to Cody. The investigator didn't look too happy. "That sounds like a rat-bastard covering his ass to me."

Greg sighed. "That's what I thought, too. We're just not sure if he's covering his ass because he acted cowardly—or if there's another reason."

Connor pulled his cell phone out of his pocket and looked at it, likely verifying that he had a signal. Then he said, "Just give me a minute, please," and he got up and went outside.

"What is it you think Pierce is afraid of?" Cody asked. "I thought it was just that he didn't want anyone thinking he'd been a coward in leaving me behind. Well, that, and the fact that he's playing up the situation to make his book worth more. Nothing sells a story like making it seem larger than life. "

"I got thinking about it, and another possibility occurred to me," Greg said.

Connor Talbot reentered the cabin. "I have people on it. I don't think it will take very long to verify if what you suspect is, indeed, fact."

"Okay, can someone fill in the clueless among us?" Rebecca asked.

"Benedict suspects that Pierce arranged for the kidnapping in the first place. The original plan was probably that you were supposed to die, Mr. Harper. But for whatever reason, your captors went back on the deal they'd struck with Pierce, probably thinking they could ransom you and collect twice."

"Son of a bitch. *That* possibility never occurred to me," Cody said.

"Then, because he couldn't know for certain what you *knew*," Greg continued, "Pierce decided to ensure that if you ever stepped forward with accusations, no one would believe you." Then he looked at Cody. "I told you I didn't like that asshole, the first moment I laid eyes on him."

"So you did, lover. So you did." Cody rubbed a hand over his face. "Well this has been just a hell of a day, all told."

"You can say that again." Jake sounded as ragged as Rebecca felt. She hoped, very much, that their guests—as life-saving as they had been—would leave soon. She wanted to be alone with her men.

"I have other contacts in the FBI. If I get the response we all believe I will, I'll see to it that agency is put in the loop. Would that be sufficient?"

Rebecca wasn't certain she knew what he meant by sufficient, but she had an idea. Greg looked at Cody, who nodded.

"Yeah. That rat bastard gets hauled up on charges, I'll be a happy man," Greg said.

"Thanks, guys," Jake said. "It just pisses us off when someone messes with one of us."

Cody just shook his head, but there was a smile on his face. Then he looked at Greg, and then met her gaze.

"Blue Eyes, can you do me a favor, please?"

"Of course. Anything."

"Call your brother, the doc." He closed his eyes for a moment, and then inhaled shakily. When he opened them again, she saw trepidation, and resolve. "I need help."

Chapter 21

"I don't know why it had to be the community center, and why we couldn't be there, too," Rebecca said.

Greg felt the exact same way. He slid his arm around her as they headed into *Lusty Appetites*. "I don't either, babe. But I trust Robbie. You should trust him, too. He's your brother, after all."

"That's the thing about siblings. They kind of stay the same bratty siblings they were growing up—in your own mind, at least."

Greg thought about his own brothers and sister. "You may have a point."

The lunch crowd had cleared and not too many tables were occupied. They chose to sit at one by the front window, where they'd be able to see Cody when he emerged from his appointment with Robert.

"Hey, guys, how are you?" Michelle greeted them. She had menus in her hands. "Are you eating, or just munching?"

"We'll have pie and coffee. What kind of pie do you have today?"

"Pecan, apple, and sweet potato." Michelle grinned. "Kelsey will be glad someone is not on a diet!"

Rebecca laughed, and Greg felt the knot in his belly ease, just a little.

"I'm in an apple pie kind of mood," Rebecca said.

"Me, too." Greg picked up Rebecca's hand and kissed it.

Michelle was back quickly with their coffee and pie. "Here you go. If y'all want anything else, just holler."

"Robbie acted pretty fast," Rebecca said. "He must think the situation with Cody is critical. I mean, I only called him yesterday, after Adam and Jake and those investigators left."

"I think he was waiting for that call, sweetheart. I don't think it's necessarily an indication that Cody's in a bad way." Then he closed his eyes. In fact, he was afraid of the same damn thing. The moment the gunshots reached them and Cody threw himself on the floor of the truck had been playing on a continuous loop through his mind for the last several hours. "You should have seen him. No, on second thought, I'm kind of glad you didn't."

Rebecca reached for his other hand and he gave it to her. "I wish I *had* seen him. I don't want or need to be protected in that way, Greg."

"I know you don't." He sat for a moment and tried to get his thoughts in order. "I think it was the gunfire," he said. Then he shook his head. "No, I *know* it was the gunfire." He shivered then because it brought to mind the moment when he'd been afraid he would have had to choose between his lovers.

He knew that help had arrived for Becca, but he'd still wanted to get to her as fast as he could.

"When she fired at you, and then Connor Talbot and Mel Richardson fired back? Those shots came fairly close together, and it was like, suddenly, he was back there. Back to the moment the car he'd been in had been ambushed by those masked men, and they were shooting at him."

He would never forget the sight of Cody, curled up in a tiny ball, shaking in terror. He'd felt helpless.

"I have a friend who has PTSD," Rebecca said. "He was deployed for a couple of tours over in Iraq. From what I know, Cody's is a mild case. I believe he'll get better. It just might take some time."

"Whatever it takes." Greg sighed. "We'll talk, after this first session. See how he does with it."

"You know—if it's psychotherapy, which is generally recommended as the most effective treatment for less severe PTSD—

that's just talking. He's not a little boy being forced to go to a 'shrink' by his parents. He's a man, fully grown, *choosing* to reach out for help."

Greg smiled. "Yeah. I know. When he said that yesterday, I was so proud of him."

Rebecca smiled. "So was I."

They let go of each other's hands and turned their attention to their snack. Greg watched her put cream and sugar into her coffee, and then stir it. Everything she did had a kind of elegant grace to it. Even when she'd run to them yesterday, relief and joy replacing fear on her face as she'd covered the distance that separated them, she'd been elegance in motion.

They ate some of their pie and sipped at their coffee, but Greg felt unsettled. He set his fork aside and looked at Rebecca. "I have a confession to make."

"All right." She set her fork down, too.

Greg reached for her. He folded his hands over hers and held tight. "Yesterday, when those shots rang out…it terrified me, too. For one moment I froze. Cody had thrown himself onto the floor of the truck." He felt his eyes tearing, and every instinct he had told him to stop, to leave it at that.

But hadn't he always pulled up short when his emotions overflowed? Wasn't that what he'd learned to do when he'd been with Daniel?

That man had abused his trust and, in a way, abused him. He'd made him afraid to be who he was, deep inside. He'd learned to hide his heart, and had taken that abuse, until finally he'd left him that fateful Christmas season.

Greg met Rebecca's gaze and saw the only woman he'd ever loved. Even after the way he'd treated her before, she'd welcomed him, and his lover, both.

She loved him and Cody in equal measure. Maybe it was time for him to be worthy of her love. He inhaled deeply and said, "I had Jake on the phone. When I heard the other guns go off, I knew that Adam had reached you. But in those moments, I was torn. It was like I had to choose between getting to you, or helping Cody. Maybe I should have just floored it and gotten to you as fast as possible…but Cody was there, right there suffering and I…" Greg couldn't finish the sentence.

"How long did it take you and Cody to come to me? From the time those shots rang out until you reached me?"

"Two, maybe three minutes."

"I know you think you chose between us, but you were too far away to help me. I was heading for the trees, and I was going to find a rock and I was going to bash that woman's brains in."

Greg couldn't hold back his grin. "I think Adam probably saved her more than he saved you, then."

Rebecca nodded. "It was Connor Talbot who shot her."

"I knew I liked that man."

Her smile faded. "That was a tough position to be in—forced to choose between the two people you love. I don't know how I would have chosen, given the same circumstance."

"I do. You'd have trusted in the family and reached for Cody."

"Yeah, I probably would have at that."

"I love you, Rebecca. I'll love you until my dying day."

"I love you, too."

She pushed aside the rest of her pie and continued to hold his hand. They sat and just looked at each other. And he knew they were both thinking of their lover, the other part of their family, and praying he was going to be all right.

* * * *

Cody didn't know what to think as Robert Jessop led him into the community center. It was dark inside, even in the middle of the afternoon, because no lights were on—except at the far end.

As they continued on into the complex he saw a large, round table with several other men sitting around it. There was country music playing, muted, but recognizable.

As were the men. He easily put names to faces. Adam Kendall, Morgan Kendall, Dev Wakefield, Drew James, and Joe Grant all seemed to be relaxed, chatting with each other. Two chairs were left—one next to the other.

Cody sat and nodded to the men.

"Would you like a beer, Cody?" Morgan offered.

"Yes, please." A beer might help. He had no idea what the hell was going on, but one thing helped him to relax.

There wasn't a single shrink in the place.

"Robbie?"

"Oh, you bet." Robert Jessop latched onto that beer as if it was his new best friend. He took a long pull on it, and set it down.

"It can be a scary proposition for a man to admit to being afraid," Robert said. "We tend to think we have to be strong, stiff upper lips, and act as if bullets can bounce off our fucking chests. And yet sometimes, what we have to do is that very thing we don't do easily. We have to talk about our feelings."

He said that with a higher pitched voice, and Cody, along with the others at the table, laughed. He felt himself begin to relax.

Robert said, "Women have the right idea, but men are wired differently. So this circle, here, this is a safe circle, because we all have one thing in common. We've each of us faced a moment when death could have come in the next heartbeat. Some of us have never spoken of the incidents that happened that were 'classified.' And some of us have just never talked about it, period. What we say here stays here. You can feel free to share your own personal revelations and epiphanies with your families if you want to. But only your own. Agreed?"

Cody understood in that moment that while he was there to get help, so was everyone else.

Each of the men nodded their agreement to the rule Robert had just laid out.

"I'll start," Robert said. He took another drink from his beer. "October 15, 2009, I was on duty in the ER, night shift, in the hospital I was working at in Chicago. We got a call from the police that a gang war had erupted, and there were numerous ambulances headed our way with possibly dozens of casualties. My God, that night my ER turned into its own kind of war zone. There'd been a young teen I'd patched up months before, a bright young man I'd been mentoring, since. His name was Bobby."

Robert looked up and Cody could see the sadness practically pouring out of him. "At about the moment I looked over and realized that it was Bobby lying dead on one of the stretchers, gunfire erupted. Somehow, one of those damned gang-bangers had managed to get into the ER and opened fire. Christ, he aimed right at me. There was a young woman, a volunteer I'd seen throughout the night. She was standing next to me. I grabbed her and hit the floor. It was only by the Grace of God he missed us." Robert inhaled deeply. "I had nightmares about that night for months afterward."

He looked down the barrel of a gun, just like I did. Cody felt a bond begin then and there, a special bond with this man who was a brother of the woman he loved.

"I was lost, somewhere in the mountains of Afghanistan." Morgan Kendall's voice, quiet, drew Cody's rapt attention. "I'd been sent in to do a special job, only everything went to hell, fast. My cover was blown and I thought for certain I was a dead man." He, too, took a drink of beer. "The man following me—the enemy—got too close. Bastard shot me, and I had to fight him, hand to hand. I thought I was going to die, but he slipped on some rocks and I…I had to kill him. I managed to get away and literally headed for the hills. Wandered around, lost and disoriented, for days. Finally found a deserted village, and holed up in one of the small shacks at the edge of the town. I'd activated my emergency transponder, but I didn't know if it was working. I made my peace." Morgan inhaled deeply and then exhaled the same way. "I was terrified that I would soon be dead. Was convinced, in fact, that I was going to die. " He used his thumb to point out the two navy SEALs at the table. "These guys found me. I don't recall a lot of that because I was feverish. My gunshot wound had gotten infected."

Morgan's words resonated inside Cody. *I never made my peace. I couldn't get beyond the fear. It was the way those bastards kept at me, kept threatening me.* Cody inhaled, deeply. He blinked. Like him, this man had been shot, and his wound had become infected. He knew what it was like to be so sick he didn't even know what was happening. He, too, had only been vaguely aware of being rescued. Then he'd seen Greg's face…Greg's very scared and worried face.

Morgan seemed such a strong, in-control kind of man. It amazed Cody that he'd had such similar experiences—and that he, too, had been certain he was going to die. "No one is more prepared to face these kinds of situations than we are," Dev said. "But when we were pinned down, most of our team around us dead or dying, I was scared shitless. I didn't want to die. We'd met Julia just before that final mission, and we…" He stopped, unable to go on.

"We cried," Drew said. "Because we knew she was the woman meant to be ours, and we thought we'd never see her again. Christ, I cried like a baby."

"We both did. Not to mention other bodily functions that happened without our permission in the thick of things."

That elicited a chuckle from everyone around the table.

Adam told of facing a kidnapper with a gun, only to have the kidnapper's victim save his life. Joe told of going on what was supposed to be a routine call and being shot, point blank, instead.

All these men, Cody thought. Each one of them strong, self-confident, and steadfast. And each one of them had endured a trauma, nightmares, and hell. They went through it all and came out whole on the other side.

He could come out whole on the other side, too.

There's nothing wrong with me. I'm not less than a man because I was afraid. I'm not alone in what I went through.

He wasn't alone in what he went through!

Deep inside him, it felt as if all of his emotions, everything he'd tried to hide, even from himself, began to move and stir and boil. He met the gazes of each man in turn and knew he wanted…no he *needed* to share. He wondered what he should say, and found the words erupting from him, as if they had a will of their own and would no longer be held back.

"They kept telling me they were going to kill me." Cody closed his eyes, and inhaled deeply as the memories pounded him. "One of them had an old-fashioned revolver. He had a favorite game. He'd come in, show me the bullet, and then he would put it in the chamber. He'd then spin the damn chamber. Then he'd hold the gun up to my head. Pull the trigger. I'd never been so scared, not in all my life." He felt the tears tracking down his face, but it didn't matter.

Greg had said that Lusty had claimed him, and he'd thought it a nice sentiment at the time. But here was proof beyond imagining. These men had come together, to share, to listen, to support.

Because he belonged to Lusty—and he belonged to them. Because *he* mattered.

Cody looked around the room and saw that no one was judging him lacking because of the tears. He saw compassion, and acceptance, and understanding.

He blinked but didn't bother to wipe his tears. He didn't have to hide them or what had happened to him, from these men. He didn't have to hide anything. So he inhaled deeply, and began to tell them about his nightmares.

He told them everything, and with each word marveled that the tightness he'd felt began, little by little, to ease.

Almost two hours later Cody stepped out onto the sidewalk and sighed, a sense of relief washing over him. He'd thought he didn't need to talk, and yet with just this first time, he already felt better.

Robert came out of the community center and stood beside him. They began to walk the half block to Main Street. "We'll do this again, next week. Turns out you aren't the only one who needs it. I think we all do."

"Okay, that sounds good." When they got to the corner, Cody turned to Robert. "Thank you. I mean that. Thank you for making me one of you." He held his hand out and Robert shook it.

"You're welcome." Then he nodded toward the other side of the cross street, and Cody turned to see what had his attention.

Greg and Rebecca were waiting for him. He could read the tension in the way they stood, and the way Rebecca reached for Greg's hand. Their attention, though, was fixed on him and he knew their tension was *for* him.

"You might consider telling them what you went through," Robert said. "When you let in the ones who are closest to you, the ones you love and who love you in return—well, in my opinion, that is one definition of heaven."

Cody turned to Robert and grinned. "That goes all ways, you know."

Robert looked at Greg and Rebecca and smiled.

"Yes. Yes, it does. I think you all three have gotten in the habit of putting on armor. You need to learn that when you're three—when you're one—the armor just gets in the way of the loving."

"I have a feeling we're going to be working on that," Cody said.

Robert clapped him on the shoulder. "Good. Call if you need me."

"Thanks, doc. Really."

"Anytime."

Cody watched Robert Jessop head off toward the clinic. Then he turned and began his own very short walk—toward his family, and his future.

Chapter 22

Rebecca could tell it had been a good session the moment Cody turned and looked at them. Then when he came to them, he did something that made her heart soar.

He kissed Greg, a soft gentle, lips-on-lips kiss right there on Main Street. And then he kissed her, too.

"Let's go home," Cody said.

"You've got it." Greg looked as happy as she felt.

He took Cody's right hand and Rebecca took his left. The truck was parked beside the community center, so they walked back that way. Greg got behind the wheel, and Cody bowed to her unspoken request and slid across the seat so he was in the middle, between them.

"We saw Matt at the restaurant. He said the state police will be sending Naomi Lake back to Seattle. They plan to charge her with attempted murder, but hold those charges back to allow Washington to try her first."

"I'm glad they have her in custody," Cody said. "But I'd be willing to bet they're going to consign her to a mental facility, likely for the rest of her life."

"I think so, too," Rebecca said. She leaned her head on Cody's shoulder. He put his arm around her and pulled her close. "How are you doing after your adventure of yesterday, Blue Eyes?"

"I'm okay. Worst part was right after Connor Talbot shot her and I knew I was safe. That's when I realized what could have happened—that she could have easily killed me. I wanted to throw up I was shaking so bad. Then when I saw you and Greg, that was when I *felt* safe."

"You know, Greg thought we ought to spank you for scaring us so—walking off without protection when we knew—at least intellectually—that bitch was headed our way. But in light of the whole screaming and diving for the floor of the truck thing I did yesterday, maybe we should give each other a pass—this time."

"*This* time?" Greg said. "There'd fucking well better not be a next time—at least as far as walking blindly into the jaws of death is concerned."

"That's what I mean. We get a pass, with the codicil that if we do anything recklessly stupid, from this moment on, the paddle comes out."

Rebecca chuckled. Cody was different. There was an easiness about him that hadn't been there that morning. She thought he was more relaxed, and hopefully more at peace. "That sounds like a plan. But first, we need to get ourselves a paddle."

"That's not all we need to get," Greg said. "We need to get a place to stay. Folks are going to want to start taking weekends and weeks at the cabin. Vacation season is nearly upon us."

"I'll go wherever you want to go." Yesterday, she'd promised herself she was going to say that to them first thing. She'd been distracted, first by the questions Greg had raised with the investigators about Drummond Pierce, and then by Cody's request for help.

Last night, when they'd finally unwound enough to go to bed, they'd all simply clung to each other and then gone to sleep.

Now, she said, "I mean that. I can paint anywhere, as long as I have some light. Now that I've found you both, I don't want to be anywhere that you're not."

Greg turned off the county road and stopped the truck while the gate swung open. Once they were through, he said, "As much as I want us to spend the rest of this afternoon and evening making love, I think we need to talk, first. So let's make some coffee, and settle in at the kitchen table and do just that."

"Good idea," Cody said. "I think it's time—past time, in fact—that we all laid it all out."

* * * *

"Sit down and relax, Blue Eyes. We have this."

Rebecca sat on one of the padded kitchen chairs and watched the men as they worked together to put on a pot of coffee and set out the small pastries she and Greg had picked up at *Lusty Appetites*.

Greg wasn't, apparently, the only one with a sweet tooth. While Cody bit into one of the pastries, Greg went into the great room, and came back a few minutes later with the folder his grandmother had given him.

"Me, first." Cody met her gaze, and then Greg's. "I owe you both an apology. Because I refused to admit that I needed help—because I let what happened to me when I was a kid cloud my judgment—I was unable to fulfill my responsibilities to *us* yesterday. Please forgive me. I know that today was only the first session for me. But I already know, this is going to work."

"I *told* you that love means you never have to say you're sorry." Rebecca reached for Cody's hand. "When you love someone, you love them, warts and all. That means you make allowance for human failings, and when the one you love is hurting, you hurt, too, and only want them to be better."

"What she said," Greg said. "The only thing that matters to us is that you get to where you're at peace and happy in your own self. Besides, boyfriend, you're not the only one who let us down."

Greg reached for Cody's hand, and then Rebecca's. They were connected, the three of them, which was how she liked them to be, best. "I've gotten in the habit of holding back my emotions, sometimes." Greg sighed. "Not that I lie—I don't do that. But when I feel stressed, I tend to close myself off. I know when I developed that habit, too, and why. It was during the year I spent with Daniel." He paused. Rebecca heard the catch in his voice. She understood how hard this was for him. She squeezed his hand and gave him what she hoped was a smile of encouragement.

Inhaling deeply, he continued. "Because this love that we share between the three of us is good, and positive, and uplifting, I can see now that what Daniel and I had wasn't any of those things at all. I'll never know if we might have brought it around to being a healthier kind of relationship." He shrugged. "But I do know *we both* would have had to change, fundamentally, for that to be so."

Rebecca recalled what Cody had said of what he'd learned about the way Daniel had treated Greg in front of others. She thought perhaps the one in that relationship who had needed help the most was Daniel. She wouldn't think badly of the man. Greg had loved him, and he was dead.

"Because of the way I was, I've cheated you, Cody—and you, too, Becca. I'm going to try very hard not to do that ever again." Greg exhaled heavily, and grinned. "Wow, that was a long time coming."

"It was," Cody said. "And I'm really grateful you can finally see that. Don't beat yourself up over the mistakes you've made, lover. We're all only human."

"No, I won't. But I really am going to do my best to face life with my eyes wide open from now on—and to stop withdrawing into myself. It shouldn't be that hard. I *know* I'm safe with the both of you. I don't want y'all to doubt that, not even for a moment."

"We don't," Rebecca said. "Bad habits are easy to form and hard to break."

"They are," Cody said. "You need to know, Greg, now that you've said that, we'll hold you to account if you begin to slip into that denial mode again."

"Yes, please. I expect you to." He leaned over and gave Rebecca a kiss. Then he kissed Cody, too.

"Now, as to this." Greg nodded at the folder. "This is a hell of an opportunity to do something that makes a real difference in the world."

"You've been making a difference for a long time, darling," Rebecca said.

"Thank you, sweetheart. But this could help us make an even bigger one—and we can manage this, the three of us, as a team. I think we could split our time between being here, in Texas, and being wherever we have to be to help carry out the foundation's work." He met her gaze and then looked at Cody. "I'd like to stay here in Lusty for a while, right now. I think you'd benefit, lover, from not going anyplace for a few months. The tranquility here, on top of your sessions with Robert would help you as you work on your issues. That's what I think. What do you think?"

"I think for the first time in my life I have a place that actually *feels* like 'home.' So yes, I'd like to stay for a while. But you said we'd have to leave this cabin soon."

"There're a lot of houses available in town. We could pick one," Greg said.

"Just like that?" Cody asked.

"Pretty much," Rebecca said. "Or, we could pick one temporarily, and have our own house built on one of the parcels of land just outside of the town proper."

"I like that idea," Greg said. "We could have a studio built for each of you, and an office I could work in, for the foundation. Plus, we could have some space, be in a more rural setting." He raised his eyebrows comically. "So that we could indulge in naked outdoor hot monkey sex when the urge struck."

Rebecca laughed. "I like that idea a lot." In fact, just thinking about hot monkey sex was making her twitchy. She looked at Cody and smiled when he adjusted the way he was sitting in his chair.

"How long would that take?" Cody asked. "To build a house like that?"

"I'll speak to the Town Trust, and put the ball in motion. But I think that by this time next year, we could be settled in that house.

Plus, it would give us a permanent place to come back to—and a place to raise kids. And that brings me to the biggest thing of all."

Greg met her gaze and then Cody's. "I love you both, and I want to spend the rest of my life with you. I want to marry you both. Please, say yes."

"I've been in love with you for a long time," Cody said to Greg. "And you," he turned to Rebecca. "You, I fell in love with practically on first sight. And then with each day, I discovered new things about you that just made me love you more. We all three mesh, when I didn't know that that sort of thing could happen for me. I want the three of us to be a forever family." Cody raised her hand to his lips and kissed it. "But how do you feel, really, Rebecca? Taking on two men who are in love with each other—that's a lot for any woman to consider."

"It is," Greg agreed. He brought her other hand to his lips and copied Cody's action, kissing it. "We want you to be sure it's what you want, sweetheart."

Rebecca looked from Greg to Cody. She wondered what she could say to convince them that she really did want to spend her life with them, in their own particular brand of ménage family. And then she smiled, because she just thought of the perfect way to *show* them that she knew her own mind about this, and had for some time.

She looked at Cody and said, "Do you remember that first night you arrived here—or should I say that first *morning*? Do you recall that I knew who you were?"

"I do. It surprised me, when I was no longer so dead tired and could think about it. Greg said that a mutual friend of yours had told you about me."

"That is the truth, and that's what I told him. But it kind of goes further than that. After I heard about your being in Greg's life, I looked you up online." She grinned. "I also looked up a lot of the wire service archives to have a look at the kind of pictures you'd taken—and I bought your book, of course. Being an artist, I know you can learn a lot about a person through their art." It was kind of silly to be blushing, especially after all the three of them had done together—but there it was. She looked at Greg. "Why don't you go to that room I was staying in when y'all arrived, and bring me what's in the closet, please? You'll know what it is I want as soon as you open the closet door."

Greg raised one eyebrow and she knew she'd aroused his curiosity. She said nothing when he met Cody's gaze. Both men shrugged, and then Greg got up and went to do as she'd asked.

He was back moments later and she held on to the urge to grin as he came into the kitchen holding a canvas. It measured three square feet, and she could see not only that he was looking at it, but that the painting confused him. She'd used softer colors, smudging them in places to represent the blur of motion, as well as to make the work appear more interpretive than was usual for her.

After all, she'd been painting not what *was* already, but what she hoped, one day, *would be*.

"What is it?" Cody asked.

"Lend me your photographer's eye and help me figure this out, please," Greg said. He moved a chair close to the wall, and then carefully set the painting on it. He stepped back and stared at it. Cody got up and stood beside him, and for a long moment, neither man spoke.

"My God!" Cody said at last. "It's us. It's the three of us, making love." He turned to face her, and she nodded.

"I named it 'Forever Love'."

Obviously, now that Cody had pointed it out, Greg could recognize their faces. Rebecca thought she'd done a pretty good job there, now that she could compare the actual man with what she'd rendered.

Greg also turned to look at her. "How?"

Rebecca met his quizzical gaze and answered his question. "I was trying to convey my hopes and dreams. It's really only ever been you for me. And, I knew in order for you to be happy there'd have to be another man. Because I loved you, I felt fairly confident I would also love any man you fell in love with. You've heard of speaking something into existence? I was *painting* something into existence."

"So, no doubts at all, then?" Cody asked.

"Not a one. And the answer to your questions, Greg, Cody, is *yes*. I want to spend the rest of my life with you, too. Yes, I'll marry you both."

"Come here, baby."

Greg's voice shook when he said that, and Rebecca's heart melted. As she approached, they each opened their arms. She took those few steps toward them, and then one more into them, and felt them enclose her within their heat and within their love.

"Let's go upstairs to that big-ass bed and get naked." Cody ran his hand over her back, and she could tell by the way he moved he was treating Greg to the same affectionate gesture. She let her gaze drift down and could make out the unmistakable shape of his cock pushing against his jeans. "Let's see what we can do about making Rebecca's art come to life."

Rebecca sighed. "That sounds like a lovely idea. Since we're beginning our happily ever after, can we get *completely* naked? I had myself tested before I left Seattle. I'm clean. I'm also on the pill. For now."

Greg bent down and kissed her, a gentle, questing kind of kiss. "Yes, baby. We can be completely naked. We're safe, too. And we'll discuss your being on the pill," he said. "But later."

The heat in his eyes, the reflection, love, and the lust combined, nearly stole her breath. She glanced at Cody, wanting to share that incredible sensation with him, only to find an identical passion in his expression, too.

"Yes," Rebecca said. "Later."

Chapter 23

Naked, they resumed their embrace, the three of them each with their arms around the others. Rebecca closed her eyes and inhaled the scent of her men, the musk and the sweat and the essence that marked each of her lovers as unique. Combined, their aroma created a one-two punch to her libido the like of which she'd never known. Her nipples contracted into hard buds and her cunt heated and became moist.

She looked up and met Greg's gaze and then looked at Cody. "The first time I saw you two kiss, I had an orgasm."

"We remember."

She grinned because the men had both said that at the same time, and both of them wore identical sappy grins.

Cody said, "*I* damn near came in my pants when I felt you coming."

"You weren't the only one, boyfriend," Greg said.

"I wonder what would happen if I watched the two of you do more than kiss?" Just the idea of watching them together thrilled her. The emotion between these two men was so pure, and so beautiful. She craved the opportunity to watch them, to have them trust her enough that they would love each other freely in her presence.

Greg and Cody exchanged a long look, and then Greg bent down and brushed his lips against hers. "Why don't we find out?"

Rebecca smiled and copied Cody's gesture of earlier. She stroked each of their backs, and when they moved in closer to each other, she felt the ripple of their muscles, and the quiver of their excitement and their need.

Contact created friction, and as they kissed, as their tongues intertwined and as their cocks brushed, one against the other, their body heat rose, pulsing their mouthwatering fragrance into the air.

Rebecca stepped back, just a half step, so that her men could embrace more fully. She wondered if her presence would inhibit them, but she discovered almost immediately, it didn't.

They leaned in, and their hands roamed freely as their kisses seduced. Fingers brushed shoulders and necks, and caressed against nipples. Rebecca could have sworn she felt the coarse hair under her own hands as they explored each other's chests. When they pressed closer, when palms cupped taut ass cheeks, Rebecca's arousal grew.

"I love you so much." Greg's words, wrapped in kisses against Cody's face and neck, swelled with emotion. Greg's hands traveled up his lover's back and then around until he cupped Cody's face. "I was so terrified, so afraid I was going to *lose* you, when I'd never told you how much you meant to me."

"You'll never lose me, Greg. *Not ever*. I love you. I will always love you."

She'd never seen a ballet as graceful as the one they performed as they moved to the bed and then moved over and on each other. They kissed and cupped, lapped and grasped and stroked. Words would have been superfluous, for the emotion shimmering between them as they loved surpassed mere words. Tiny sounds of pleasure, of masculine arousal strummed Rebecca's senses and kissed her flesh with a feather-light brush of pleasure. Unable to stop herself, she reached down to stroke her slit, her fingers dipping into her cunt, finding it wet and hungry.

Tiny little shivers of Eros raced through her as the scent of sex, hers and theirs, surrounded them all. They turned on the bed, a slow, gentle rotation until they were in the perfect position to stroke and kiss each other's cocks. She sighed when, as one, they began to lick, and then took each other's cocks into their mouths. Their eyes closed, and their cheeks hollowed as they pleasured each other. Her lovers were lost in their love of and for one another, and Rebecca bit back a moan of her own. She'd never seen anything so beautiful, and so erotic, in her life.

She knelt on the corner of the mattress, lost in the passion of their loving. Watching them made her hotter, and she continued to pinch her nipples and tease her cunt with her own hands. Her fingers delved into her pussy, a slow fucking motion that she unconsciously synced with the rhythm she could see in their cheeks.

Movements slowed, became sinuous and lithe and graceful, as hands stroked and mouths loved. She heard their desperation, their growing need in the deep, resonating moans and sighs and growls they made. Their breathing hitched, and Rebecca knew she wasn't alone in approaching orgasm.

Grace and patience fell away, replaced by a fine desperation that coated their flesh with sweat. Fast and furious now, they gave, they took, and Rebecca stared, transfixed, as the excitement, and the arousal, and the drive toward completion took over. Her breath caught as their race to pleasure heightened, as they both stiffened, and reached their climaxes together. Rebecca pinched her nipple hard with the fingers of one hand and her clitoris with the fingers of the other. Everything coalesced, drew together, and became sharp and shivery as she joined them. Her rapture gushed from her in tiny waves of celebration, spilling out onto her hand.

Rebecca slid to her haunches as she tried to catch her breath. On the bed before her, Greg and Cody still held each other, arms around hips, faces turned to the side against bellies, their breathing ragged.

Greg turned his head slightly and met her gaze. "Well?"

"Hot. Holy. Hell." Rebecca sighed. A tiny shiver of aftershock washed through her.

Cody snickered. "It was pretty hot knowing you were watching us, Blue Eyes."

"And playing with yourself while you did," Greg said.

Rebecca smiled. Her orgasm hadn't been as good as it would have been if it had been *their* hands pleasuring her, but it had been pretty darn good nonetheless.

"Come here, sweetheart."

Rebecca really had no time respond to their request on her own as both men moved, and reached for her at the same time. Before she could blink, she found herself lying between them, facing Greg with Cody spooning her. Despite the orgasms both men had enjoyed, their cocks were already stiffening against her flesh. It wouldn't take much, she knew, to get them as hard as steel.

Cody kissed her shoulder. "It means a lot to me that you enjoyed that." He stroked his hand down her body, and when he reached the top of her left leg, he lifted it and guided it back, over his hip. "You didn't just get off on seeing us pleasure each other. There was joy in your expression as you watched us."

"How could there not be?" Rebecca stretched back and kissed him.

"Very easily," Greg said.

"Knowing you love each other so deeply simply moves me." Rebecca sighed and snuggled into both men.

"You have no idea how special you are, Blue Eyes." Cody hugged her and she fully relaxed into his embrace.

She loved the sensation of being snuggled between her men. The strength of their bodies bolstered her, and the heat of their bodies warmed her, so that no part of her, inside or out, remained cold, or lonely.

Rebecca met Greg's gaze when he lifted her chin with his hand. "You're perfect for us, Becca. I think we were meant to be together, the three of us."

"Then let's be together, please. I need to feel you both inside me at the same time. I want our forever to begin here and now."

"*Sweetheart.*" Greg laid his mouth on hers, his lips coaxing as he kissed her.

She opened to him, unable to resist. His tongue slid into her mouth and coaxed hers into a slow and sultry tango. She could taste the remnants of Cody's nectar on Greg's tongue, and the combination of flavors made her hot.

The warm and the wet of Greg's kiss made her heart pound and her blood heat. Cody had laid her leg over his, effectively opening her for their lover, and Greg wasted no time taking advantage. His fingers stroked back and forth across the lips of her pussy. She could feel her dampness on his fingers and shivered as he spread that natural lubricant over her swollen folds, and then up a little higher to tease her clit.

Greg lifted his mouth from hers, and Cody used his hand to bring her face closer to his. She stretched her neck back again and kissed him, sucking his tongue into her mouth, stroking it so he would have no doubt that she wanted to suck his cock.

I can taste Greg's cum in his mouth. The reality of this level of intimacy at once excited her and filled her heart with joy.

When Greg inserted two fingers into her pussy and began to finger-fuck her, she broke her kiss with Cody.

"Oh, yes. Mmm, yes *fuck me*, baby." She moved her hips in time to Greg's movements, her back pressing against Cody, using him as a brace.

"We're both going to fuck you, *wife*. We'll fuck you so thoroughly, you won't know where you end and we begin." Cody's dark promise thrilled her in a way she couldn't explain.

"I want you to stop taking those pills," Greg said. "There's nothing we'd like better than to see our child growing inside you." He flicked his gaze over her shoulder. "We don't care which one of us is the biological father," he said. "Because we'll both be the fathers of all your children, in our hearts and in our minds."

"Yes, please. I want your babies." Rebecca caressed Greg's face, then turned and reached for Cody's. "I want both your babies."

“God, that makes me hot, hearing you say that.” Cody nuzzled her neck. “I love you, Rebecca.”

“I love you, too, Cody. Now, enough talking.” The feelings swirling through her demanded action. Her voice caught when she spoke. “Fuck me, now. Fill me with your cocks and your love. I need you. I need you both *so much*.”

“Hush, now.” Greg kissed her cheek and she felt the dampness of tears she hadn’t known she’d spilled. The emotion within was painted on her soul in vibrant colors and bold strokes. This emotion cried out for expression. It refused to be contained.

Rebecca combed her hand through Greg’s hair and pulled him into her kiss. Hot and hard, wild and wonderful, her tongue claimed his mouth, tasting and teasing, and yes, *begging*.

Without letting her lips go, he wrapped his arms around her and turned them on the bed so that she lay atop him.

“Take my cock inside your sexy cunt, Becca.” He slid his hands to her waist and lifted. She reached beneath herself and placed his cock at the entrance of her pussy.

“You feel so good sliding into me.” Rebecca shivered in pleasure. “I’ve never had a naked cock in my cunt before. Oh, *yes* you feel fabulous!”

“You feel pretty damn wonderful surrounding my cock,” Greg said.

He pulled her down, so that her head rested on his chest, and stroked his hands over her back.

“Squeeze me, baby.”

Rebecca did as he asked, even as she looked over her shoulder at Cody. He winked at her as he opened the lube and squeezed a generous amount onto his fingers.

Then as he spread the cool gel over her anus, his expression changed, leaving playful behind, edging into hunger.

He took a moment to stroke his cock, so that the lubricant coated that magnificent organ, too.

"Fuck me, Cody. I need your cock in my ass. I need to feel the both of you inside me."

"I will. I am. I need to feel both my lovers at the same time, too." He moved in behind her, fitting himself between Greg's legs.

She felt the brush of his hot cock across the rosebud of her anus and sighed when he centered himself there and began to push.

The heat of contact turned into the burn of his penetration, and Rebecca felt her pussy convulse around Greg's cock as it gushed her arousal.

"Mmm, your cunt is getting tighter and wetter and…ah, *yes*." Greg kissed the top of her head and smoothed his hands over her back.

Cody's cock slid slowly into her ass so that he was buried to the hilt. The sensation of his scrotum brushing the bottom of her slit sent ripples of pure pleasure through her.

"Can you feel it?" Greg whispered the words, almost as if he feared disturbing the shimmering aura that enveloped them. "Sacred," he said. "Right here, the three of us, no longer only three, now we're *one*."

"Yes." Rebecca knew no moment would ever be as special for the three of them together as this. When they came together, joined together as one, their bond became spiritual, so much more than just physical and emotional.

"Lord." Cody leaned over and kissed Rebecca's shoulder. Then he leaned forward even further and brushed his lips over Greg's. "I never even knew intimacy this prime existed."

Rebecca's heart filled with so much love she didn't know how she could hold it all in. She rolled her hips, tiny little movements, down and in, and then up and back, a dance of passion and sex. Driven by the need to give to both of her men at the same time, she let her body take what it would, how it would.

No music played and yet the strings of a powerful opus played within their hearts. They began to love, to give and take and share, and Rebecca had no words. Thoughts shattered, and civilization vanished. There existed now only the need to love. Rapture beckoned, the siren song compelling and irresistible. The urge to mate, to strive for ecstasy consumed her, consumed them all.

Heat and heart, purpose and a ripe, burgeoning pleasure surrounded them and drove them closer, then closer still to the edge.

Rebecca loved the sensation of these hot, hard cocks inside her, but loved more the connection, the emotion that bound them together.

"Let go, Becca. Let us take over, my love." Greg's words practically hissed out of him. So close to the edge, she sighed, and relaxed every muscle, giving over complete control of her body, and their loving, to her men.

"Oh, yes, that's it." Cody shivered as he began to move in her, as he and Greg timed their thrusts to counter the bulge of each other's cocks inside her body. Friction built and Rebecca cried out as all control of her arousal evaporated. It danced and dipped, swirling and churning, a feast beyond anything she'd ever tasted.

Growing, soaring, her orgasm spiraled out of control. Stroke for stroke her lovers fed it, freed it, so that every part of her quivered as bliss consumed her completely.

Consumed her, renewed her, and spilled over as she felt the men inside her stiffen, as she heard their shouts of completion and felt their hot seed pulse into her body.

In her ears, three hearts pounded an identical rhythm. Her lips stretched into a smile that felt full and sweet as she struggled for breath, and knew she wasn't the only one transformed.

Damp perspiration coated her, and she reveled in the essence of their combined labor. Her heart overflowing, and her soul at peace, she knew this was their forever, and it would last until the end of time.

Cody kissed her shoulder. "Don't move, Blue Eyes. I'll be back in a bit."

"Can't move." Satiation became a heavy blanket that covered her. Greg's heartbeat beneath her ear continued to surge strong, and she allowed herself to be wooed by that steady tempo, toward sleep. She heard the shower come on, and then go off, but continued to lie still.

Then Cody returned and cared for her, the cloth warm and damp, his touch gentle.

She sighed when he lifted her off Greg and laid her in the center of the bed.

"I can see Greg's cum glistening on the lips of your cunt. Sexy as hell."

She felt Greg move, and knew he was having a look for himself. "Kind of makes me feel all he-manish and territorial," he said.

Rebecca giggled at this display of the chest-beating alpha male. She guessed if she didn't love these men so very much, such words would irritate the hell out of her. But she did love them, and she understood that men experienced their emotions in different ways than did women.

"I love you both so much." She rolled onto her back so that she could see them both at the same time.

Each of her lovers looked down at her. Cody picked up her right hand and brought it to his lips. He kissed it and then laid it on her abdomen. Greg's hand covered Cody's, and here was another symbol of the connection between them.

"I never dreamt I could have a real family," Cody said. "But I do—the two of you *are* my family. The two of you and however many children we may one day have between us. I've never been happier."

"I love you both." Greg bent down and kissed Rebecca. Then he stretched out toward Cody. The men kissed over her, and she couldn't hold back her smile. "I thought I'd ruined my chances for a happy ending," he said. "I'll spend the rest of my life being grateful for you both."

"I wanted you—I wanted this forever." Rebecca looked at each man in turn. "I was certain I'd screwed up, too. I was afraid to reach out to you, to set aside my useless and empty pride. And yet the prospect of living my life alone frightened me more. Thank you, both of you, for loving me. Thank you for giving me a future to believe in."

Greg grinned. "You're going to spend the rest of your days making love under two adventurers," he said.

"That sounds pretty darn perfect to me." Rebecca yawned, and then giggled. Cody and Greg looked at each other, and then moved as one, snuggling down, pressing close on either side of her, cocooning her.

Warmth, and love, and total peace surrounded her, just as their heat surrounded her, and she knew she'd found heaven on earth.

Chapter 24

"I think I'm getting used to the concept of extended family." Cody slipped his arm around Rebecca, pulling her close.

They stood inside *Lusty Appetites*, as people began to arrive to celebrate their engagement. It hadn't taken them long to get here from their new, temporary home—a two-story house two doors down from the Parkview Inn.

The Town Trust had approved their request to build a house, and they'd chosen the parcel of land they wanted—one that had a grove of trees, a babbling stream, and a field that Rebecca knew, for a fact, would sprout a million bluebells come midsummer.

Cody's words tickled her sense of humor. She giggled and laid her head on his shoulder. "Good. I don't think there can be any doubt whatsoever that you've been accepted here."

"Hell, no. It's actually kind of cool, in fact."

"What were you and Aunt Anna whispering about a few minutes ago?" Greg asked.

"Oh, just this and that." Cody's eyes twinkled in merriment.

He'd only had three sessions in total so far with Robert, yet the change in him was remarkable. Greg had told her this was the Cody he'd fallen in love with, and she believed it.

"Come on, lover, give," Greg coaxed.

"Okay. For the next month or so, I'm going to be haunting the town with my camera at the ready. Aunt Anna wants some pictures taken of current family members, for posterity. Not posed photographs, but impromptu, random images that will reveal the heart and the soul of the subjects."

"That is a wonderful idea!"

Rebecca's heart swelled when she saw the smile cross Cody's face. He was the first to reach for Grandma Kate and give her a hug.

"I'm so glad to see you, Grandma."

Kate Benedict laid her hand on Cody's cheek. "I'm delighted to be here, and very pleased that you're going to be my grandson."

Rebecca reached for Greg's hand, because the look on Cody's face simply melted her.

"Thank you. I'll make you proud of me."

"Oh, sweetheart, I already am." She tilted her head to the side. "I'm so looking forward to the pictures you're going to take. Tell me, will they all be random samples? Will you take some portraits?"

"I'll take both kinds, I think." He looked around the restaurant, already more than half full of family. "I'd love to recreate the portrait of the family Fourth of July picnic. You'll have similar pictures, of everyone who was in your family then, and now. Imagine what it would be like, having them hang side by side?"

"Oh, I like that idea. It would be like a tribute to Sarah and Amanda and their men! It would be a way to show that their dream came true in a big way. Yes, let's do that!"

"We'll have to figure on a day and time. I expect it'll be an enormous picture."

"The Town Trust will arrange everything, don't you worry." Kate took his hands in hers. "We're not any of us perfect," she said, her voice soft. "Perfection doesn't really matter. What matters is what's in the heart. You remember that, Cody Harper. You remember that and ease up on yourself, just a little."

Cody smiled. "Yes, ma'am." He bent down and kissed her cheek.

"Now, if you'll excuse me, there are a lot of babies here, and there is nothing I like more than getting my hands on them."

They watched as she made a beeline to the back corner of the restaurant. Adam, Jake, and Ginny had settled in next to Julia and her SEALs, and Tracy, Peter, and Jordan. They'd grabbed another couple of tables, and Rebecca figured that pretty soon, most of Lusty's next generation would be gathered in that one area.

Michelle and Emily Anne had filled the buffet, and Carrie Benedict emerged from the kitchen to give everything an inspection. She caught Rebecca looking at her and grinned.

"The boss will be here shortly and I don't want her thinking she needs to be doing anything here, tonight."

Greg overheard his sister-in-law's comment. He laughed. "Our cousin does like to keep her finger on every pulse point," Greg said. "Guess I can't blame her. Pride of ownership, and all that."

Carrie came over and gave him a hug. "Well, *I* can blame her. Today is supposed to be her day off."

The door swung open and Abigail, Carson, and Michael Benedict entered, followed closely by Pamela, Adam, and James Jessop.

"What a happy occasion!" Abigail said. She hugged Rebecca, and then held her at arm's length. "I can't tell you how delighted I am to welcome you as a daughter. I've loved you since you were just a tiny little thing." Then she looked at Cody. "And I'm very pleased to get another son."

Cody stepped into her hug. "Thanks, Mom. That means a lot to me."

Abigail hugged Greg, and Rebecca saw such love and relief on her face. She'd confessed once that she'd worried about Greg the most, because even as a child he'd seemed to need something she hadn't known how to give him.

No, none of us are perfect, and this place isn't a perfect place. But here, Rebecca thought, love was encouraged to grow as love would. Openheartedness made up for a lot of imperfections, as far as she was concerned.

The men—Benedicts and Jessops alike—bestowed hugs and backslaps on Greg and Cody, and kisses on Rebecca's cheek.

Her father, James, cupped her face. "Now that you have two good men to look after you, I won't worry quite so much."

"Oh, dad, you're such a fibber. You're going to worry about me when I'm fifty." And that was really fine with her.

James smiled, and Rebecca thought, not for the first time, how young-looking her fathers looked for men in their late sixties.

Kelsey, Matt, and Steven arrived with little Amanda Rose. As she had with all of the babies that arrived with parents in tow, Rebecca scooped Mandy for a moment and then passed her on to Cody.

"Good-sized crowd," Kelsey said. "Maybe I'll just—"

"Hug your present and future cousins and then come and sit with us," Steven said. "I'm sure everything's going well. Probably Carrie will slip out of the kitchen and give you a full report before long."

Kelsey laughed. "Okay, okay, I get it." She sighed. "I have to learn that day off means *day off*. I am a work in progress."

"We all are," Cody said. He handed Mandy over to Matt and then hugged Kelsey.

Rebecca's brothers all arrived en masse. Robert and David, with Jillian, stood just ahead of Grant, Andrew, and Chloe.

"I'm delighted to pass the torch, as it were," Robert said, directing his comment to Greg. "And anytime you want to come and check out *The Lyon's Den*, you just let me know."

Greg laughed, and then gave his future brother-in-law a hug. "I don't think that's going to happen any time soon," he said.

"I can also give you the name of a good club in Dallas—in case the possibility of running into family at the *Den* is an issue."

"We'll talk," Greg said.

"Isn't the idea of your passing the torch supposed to mean that you stop being a bossy, arrogant Dom?" Rebecca asked. Beside her, Cody snickered.

Robert said, "I'm sure I don't know what you're talking about. Bossy? Arrogant?"

"Right." She hugged her brother anyway, because whether he was bossy or not, he did love her—and he was being very good with and for Cody.

Grant and Andrew towered over their fiancé, Chloe, and yet Rebecca couldn't say she'd ever seen two men, anywhere, be as gentle as they were being with her. She'd come to the conclusion that the two had finally evolved beyond the Neanderthal stage. She hugged her future sister-in-law.

"Every time I come to one of these parties, I'm in awe, all over again, that everyone here is family," Chloe said.

"I know. Even though I grew up with so many relatives, I've traveled so I know how unique we truly are, here."

Rebecca noticed Emily Anne moving about the room, a pitcher of sweet tea in hand. And yet, even as she chatted and filled glasses, her gaze kept straying to the large, plateglass window and the sidewalk in front of the restaurant.

She didn't wonder who the woman was waiting for. She knew.

As if summoned by the waitress's thoughts, the door opened and two big, tough-looking men came in.

She'd last seen the private detectives at the cabin, the day Naomi Lake had attacked. That woman had already been returned to Seattle. Although she was charged with several counts of murder, Rebecca knew she'd likely never stand trial.

She'd heard from Adam that the woman's mental state had deteriorated considerably since her failed attempt on Rebecca's life.

Rebecca felt sorry for her. She'd been damaged while still a child, and had never really recovered.

"Congratulations." Melvin Richardson shook Greg's hand, and gave Rebecca a hug. When he got to Cody, he shook his hand and said, "Aside from coming to celebrate your engagement, we bring you some good news."

Connor Talbot had greeted Greg and her, and joined his partner in front of Cody. "The US attorney in New York City has issued an arrest warrant for Drummond Pierce. It's being served on him as we speak." Connor looked at Greg. "You were right. He did arrange for the entire 'kidnapping' adventure." He shook his head and met

Cody's gaze. "According to my sources—who were willing to go on the record—he paid ten thousand dollars to the men he hired. They were supposed to have killed you, Cody. But they were greedy little bastards, and decided to hold on to you and see if they could collect a ransom for you, instead."

"Thank you. I'll look forward to testifying at that SOB's trial."

"I imagine the story will be covered on ANN tonight. You should likely get ready for an influx of media here in Lusty."

"Thanks for the heads-up," Cody said. "I hope you'll stay for a while and celebrate with us."

"That was the plan," Connor said. "We need to report to Jake, but we'll do that in the morning. We've booked rooms for the night at the Parkview Inn."

"I know you've been putting in a lot of time trying to track down the man who stole Chloe and Carrie's inheritance," Rebecca said. "I won't ask for specifics, but I was wondering if you were getting any closer?"

Melvin Richardson nodded. "We have a lead—a big, complicated lead. Detective work is mostly details and boring, time-consuming checking of those details. We expect this case to start picking up steam, soon."

Because she'd been sort of keeping an eye open for it, Rebecca saw the moment that Emily Anne Bancroft realized the investigators had arrived. She blushed, and bobbled the tray she held. But then she seemed to get a grip, not just of the tray but her emotions, too.

When the men both smiled at the young woman, she gave them a cool look, a slight nod, and went back to doing her job.

"Looks like you men have your work cut out for you," Cody said.

"That's all right," Melvin Richardson said.

"Some things just aren't meant to be easy in life," Connor Talbot agreed.

Rebecca watched as they headed toward the back of the room, where the babies were holding court. The two men were welcomed easily and seemed to enjoy getting in the midst of what many might consider chaos.

When Connor Talbot accepted one of the twins from Jake Kendall, Greg chuckled. "Now that was a smooth move."

Rebecca understood immediately what he meant. What woman could resist a man who had no problem cuddling a small baby to his big chest?

Out of the corner of her eye she watched as Emily Anne's face softened. And then chuckled when she shook her head and turned her back on the scene.

"I'm kind of glad we'll be staying in Lusty for a few months," Cody said. "I think I'm going to enjoy watching *that* story unfold."

Greg moved so that he stood between the two of them. He placed one hand on Rebecca's shoulder and one on Cody's. "You know, the cousins were all full of dire warnings about Grandma Kate and her matchmaking ways. But if you think about it, we have Robert to thank for our getting together. I really don't see how she has had anything to do with those two private dicks falling for Emily Anne, either. And the ones who became engaged just before us—that would have been Grant and Andrew, and Chloe. They all met because Carrie got hired here, and the cowboys realized she was the woman meant to be theirs. I think Grandma's penchant for bringing lovers together has been reported all out of proportion."

Carrie had come out of the kitchen to inspect the buffet, and had obviously heard Greg's softly spoken comment.

She came over to them and flashed a grin that looked young and full of fun. "You know, big brother, you ought not to doubt the reach—or the intelligence—of our grandmother," Carrie said. "She was the one who suggested the firefighters be assigned to watch over Chloe when the town was rallying to protect me from George Lockwood, and she was the one who suggested those two private dicks be put on the case of our stolen inheritance."

"And I'd be willing to bet she'd had a heart-to-heart with Robert before you even called him," Rebecca said quietly. "Because my brother the bossy, arrogant Dom would do a lot of high-handed things, but setting events in motion so that you would be left *alone* with his baby sister really isn't one of them."

"And," Cody said, "she is the one who gave you *Maria's Quest* to run."

Greg met her gaze and then laughed. "All right, I give. I will never doubt my grandmother again."

Carrie gently patted his face. "Probably wise."

Music played quietly on the sound system, and darkness descended upon the town. Inside *Lusty Appetites*, people chatted and mingled and munched. They lived and they laughed and they loved.

Rebecca noticed how Emily Anne, likely despite her best intentions, kept turning and watching Mel Richardson and Connor Talbot. The look on her face was, Rebecca judged, half wistful and half lustful.

It *was* going to be interesting to watch that story unfold. Rebecca snuggled in next to her men, content, at least for now, to be home.

THE END

WWW.MORGANASHBURY.COM

ABOUT THE AUTHOR

Morgan Ashbury, also writing as Cara Covington, has been a writer since she was first able to pick up a pen. In the beginning it was a hobby, a way to create a world of her own, and who could resist the allure of that? Then as she grew and matured, life got in the way, as life often does. She got married and had three children, and worked in the field of accounting, for that was the practical thing to do and the children did need to be fed. And all the time she was being practical, she would squirrel herself away on quiet Sunday afternoons, and write.

Most children are raised knowing the Ten Commandments and the Golden Rule. Morgan's children also learned the Paper Rule: thou shalt not throw out any paper that has thy mother's words upon it.

Believing in tradition, Morgan ensured that her children's children learned this rule, too.

Life threw Morgan a curve when, in 2002, she underwent emergency triple bypass surgery. Second chances are to be cherished, and with the encouragement and support of her husband, Morgan decided to use hers to do what she'd always dreamed of doing—writing full time.

Morgan has always loved writing romance. It is the one genre that can incorporate every other genre within its pulsating heart. Romance showcases all that humankind can aspire to be. And, she admits, she's a sucker for a happy ending.

Morgan's favorite hobbies are reading, cooking, and traveling—though she would rather you didn't mention that last one to her husband. She has too much fun teasing him about having become a "Traveling Fool" of late.

Morgan lives in Southwestern Ontario, Canada, with a mysterious cat, a new Morkie puppy who thinks he's a German Shepherd, and her husband of forty years, David.

For all titles by Cara Covington, please visit
www.bookstrand.com/cara-covington

For titles by Cara Covington writing as
Morgan Ashbury, please visit
www.bookstrand.com/morgan-ashbury

Siren Publishing, Inc.
www.SirenPublishing.com

CPSIA information can be obtained at www.ICGtesting.com
Printed in the USA
LVOW12s0001240813

349377LV00035B/2307/P

9 781627 401135